The Dream Wedding

ALSO BY RENITA D'SILVA

STANDALONES
The Neighbours
The Dream Wedding

July '25

THE DREAM WEDDING

Best wishes,
Renita D'Silva xx

RENITA D'SILVA

JOFFE BOOKS

Joffe Books, London
www.joffebooks.com

First published in Great Britain in 2025

© Renita D'Silva

This book is a work of fiction. Names, characters, businesses, organisations, places and events are either the product of the author's imagination or are used fictitiously. Any resemblance to actual persons, living or dead, events or locales is entirely coincidental. The spelling used is British English except where fidelity to the author's rendering of accent or dialect supersedes this. The right of Renita D'Silva to be identified as author of this work has been asserted in accordance with the Copyright, Designs and Patents Act 1988.

No part of this book may be used or reproduced in any manner for the purpose of training artificial intelligence technologies or systems. In accordance with Article 4(3) of the Digital Single Market Directive 2019/790, Joffe Books expressly reserves this work from the text and data mining exception.

Cover art by Nick Castle

ISBN: 978-1-80573-100-9

*For the Adamses: Sylvie, Mike, Nikita, Natasha,
Dylan, Peanut and Snoopy.*

Thank you for your wonderful friendship, for the joy, the laughter, and, especially, the magic you bring into our lives. For the fun times, the themed parties, the quiz nights and magic shows (conducted via Zoom during the pandemic). For your generosity and kindness. For being there through ups and downs, tough times and good.

With all my love.

*'How many of our daydreams would darken into nightmares,
were there a danger of their coming true!'*
Logan Pearsall Smith

PROLOGUE

When the mutinous glower of storm clouds finally breaks, it does so to thunderous applause. The heavens are split open, silver tridents sent forth by a raging army intent on destruction. Whipping the sea into a frenzy, waves the size of mango trees growl and crash in tempestuous outrage.

Just visible on the horizon, a lone boat struggles to stay upright, thrown this way and that at the whim of the weather, a plaything in the hands of a giant. The solitary figure at the helm is knifed by the sabre-edged torrent, beleaguered by spray and tossed by the raging sea swell as he tries to gather his fishing nets while struggling to control his boat.

It's a losing battle. The vessel is battered from all sides at the hands of the scowling monster that the sea he's lived beside and fished upon has become. There's no reasoning with it now, no point asking it to show mercy. It's too far gone, heady with its own power.

And so he closes his eyes and tries to gain purchase on his boat, which is cleaving apart, sundered by the relentless beating of the waves. As the nets slip from his hands and the water pulls him into a spiralling whirlpool, his thoughts travel to his three loves: his wife and his children. And as the water enters his lungs, he finally finds peace in the imagined comfort of his family's embrace.

* * *

She runs after the car, assailed by the hail of pebbles thrown up by the wheels, blinded by the orange dust, suffocated by the fumes, tasting gasoline and grief and rage hot as chillies. She runs until it's a dot in the distance, until her legs give way and she sinks to her knees on the mud road, until gentle arms lift her and carry her home. Her home, empty now without him, yawning with grief for him, for her husband, the father of her children, who is never coming back.

You did this! she screams in silence at the empty road. The car must have reached town by now. The taste of mud still on her lips, tears of wrath and sorrow spill onto the old sari that serves her as a pillow. She lacks the strength to raise her head from the damp, to open her eyes, even as her children call, 'Ma, Ma,' even as their small hands try to shake her awake, put their tiny arms around her, their eyes wide in innocent confusion.

'You did this!' she shouts after the car.

But the car is long gone. What remains is the image of a laughing, unrepentant face. As if the life of a father and husband, tragically cut short, is nothing but a joke. Words flung at her in the mud, in the spice and smog-suffused breeze: 'No point blaming me, he lost his life to greed. I'm doing you a favour by not demanding my money back. Where's the fish I paid for?'

PART ONE

CHAPTER 1

Now
The locals

Picture this.

A swish seven-star seaside holiday resort in Cornwall, favourite haunt of the mega rich, all set to host the most talked-about wedding of the year.

The richest man in India, in England, some even say the world, heir to countless billions, is about to marry a nobody, or, to put it more kindly, an ordinary girl next door from Essex.

What nobody knows — not the embittered locals, not the enchanted public, not the on-the-hunt-for-an-exposé paparazzi, not even the wedding party itself — is that this wedding, already trending worldwide, is going to become the most talked about *ever*. Nobody is going to forget this unlikely union, this wedding of the year, of the century, in a hurry.

The resort, all several hundred acres of it, is so exclusive and protected that the airspace above it is designated a no-fly zone between the hours of 10 p.m. and 6 a.m. Only certain select media, carefully vetted by the groom's PR outfit, and, separately, by his security detail, have been invited to cover the wedding. Of course, the people living on the doorstep have no access at all, unless they work at the resort, and even then they have to sign a non-disclosure agreement several pages long and peppered with countless carefully worded threats regarding what will happen to anyone daring to breach its numerous caveats.

The locals, however, are not to be outdone. They've figured a way to get a scoop on the wedding. They live here, after all. They were here before the resort was built — in fact, they protested, loudly and vehemently, when it was first mooted. They know the area well. They've walked every inch of these acres with their dogs and their lovers, have grazed their sheep where the world's richest now swim and drink and dine their stresses away. As advertised in the glossy brochure, these guests are waited upon hand and foot, their every whim catered for, their every desire fulfilled before they even know what it is that they want.

The locals are aware of every secret ingress and hidden pathway in the vast acreage that makes up the resort. They know that the wedding will likely be held at the cove, whose pristine golden sands sparkle as if kissed by the gods, where the sea, sheltered on either side by craggy cliffs, is always calm and perfectly blue. They picture it taking place at that magical time when the sun dips into the sea and the horizon blushes like a woman in love, when the sky is a kaleidoscope of crimson and rose, and the golden sand gleams, winking as if it holds treasured secrets, and the bride will glide down the path between the cliffs and onto the sand. Their own children were married there, before the resort appropriated that stretch of the coast. Their daughters walked barefoot along the path lined by bright yellow gorse, the nutty brine of the air electric with anticipation and celebration. This particular bride, this ordinary girl from Essex, will follow that same path. Unlike them, once the waiting groom takes her hand and they face the chaplain (naturally, not one of theirs, nobody local — a famous churchman, somebody they've all seen on TV) she will never be ordinary again. With her vows she will shed that life and tread an extraordinary, fairytale path, one of the chosen few.

Why was she chosen? Nobody knows.

There's a lot of conjecture, of course, but that's all it is.

It could have been anyone, anyone at all, even one of their daughters. Why her, this girl from Essex, earmarked for a life in the public gaze, every move interrogated, judged?

Now, as to where the wedding ceremony will take place, it's not just a lucky guess. There's a lookout on Mr Swain's property, from where, if you have good binoculars, you have a bird's eye view of the beach and the secluded cove — not so secluded now, eh? Oh, they try to put up walls, post signs to keep the locals out, but can they really? According to Mr Swain, there's been a constant hum of activity down at the cove since it was announced that the wedding was to be held at the resort. A steady stream of vehicles arriving and reversing. There've even been helicopters landing upon the cliffs, Mr Swain reports to his avid listeners, revelling in the attention he's commanding.

'Ah, I did see them hovering. The wedding's taking place in the cove for sure,' former postmistress Mrs Ramsbottom agrees thoughtfully, thus making Mr Swain's conjecture fact as far as the others are concerned.

Emboldened by this, Mr Swain issues daily updates.

'I seen people walking up and down the beach, taking measurements. There's a woman with a clipboard directing. They lowered an arch from the back of one of the lorries to put at the head of the cove.' He chuckles. 'It was so blustery it was nearly knocked down. I reckon they were only checking, to see if it passed muster, like.' Mr Swain takes a breath. He isn't used to talking so much, or being the centre of attention. He decides he quite likes it. He takes a handkerchief out of his pocket and pats his moustache — not as bushy as it once was, but passable all the same. Pinned under the gaze of the women of the village, all the beauties of yesteryear he once fancied, he has become quite flustered, and when he's nervous, his moustache gets sweaty. 'Everything has to be perfect, don't you know, for these rich out-of-towners. They were even measuring for a carpet, I reckon.'

His audience tuts, and Mrs Lewes, sniffing loudly, voices what they're all thinking. 'Whoever heard of a carpet on a beach? What do they think this is, the Oscars? *Aladdin*?'

The women all snigger, and Mr Swain joins in, basking in the rare camaraderie of his fellow villagers. His cottage being where it is, at the outer bounds of the village, he's always felt like an outsider, hovering at the edge of things. Well, no longer. Now, his property with its lookout — the shepherd's hut that's been in his family for generations — is the centre of the action.

Taking a deep breath, he says, before he loses his nerve, 'You're all welcome to the lookout anytime, you know, to keep an eye on things, as it were.'

And the women beam, Mrs Lewes going so far as to give him a peck on his cheek. She smells of talcum powder and mothballs, making him think of his mother.

Thanks to Mr Swain, the locals now know the wedding will be held at the cove. But the details of when and at what time it will take place have not been released to the general public — they don't want the locals, not to mention the media, to try and get a look-in. Yes, they've put up walls and fences but there are always drones.

'There are pages and pages of rules about drones,' reports Mrs Lewes's son, who works as one of the sous-chefs at the resort.

'So, what did you cook today, then?' Mrs Lewes asks casually, trying to hide her curiosity.

It's no good. Her son sees right through her. 'You know I can't tell you that. It's in my contract.'

Mrs Lewes snorts, unimpressed. 'Contract! I don't understand why the secrecy around what they eat, for God's sake.'

'Perhaps because it's nothing to write home about. They might be fancy but their tastes are crude, Mum.'

'What, cruder than deep-fried Mars bars and greasy chips?' Mrs Lewes teases. Young Harry might be a chef concocting 'fancy' food, as his mother thinks of it ('Foie gras and ceviche — what's that when it's at home?'), but his personal tastes run to anything deep-fried and battered, the greasier the better, and his mother never misses an opportunity to remind him of it.

'You don't want to know.' Harry strokes the beard he's cultivating — still straggly, despite all the products he secretly uses. How come it isn't bushy and prolific like his mate Ralph's? The lucky bugger doesn't even have to *try* — he shaves in the morning and wham, by evening he has a beard thicker than Harry's, who has just spent the last two weeks carefully massaging his chin with Boots' best (and most expensive) products.

'I do, son, believe me,' his mother is saying.

'I've signed a non-disclosure agreement, Mum. I can't tell you.'

'You know my lips are sealed.'

'Ha, I've heard *that* before.' Harry chuckles, while his mother sucks her teeth in that annoying way she does.

'Tell me this,' she says after a bit, 'is that woman, the mother of the groom — now, what did the *Sun* say? — ah, "one of the top ten most beautiful women in the world"? Well? Is she?'

He only came down for a slice of toast, and here he is being subjected to an interrogation. He takes a huge bite of his toast (white, slathered with butter — nothing quite like it) and considers. 'She's all right, I guess — for an old biddy.'

His mother cackles and he can't help smiling. He takes another huge bite. 'Not as old as you, mind.'

'Don't be cheeky, now,' his mother scolds.

'She's a bit snooty, she is. Nose in the air.'

'That lot all are,' his mother agrees. 'And what about her diamonds? Are they really as big as fists, like the *Sun* says?'

'I suppose I can tell you, being as the *Sun* has already reported it — they are *huge*. You can't take your eyes off them. I used to think you can't tell fake from real, so why spend so much on a tiny real diamond when you can get a huge fake?'

His mum snorts. '*Pshaw.* Only a bloke would think that.'

Harry puts another slice of bread in the toaster.

'But now I've seen the real deal — well, you can absolutely tell the difference.'

'Course you can,' his mother says. Then, wistfully, 'What I wouldn't give for diamonds as big as my palm.'

'Dream on, Mother.' Harry laughs, applying a generous helping of butter to his toast.

In any case, since Mr Swain issued his invite, the locals have taken to gathering every evening at the Swain family shepherd's hut. Those with a bit of time on their hands — the retired and the work-shy — drop in throughout the day. They've practically set up camp there, to Mr Swain's secret delight. He's no longer lonely, no longer counting down the endless hours of each monotonous day to the growl of the waves and the rhythm of the tides. Who would have thought that his solitary cottage at the very edge of the village would, thanks to this wedding, be the headquarters (for that's how he privately thinks of it) of the local rebels and insurgents who want in on the most talked-about event of the year? And who would blame them — after all, isn't this *their* town?

Even the youngsters have started dropping by, putting much-needed life into Mr Swain's old bones, bringing back fond memories just by watching them nudge one another and mess about. He used to be like that once, with a full head of hair tousled by the briny sea breeze, a growly voice prone to breaking at the oddest of times, skin that was always coming out in a rash of pimples, especially when there was a girl he fancied, and there always was . . .

Ah, the glory days of youth! How naive he was then, much like these sproglets with their incomprehensible jargon — TikTok and Insta, whatever they were.

'Hashtag SamWedsSuraj is trending on social media but even there the details are scarce and tightly controlled by the mega-rich billionaire's media outfit,' the youngsters say.

'Word is Taylor Swift is serenading the newlyweds. We might even get to see her arrive!' they exult.

Mr Swain now knows who will drop in when. The youngsters descend in a big swarm once school is out, the retired throughout the day, whizzing through their chores so they can have a go at the binoculars. There are two pairs, both kindly donated by Mr Swain. The smaller, less fancy one he's kept for himself. The other, bigger and much more powerful — Great Uncle Tobias was a serious birdwatcher — he's handed to the locals to take turns on.

'Quit hogging it, our Brenda, and give us a go. Don't you have chores to do?' Mrs Lewes tuts.

'Chores can wait. Spying on them lot is much more interesting.' Brenda cackles so hard her false teeth drop, coming perilously close to falling out.

The youngsters snigger among themselves.

'Wait till you reach my age, you lot, then we'll see who's smirking,' Brenda mutters, waving her cane at them, even as Mrs Lewes snatches the binoculars from her.

'Och,' Mrs Lewes complains. 'Am I doing this wrong? Can't see anything except sand and sea. What's going on, Brenda?'

'Nothing, that's what. I've been watching till my eyes are sore. Having a good old nose even when there's nothing to see. It's nice to rest my peepers a tad, let me tell you.' Brenda sighs, leaning back and resting her head against the wooden wall. After a moment or two, small snores can be heard escaping her partly open mouth, and the youth nudge one another and snigger some more.

A vigorous snore sends Brenda's head bumping against the back panel, causing an avalanche of giggles among the teenagers. 'Tell you what, it's very cosy in here,' she says.

'It was my great-great-grandfather's,' Mr Swain declares proudly. 'He was a shepherd. He would sit here all day watching his sheep graze.'

'Much like we're doing now.' Brenda helps herself to one of the rock cakes Mrs Lewes has brought. 'These are ever so good, Margaret,' she says through a mouthful.

Mrs Lewes beams. 'Try my tiffin bites, go on. Nigella's recipe. That woman truly is a goddess. Once you've tasted one of mine, you won't be buying them at Tesco's again, even if I say so myself.'

Brenda sighs. 'They're all gone, only crumbs left.'

Margaret Lewes smiles. 'What did I tell you?'

It's like an impromptu party, Mr Swain thinks, secretly hoping the wedding won't take place for another two weeks at least. He's never been more popular or felt more part of a family than he does now. All those girls he fancied, all those chances missed because of his cursed shyness. Speaking of which . . .

Mrs Ramsbottom, who used to run the post office, now retired, comes panting in. 'Have I missed anything?'

'Not as yet,' Mr Swain tells her, grinning goofily and putting his binoculars down for a minute. He had dated her, back in the day, before Ramsbottom swooped in with a better offer. Mr Swain didn't blame her for choosing Ramsbottom — who in their right mind turns down a post office and the chance to know the goings-on of the entire village? He's never held it against her. She's aged well, he thinks, not as apple-cheeked as before, but those sparkling eyes are still the same. And in any case, to him, she will always be that bonny, apple-cheeked young lass he fancied rotten, and he wouldn't hesitate to tell her so, given the opportunity.

Ramsbottom, on the other hand . . .

He huffs and puffs into a seat, which, with one look from Mr Swain, the young whippersnapper who was hogging it relinquishes hastily. Mr Swain was PE master back in the day and he's still got it — not the stamina, but he still knows how, with a look, to get even the most recalcitrant teen to do his bidding.

Ramsbottom waves his cane at Mr Swain, looking at him from over the top of the thick glasses balanced upon the bridge of his bulbous nose. 'I tell you, this young lady over here, my good wife . . .'

The teenagers roll their eyes and double up with laughter, mouthing 'young' to one another.

'She's obsessed with this wedding. Rushing through her chores, she is.'

Mrs Ramsbottom tuts at her husband.

As she should, thinks Mr Swain.

'She's the best cook in the village, but today the mash was lumpy, the sausages undercooked...'

Mrs Ramsbottom rolls her eyes, just like the teenagers moments before, and turns her ample behind towards her husband.

'And she hurried me through dinner too. I almost choked on the undercooked mush...'

Her back to her husband, Mrs Ramsbottom huffs loudly.

I bet you wish you'd married me now, Mr Swain thinks, sitting up straighter in his chair.

'I, for one, will be glad when it's all over and that lot over there—' he waves his cane in the general direction of the cove — 'go back where they came from,' Mr Ramsbottom declares.

Now it's the teenagers' turn to tut. 'You're not supposed to say that.'

'And why not, eh? Neither of them is from round here. So why did they choose Cornwall to get married, I ask? What memories tie them here? What sentimental attachment? None. They're only here for the seven-star resort. Seven stars, indeed. Let me tell you, it's no different from four- or three-star, except for the cost. The stories I hear from the staff...'

Mr Ramsbottom once stood for local elections, and the habit of pontificating has never left him.

His wife is shaking her head. The teenagers are grinning among themselves and fiddling with their phones, probably recording Mr Ramsbottom's rant and live-streaming it. Mr Swain might not know much about social media, but he does know that teenagers are notorious for advertising their lives for the world to see. Now they have the means, whereas in his time...

'In my time,' Mr Ramsbottom is droning, 'couples got married in their local church with their loved ones around them.' He shakes his head so hard he dislodges his hairpiece.

The teenagers fall about laughing.

Mr Swain stares. *Hang on a minute!* A wig! A bloody wig! So that's the secret to the luxuriant mane that Mr Swain has always been envious of.

Ha!

And there he is, still expounding, his wife turned away, the teenagers laughing at him, not having a clue that his secret is out.

Feeling very pleased with himself, Mr Swain lifts his binoculars to his eyes again, and in an instant the wig is forgotten.

'Something's happening,' he says, and a hush falls over the assembled villagers. 'But I can't quite make out what it is. Who's got the bigger binoculars? What's going on?'

Mr Stone, who happens to be holding the binoculars at the crucial moment, will never forget what he sees then. For the rest of his life, whenever he closes his eyes, it will rise up before him, the terrible, terrible sight . . . The figure, limbs flailing, thrust ruthlessly against the rock face, then hurtling down the steep cliffside to the thundering sea below, arms spread out, cries of pain swallowed by the briny wind — *Help me! Please.*

Gulls wheeling overhead screech a warning.

'H—Help,' Mr Stone stammers, shocking his fellows, the little clutch of locals gathered at the one place where outsiders are assured, with the aid of binoculars, a clear view. Tears of horror sting his eyes like the salty wind battering those poor limbs. The pleas for deliverance, swallowed by the sea — sacrificed to the remorseless whim of destiny, fate . . .

Fate? Or was there another, altogether more human hand involved? Those questions will come later. They will be for the police — even that will give rise to controversy, like everything to do with the resort and the wedding that was supposed to be the event of the year.

Because nobody, apparently, can agree as to who should be involved: Interpol? The CID from India (given the Sharmas' base there)? Scotland Yard, or indeed the local police?

'There's even talk the FBI might pitch in,' Mrs Ramsbottom will declare, breathlessly, having learned this snippet from Roy, who delivers the post to the local constabulary.

Mr Swain will smile gently at Mrs Ramsbottom and say, sweetly, 'You all right, Juliet? Here, have this cuppa, nice and hot with two sugars to perk you right up.'

Mr Swain, despite being just as upset about the tragedy at the resort as the next person, will also secretly be pleased that the shepherd's hut, far from being abandoned, is now in more demand than ever, with locals *and* the press — national and even international — having realised what a good lookout point it is.

Afterwards, when the dust has settled somewhat, the locals are to be rocked by the new scandal that has been developing right before their eyes, but which none of them had the wherewithal to notice, distracted as they were by the goings-on at the resort. Mrs Lewes and Mrs Snow will grumble that, wouldn't you know it, Mr Stone would have the luck of the draw, get to see the moment when it all happened.

He will be the one the police will want to interview, but of course, his wife will take centre stage, saying he's 'too traumatised'.

'Traumatised!' the local matrons will scoff. 'Mr Stone? I'd believe it of anyone but him!'

For Mr Stone, true to his name (and his wife and children's annoyance) has never, to anyone's knowledge, cried or even laughed loudly or indeed displayed any other unruly emotion in his entire adult life.

If Mr Stone knew what they were thinking, he would have been appalled. Ever since it happened, he's been cursing himself for having given in to the avid curiosity infecting his fellows and gone along to see what the fuss was about.

If Mr Stone had known what would happen, he would never have looked. He would have thrust the binoculars at one of the others. The others, even his wife, would rather *they* had been the one to see it, while Mr Stone would give anything to unsee it. They'll think he's milking it, making far too big a deal of it. Even his wife — in secret, especially when she's woken by Mr Stone's nightmares — will think the same. After all, haven't they all seen sheep fall from the cliffs? That's the nature of the coast they live on. It's beautiful but rugged and precarious, they all know that.

But all that is to come.

Now, in this moment, Mr Stone shocks the others by letting out a small whimper, giving them a glimpse of the boy he once must have been, so very long ago. 'S—Someone please call 999.'

The ambulance arrives in record time, mere minutes after the call is logged.

'One rule for them, one for us,' Mrs Lewes tuts. 'When I called the ambulance for my poor Fred, it took twenty minutes, by which time he was cold.'

More ambulances follow, and, on their heels, the best doctors, helicoptered in from different corners of the world, never mind the cost.

All to no avail.

They're too late.

Far, far too late.

CHAPTER 2

Six months previously
Sam

The letter is waiting for her when she opens up the shop. She looks at her name, the new one to go with her new life, and feels a coil of unease spiral down her spine.

Sam leads a quiet life. Work. Home. Dinner — beans on toast, usually, an omelette if she's in the mood for cooking and if there are eggs going spare. Afterwards, she reclines in her armchair and reads one of the books she always has on the go, a cup of tea going cold by her side.

Working in a charity shop means people are always bringing in book donations and so she never has to worry about running out of reading material. Sometimes, if the book is very good, she reads late into the night, while outside her window dusk falls and violet blades of grass emerge from velvet shadows, teased into a languidly swaying dance. She used to watch telly — just the news, but it's all doom and gloom nowadays. And in any case, the telly is always on at work, in the room where she sorts through all the junk people kindly bring in, so she stays up to date on world news.

As for local news, the regulars frequenting the shop take care of that, and Sam is always in the know about village goings-on.

The first to arrive is always old Mr Venables, who comes in every day without fail, bang on 10 a.m. 'Now, has anyone donated anything I'd like today, dear?'

He never buys anything, does Mr Venables — he just wants to get out of the house, talk to people. 'The doctor said I should give these old legs a turn.' He frequents every shop on the small parade that serves their village, and then makes his way home around half twelve to have a cuppa and crackers with cheese, and sometimes, if the local Budgens has a deal, a slice of his favourite fruit cake. 'Nothing like my Maud used to make, God rest her soul. But it's passable, mind, and it makes the news — all war and hatred, the pain humans inflict on one another — more palatable, my dear.'

Then there's posh Mrs Arbuthnot, who speaks like the BBC presenters of old, an accent like tinkling glass, coming for a nose for items she can pass off as inheritances from her illustrious family. 'My children,' she'd grumble, 'ran the family fortune to the ground, sold off the manor and installed me here, among the commoners.' And yet she counts each coin carefully as she buys those of the 'commoners'' donations that look suitably classy to pass off as treasures from her august past.

She's followed by the twins: 'Call us Edie and Edna, everybody does, otherwise it gets confusing, as we're both Miss Crump.' Neither Miss Crump has married, and they still live together in the house they grew up in. Well into their eighties, they giggle like teenage girls whenever Mr Venables is present, blushing to the roots of their sparse hair, their faces redder than the rouge each has applied so carefully to their weathered cheeks.

Crossing paths with Mrs Arbuthnot, the two of them scowl. 'Hoity toity, that one. Gives herself airs and graces — what for, we'd like to know. Looks down her nose at us.'

To say Sam loves working at the charity shop is a bit of an overstatement, but, truth be told, it's all right — it gets her out of the flat, gives meaning to her days. As it is, she's lucky to have a job at all. Back when she started, she was an assistant, watched hawk-eyed at all times by Manda, the manager, but Sam didn't mind. She was grateful for the job and determined to keep it.

It took years, but Manda did in the end come to trust her, and now Sam is manager, Manda having moved to Hertfordshire to be closer to her daughter and grandchildren.

Sam likes being in sole charge, the only employee, apart from the times, usually towards the end of the school year, when sullen teens 'help' as part of their Duke of Edinburgh volunteering scheme.

She walks to the shop and back — it isn't far, fifteen minutes each way — and it comprises her constitutional for the day. She works six days a week. Sunday, her only day off, is spent reading more books. After all, what else is there to do? Her only friends are the regulars at her shop, all octogenarians. She's chosen to lead a solitary life since it all happened, and it suits her.

Or so she tells herself.

But now when she opens up, there is the letter, waiting, alongside the torn and scattered bags of donations propped against the outer wall — no matter how many times she puts up a sign asking patrons politely to please not leave donations outside but to bring them in during opening hours, her requests are always ignored, and she spends half an hour each morning cleaning up the ripped bags and collecting the items strewn along the street by the foxes that have got at them in the night.

She almost discards the letter, thinking it's fallen out of one of the bags. But then she turns it over and sees her name.

Her spine tingles with fear, her brain urges calm.

It *looks* innocuous enough. But there's no clue as to who has sent it.

She examines it with trembling fingers, while every instinct compels her to throw it away, burn the thing.

Taking a deep breath, she decisively tears it open.

An invitation from the bookshop in town: *You have won a signed copy of author Rohan Garvi's new novel,* The Grief Malady. *You are invited to his book launch on Sunday . . .*

She doesn't recall entering any competition, book related or otherwise.

And how do they know her name and place of work?

Someone who came into the shop must have entered on your behalf, she thinks. *Everyone who comes in the shop, or even peers through the windows, will know you like books. You're always reading.*

Her heartbeat gradually settling, she sets the letter down and switches the kettle on — she has half an hour before Mr Venables arrives.

As she drinks her tea, she looks at the letter again. She likes Rohan Garvi's work, and to have her own signed copy — a new book instead of one that's second-hand — is tempting. She could take the bus into town and meet him, she muses.

It isn't her usual way to spend her only day off.

What will you do otherwise, eh? Curl up in your armchair and read, only stirring when your stomach complains or to make a cuppa, or when you need the loo.

When she was younger, Sam never thought that she would one day find herself living a life like this. She looked down on people who were content with so little, pitied the smallness of their lives.

But she doesn't consider her life small. At the charity shop she meets people from all walks of life. And through her reading, she travels, absorbs knowledge, has adventures galore. She is content. It is enough.

You are young, and yet you live like an old woman.

The old women who frequent the charity shop, smelling mustily of mothballs and memories, often ask her, 'Is there anyone special in your life, dear?'

'Only the latest hero from the book I'm reading,' she always replies.

'You should go out, have fun, live a little. You're only young once.'

She doesn't want to go out, have fun, live a little.

She's done all that, and it caused her enough pain to last a lifetime.

But this, the book launch, is different.

For the first time in a long while, in for ever, she wants to go out.

And so, on Sunday, she makes an effort. She wears her only good dress. It's a bit tight around the waist. Too much sitting around and reading and snacking on Jaffa cakes, too many mugs of sweet tea.

Then there's the question of what to do with her hair. It needs a cut. It's too long, straggly and full of split ends.

She thinks of her sister, two towns away, who runs her own hair and make-up business. Sam is in awe of Georgie, of the way she got back on her feet after everything that happened. She's made something of herself. But Sam hasn't been able to tell her so. They speak rarely and when they do, Sam's mouth clamps up, her throat choked with too much that is unsaid. The only words she can manage are 'I'm sorry, Georgie, so very sorry.'

And that puts an end to the fledgling conversation before it has had a chance to take flight.

Sorry is not enough. It never will be.

'What's the point of saying sorry now?' Georgie would ask stonily. And that would be that — yet another stilted conversation with her sister.

When was the last time they spoke? A year ago? About that.

'I'm proud of you,' Sam wants to say, but they never get that far. They can't talk anymore.

Her eyes prickle and she squeezes them shut.

Ah well, nothing she can do about her hair except wear it the way she does every day for work. She twists it into a bun and pushes a pencil through it to hold it in place.

Then she checks the bus times and walks to the bus stop. She stopped driving after that night.

Don't go there.

But her mind goes there anyway. It has never really moved on, that's the problem.

CHAPTER 3

Sam

The bookshop is packed.

There's a queue a mile long, snaking into the town square.

Sam is intrigued. She's underestimated the popularity of the author, who writes rambling literary tomes, which she assumed were not to everyone's taste. Clearly, she was wrong. There are people of all ages here, a cross-section of society.

She taps the person in front of her on the shoulder. 'You're here for Rohan Garvi?'

'Who?' The girl — barely out of her teens — wrinkles her nose.

Sam knows she shouldn't judge, but joining the queue behind this girl, busy TikToking on her phone, she did wonder why she should be attending the book launch of a literary author who writes about grief and loss.

It seems she was right in her judgement.

Her trip to town is a waste. She would have been better off at home rereading Rohan Garvi's books. She must have got the wrong end of the stick. Or perhaps she's in the wrong queue.

'The author?' she tries. 'Rohan Garvi? He's supposed to be launching his new book here, *The Grief Malady*.'

The girl continues to stare blankly at her.

'This is the queue for the bookshop, isn't it?'

'Yes.'

'The author isn't going to be here?'

'I don't know what you're talking about.' The girl shrugs and returns to her phone.

Sam feels, inexplicably, like crying. Tears prick her eyes again, like when she thought about Georgie. What is wrong with her? She'll just take the bus back home again. Nothing lost, except time.

You have only time on your hands, nothing else, her conscience points out.

'Excuse me.' It's the woman behind Sam in the queue. 'I couldn't help hearing your exchange with the girl in front.' The woman is middle-aged, her eyes crinkled with laugh lines. 'Some author is launching his book, yes,' she says kindly.

Sam smiles at her. 'Oh, thank goodness, I thought I'd got the date wrong. But you're not all here for that?'

'No. You see, it's his friend we're waiting to meet.'

'His friend?'

'Suraj Sharma,' the woman says as if Sam should know who he is.

She has truly been living under a rock. It's the first time Sam has heard his name.

CHAPTER 4

Sam

Sam waits patiently in the queue, and eventually a roar rocks the crowd. A cavalcade of cars — limousines, mind you — pulls up and ejects a battalion of men in black, who look just like the men in the movie — black suits, sunglasses and inscrutable expressions.

The surging, impatient crowd, who were rustling and complaining and texting and, a moment ago, cheering, are now silent, agog, waiting. Sam is caught up in the general mood, the heady flutter of anticipation.

Sam is expecting Rohan Garvi to look a bit different from the author photo at the back of his books, but the unassuming man who emerges from the most ostentatious limo to a murmur of disappointment from the crowd is unmistakable, hair perhaps a little thinner, greyer. Slight and hunched forward, he seems to be apologising for his presence. His expression is one of utter confusion. Actually, he looks terrified as he takes in the waiting horde.

Sam notices him glance with longing at the car he's just emerged from, as if he wants to escape back inside and shut the door on the waiting mob.

She absolutely understands, even though she's happy to see him.

The crowd surrounding her, however, is not.

They all have their phones out, ready to click, and they're waiting, the buzz of excitement electrifying the air.

And then a huge celebratory cry surges through the gathering. 'He's here. Suraj Sharma, over here!'

Sam feels sorry for Rohan Garvi, his book overshadowed by his famous friend.

But then she sees this friend, briefly, before the coven of black-clad men converge upon him and lead him inside, snug within their protective fortress, and that brief glimpse is enough for her to understand why the crowd is so wild.

While Rohan Garvi is ordinary — interchangeable with any other man — Suraj Sharma stands out. Perhaps it's his aura of charm and confidence in his good looks, that special something that actors and certain politicians possess.

Before he's surrounded by his towering bodyguards, Suraj Sharma's languid yet piercing gaze sweeps over the crowd and connects, so briefly that Sam thinks she must have dreamed it, with hers. He raises his eyebrow ever so slightly and smiles, his wonderfully full lips curving upwards subtly, as if they're sharing a very private joke.

She turns round, wondering if the look was aimed at someone else.

But no . . . everyone has their phones raised, capturing the moment. Only she is gazing, empty-handed, wondering at the jolt she's just experienced, the kind she's only read about in books.

Did it really happen?

When she turns back, he's hidden from view. All she can see are the backs of the bodyguards leading him and a bewildered Rohan Garvi into the bookshop, keeping them well away from the surging crowd that's now chanting Suraj's name.

Again, Sam feels sorry for Rohan Garvi, having his event so thoroughly overshadowed.

Oh, never mind, he'll sell a lot of books. The publisher must have jumped at the opportunity to have Suraj Sharma attend his friend's book launch.

As Sam is carried along in the swell of the crowd, the back of her neck prickles with unease, every instinct on high alert. She feels uncomfortable. Claustrophobic.

You're just not used to being surrounded by so many people, that's all, especially given your history.

But this physical discomfort, the feeling of nausea, like she's going to be sick? She's only ever experienced that in prison.

She wants to run but she can't, just like she couldn't then, but there it was locks and gates and walls holding her hostage. Here it's people — she's hemmed in from all sides.

She looks around, choking, a silent scream trapped in her throat, trying to get a sense of why she feels this way suddenly — as if there is something, *someone* evil here, someone who wishes her harm.

Her attempt at escape is met by tuts, grumbling, the security guard who is ushering people in repeating in a firm monotone, 'Please keep moving.'

And then, just as she reaches the entrance to the bookshop, she feels it.

A hand at her back, pushing, hard. She stumbles and would have fallen had the lady who stood behind her in the queue not caught her just in time.

'Careful there. It's packed, isn't it?'

She gets a whiff of her rescuer's perfume, something flowery, mixed in with sweat.

And then the dizziness overpowers her and she feels nothing at all.

CHAPTER 5

Now
Blog post — Starry-Eyed Gal
Destination Murder!

I'm a sucker for weddings, especially grand, showy celebrity weddings.

There's something about weddings, isn't there? The beautiful dresses, the matching hats and corsages and flowers in buttonholes, the shiny suits and polished shoes, the hope, the promise of a joyful lifetime together tapping into our childhoods when we dreamed of princes and princesses and grand, romantic gestures and happy-ever-afters.

The union of Sam Reeve and Suraj Sharma had all these fairy-tale elements — it was straight out of a Disney movie, capturing the world's imagination, warming all of our hearts. The ordinary girl and the ultra-rich, super-handsome boy meeting by chance and falling in love . . .

If you're anything like me, when you think *weddings*, you think new beginnings, the start of a glorious future together for the happy couple, of honeymoons and champagne under the stars, of everlasting love.

You do *not* think of death, accidental or — whisper it — *otherwise*...

Yet this is just what happened at the wedding of the decade set to take place at the controversial seven-star Dream Resort in Cornwall.

Now, Dream Resort is no stranger to being in the news for all the wrong reasons.

But this... death at the wedding of the scion, the lone heir of one of the wealthiest families in the world, is on another level altogether.

Detectives (and there has been controversy surrounding this too — over which police force is to conduct the investigation) are 'not ruling out foul play'.

Which means, of course, that this is murder.

Now, as I said, Dream Resort has made the headlines since it was nothing but an idea proposed by the megalo-billionaire and world-renowned businessman who recently made a much talked-about (and much reviled by many, cheered by even more) leap into politics. But since this blog is not about politics, I will not waste my breath naming him — anyway, unless you've been hiding under a very big rock, you'll all know who he is.

When he bought the huge, sweeping, prime track of land (a whopping hundred and fifty acres, no less) overlooking the sea with its own private beach and woodland near Looe, and announced his plans to transform it into an exclusive seven-star resort and wellness centre, there was outrage.

The local community was up in arms. 'We don't want this kind of exclusivity here. Cornwall should be accessible to everyone, from all walks of life. This man is fostering inequality, increasing the gap between the stinking rich and the working classes by building this resort on our beautiful, unspoilt doorstep, and rubbing it in our faces. Not to mention spoiling the natural habitat of thousands of woodland creatures and ruining the landscape.'

Environmentalists and nature lovers decried the cutting down of trees and the desecration of nature and wildlife just so the resort's celebrity guests could enjoy their exclusive 'lodges'.

'Rubbish,' the tycoon protested. 'I have environmentalists on my staff who will be advising me on the best, most sustainable way to build the resort, so the animals and birds whose habitat this is are not endangered. I will plant two trees for every one that is cut down, that's a promise. You can hold me to it. And the resort will be creating jobs for locals — I plan to hire local staff. And what's more, I will put Cornwall's name on the map. My resort will be the best in the world.'

He certainly did that. Dream Resort is mentioned in the same breath as the seven-star hotel in Dubai and all the other exclusive hot spots favoured by mega-celebrities.

Boasting a helicopter pad, several world-class spas, palatial suites with infinity pools and seven-star restaurants serving every cuisine you can think of, the guests' every desire catered to, with a few hundred — yes, you read that right — members of staff on its books, it has boosted the local economy and provided jobs for the locals.

Of course it still has its detractors — people grumble about the posh cars clogging the local roads, the spoiled brats who expect people to kowtow to them on the rare occasions they are chauffeured outside the resort to take in the quaint local vibes . . .

So, all in all, the Dream Resort hasn't been without controversy. In fact it has almost always, since its inception, been in the news for one reason or another — but none has been nearly as controversial as this latest.

I have it on good authority that detectives from London are at the resort interviewing staff and guests, trying to get to the bottom of the tragedy. There's also talk that Interpol and the Indian CID are to be involved. The higher-ups maintain that this job is not one for the local police, who are more used to dealing with minor infractions — rowdy teenagers, shoplifting tourists, missing pensioners who've wandered off in a forgetful doze, unruly pets and the like — which has, without doubt, caused more controversy. But the fact remains that no matter how competent the police force, whether Indian, British, international or indeed local, anyone can be bought — for a price. The Sharmas and their super-rich friends have lawyered up, of course, so whether the truth will out or we will be fed carefully curated, legally advised fiction is another matter.

But rest assured, my dearies, I have a source in the know, and I will make sure to find out as much as I possibly can and report back here.

The news that detectives from London have arrived to investigate the tragedy will, and already has, rubbed some in the local community up the wrong way.

'What's wrong with our own police force? If this had happened to one of the workers at the resort, would they summon someone from London too? No, of course not. I bet they wouldn't bat an eyelid,' says Mrs Lewes, who runs the corner shop in the village, a mile from the resort. 'I get their sort coming in here once in a while. Accompanied by bodyguards.' She gives a loud snort. 'They want to take pictures. They say my shop is charming, "quintessentially" British. They want the local flavour.' She sniffs.

'Do you refuse to serve them?' I ask.

'Of course not, why would I? And if they want to take pictures, they're welcome,' she mumbles, busying herself with something at the counter suddenly requiring all of her attention.

I expect the hefty tip helps too, not to mention the free publicity.

In any case, my lovelies, what a mess, eh?

A new beginning in an idyllic setting has sadly become a very tragic ending. Was it, as the police likely suspect, murder? If so, what's the motive?

This just goes to prove that even the most exclusive settings are not exempt from tragedy — money might cushion you to a great extent, but baser human instinct will nevertheless prevail.

I will attempt to keep you updated — as I said, I have a friend with their ear close to the ground and I will share what I can without getting them in trouble, that's a promise.

Meanwhile, post your comments/thoughts on what's happened.

Let's keep the conversation going.

Until next time, adios. Keep safe, lovelies.

Sending all good vibes.

CHAPTER 6

Six months previously
Sam

'Miss. Miss?'

Sam opens her eyes and thinks she's arrived in heaven.

She's looking into a pair of divine eyes, the hue of molten chocolate, liquid with concern.

She's aware of noise in the periphery, rustles and murmurs, the hum of conversation.

She's lying on a sofa surrounded by men, pacing and talking into radios that boom static and crackle into the room.

A slight man is hovering over her, anxiously pulling at his collar as if it's choking him.

He looks familiar . . .

Ah, the author. Rohan Garvi.

And suddenly it comes to her, where she is and what happened.

She sits up.

Her throat is dry, parched. It's hard to form the words. 'Someone pushed me,' she says.

And the man she thought was an angel sitting next to her smiles. And the smile *is* angelic, bestowed on her like a gift.

'Ah, a rowdy crowd. They always are overexcited, I'm afraid. Speaking of which, I'd better go and meet them.'

He sighs, gets to his feet. 'But please stay here, Miss . . . ?'

'Reeve,' she says. 'Sam Reeve.'

'Miss Reeve, a pleasure to meet you, although I wish it had been in better circumstances.' He says it like he means it, smiling warmly, those chocolate eyes twinkling. 'I would like to take you for a coffee afterwards, to make it up to you.'

And with a smile, Suraj Sharma is gone. Rohan Garvi follows, a tad reluctantly it seems, still pulling nervously at his collar, his eyes darting with longing towards the sofa, where he casts an envious glance at Sam.

She drinks the bottle of water that one of Suraj Sharma's black-clad posse offers. She understands that she's in the storeroom at the back of the bookshop — her kind of room, packed with books, their musty scent of ink and knowledge all but obliterated by the people crowding the small space.

From the main part of the bookshop wafts the wild, ecstatic roar of the crowd as Suraj Sharma appears.

Did she hear him say he was taking her for a coffee after?

* * *

He keeps his word.

After he bids goodbye to Rohan Garvi, who dutifully hands Sam a signed copy of his book, Suraj Sharma ushers Sam out of the bookshop. 'That's one way to get my attention. Fall in a dead faint. Scare us all half to death.'

Colour rushes furiously to her cheeks. She starts to say, 'I didn't mean . . .' and steps out the door, only to stumble backwards, startled by the fusillade of cameras going off in her face.

'Another hazard of being in the public eye, I'm afraid,' Suraj, steadying her, whispers in her ear, the soft caress of his voice raising goosebumps along her arms. 'I should have warned you. This is a side entrance but no entrance or exit is safe from the paparazzi.'

That picture of her — her hair in a knot barely held together by a pencil, sweaty strands framing her bright red, blotchy face, falling backwards into Suraj's arms — will be everywhere.

Later, she finds out that, for the first time, she has trended on social media. It seems some of the sites even broke briefly, because they couldn't cope with the sheer volume of hits they received. All of them were united in their outrage. 'What is *he* doing with *her*?'

Next time you want your hero to take you out, the newspapers and webzines will declare, *faint in the queue, making sure he sees, and stumble when he opens the door for you so he can gather you in his arms!*

Suraj takes her to the best coffee shop in town. His bodyguards have emptied it of patrons for them — a couple of calls as they set off from the bookstore were all it took.

'No paparazzi here. We can relax, finally.' He smiles at her, stretching his arms expansively across the back of the sofa.

'My, it must be so hard to live in the glare of public opinion all the time,' she says.

He beams at her. 'That's it exactly. You have to be on your guard every minute.'

Their coffee arrives, with carrot cake. 'Compliments of the chef, sir,' the barista says, smiling exclusively at Suraj.

'Tuck in,' Suraj tells Sam.

She does. 'This is delicious, the best cake I've eaten,' she says between mouthfuls.

He laughs. 'You're easily pleased.'

'Oh.' She's suddenly, mortifyingly aware that she's nearly finished the cake and Suraj is yet to take a bite. She pushes the plate towards him. 'Here, have the rest, please. I'm sorry, I got carried away.'

'I like it.' He grins. 'All the other girls I've been out with are always on a diet.'

'I should probably go on a diet,' she says, 'but I like food too much.'

'You're perfect,' he replies, eyes bright, glowing in the romantic, dimmed lights.

She blushes, tucking the compliment away to cherish later, even though she suspects he's only being polite, this whole thing an exercise in preserving his image and forestalling a complaint or, God forbid, a lawsuit. She tells herself he's just taking out a fan who thought someone had pushed her at his event (well, Rohan Garvi's) so she won't make a song and dance about it.

Being in close quarters with a celebrity is a surreal experience. Sam enjoys it more than she expected. Away from the public eye, Suraj Sharma is nice. Surprisingly real and easy to talk to. He listens to her, and appears genuinely interested in what she has to say.

She finds out that Suraj has not really read any of Rohan's books. 'I'm not a reader. I prefer watching TV — especially when I'm on,' he says, winking at her.

She laughs, not sure whether he's joking.

And through it all her mind is going haywire. *What am I doing here with this man, instead of at home, curled up on my armchair with a book?*

I must make the most of this, she tells herself, her hand shaking as she picks up her mug. *At least I will have something to tell the regulars tomorrow when they ask me how my weekend went.*

When she gets home, refusing Suraj's offer of a lift, not wanting the mob to know where she lives, she has a warm bath and goes straight to bed, too excited to read.

She falls asleep going over their conversation in her head. It felt so natural, so good.

She wakes up from a nightmare gasping and struggling to breathe, experiencing afresh that sinister feeling, evil and malevolent, the hair at the back of her neck standing to attention, the hand at her back — pushing. Yes, she was definitely pushed. Was it, like Suraj claimed, just one of the rowdy crowd, impatient to get inside?

In the excitement of Suraj taking her out, she forgot the incident that had caused it. She can't get back to sleep, so she switches on the bedside lamp and picks up her signed copy of Rohan Garvi's book, made out to her.

She touches the cover reverently.

Opens it.

To Maisy,
Happy reading,
Best wishes, Rohan Garvi.

The book falls from her hands, which are suddenly slack. Her throat is constricted. She feels strangled. She's short of breath again.

That name. It's a shock, a slap, a shot from the past. She hasn't used it since she came out of prison and started a new life in a new town, with a new persona and a new hair colour to go with her brand new name — although she couldn't help choosing one that had an echo of the old one.

Her old name, the one she was born with, the one that was splashed all over the newspapers.

How does Rohan Garvi know it?

CHAPTER 7

Two days before the wedding
The sister of the bride

In the bridal suite, it is mayhem. A mess of discarded finery and make-up, jewellery scattered everywhere.

'I can't find the brushes. Bloody hell, where are the make-up brushes? I swear I brought a bloody ton. Sam, can you see them anywhere?' cries Georgie, sister of the bride-to-be, through a mouthful of hairpins.

She's feeling the pressure. It's her salon that's going to be advertised, she who's taken responsibility for the bride's make-up and hair.

And she has her work cut out for her. If she'd known Sam would be like this — pale, wan, her skin blotchy and coming out in hives that no amount of slap can fully hide — Georgie wouldn't have volunteered. Sam gets like this when she's stressed. Although they're no longer close, Georgie should have remembered this, her sister's childhood trait that she appears to have carried into adulthood.

What has *she* got to be stressed about? Georgie would like to know.

Everything is taken care of, Sam's billionaire in-laws-to-be throwing money left, right and centre, making the slightest irritation disappear before it has time to become a problem.

But judging from the way her sister is moping, anyone would think it was Sam's funeral rather than her wedding to the love of her bloody life.

Come to think of it, this room, with its haphazard collection of items — Georgie's make-up trolley spilling its contents (but no make-up brushes — where the bloody hell are they?), the bed strewn with the remnants of a hasty lunch, the wedding trousseau: silk saris, cashmere shawls, expensive one-of-a-kind designer outfits, all peppered with (real) pearls and emeralds, rubies and diamonds — looks like a murder scene, and Georgie's sister like death warmed up.

Georgie sighs.

Sam is making no move to help, just sitting in front of the mirror and looking at her reflection with tragic eyes.

Georgie wants to shake some life into her.

Her sister, about to marry the wealthiest man in India, England, perhaps the world, looking for all the world like a wronged heroine facing her untimely demise.

Georgie sighs again, then spies something that looks like a fox's tail under a pile of make-up.

The brushes!

'Found them!' she cries and the hairpins scatter across the floor.

Her sister doesn't move, makes no sound. A wax maiden.

Georgie sighs for the umpteenth time that hour.

They say blood is thicker than water, but right now Georgie could happily murder her sister.

'So, what are you wearing for the Mehendi, then?' Georgie asks. She's trying, God help her, to get her sister's face done for the Mehendi ceremony this evening, which involves henna being applied to the bride's and guests' hands and feet. Georgie has heard that the best henna artist in India is being flown here by helicopter right about now.

Sam is quiet, to all intents deaf as well as miserable.

'I want to do your make-up in a matching style,' Georgie says, trying for patience, taking another gulp of her champagne — room service, everything billed to Sam's in-laws. Oh, but this uber-expensive vintage grog slides down her throat so smoothly. She could very easily get used to this.

Finally Sam speaks. 'My lehenga. Gifted by my in-laws especially for the Mehendi.'

'Ah, all right. Where is it, then?' Georgie looks about the room, wondering where and how they'll find it in this mess.

'Um . . .' Sam looks round, huge bags under her eyes.

Has she not been sleeping? Honestly, if she can't sleep here — goose-down pillows, thousand-count sheets — then where on earth will she?

Sam stands, goes to the wardrobe that takes up one entire side of this huge room. She opens it. More outfits studded with jewels catch the light and shimmer rainbows. Georgie experiences a stab of envy — not her first since they arrived at this resort either.

None of the colours — burnished saffron, iridescent violet, sunset orange, rose-petal scarlet — suit Sam's complexion. They would only serve to make her look more anaemic. Georgie, on the other hand . . .

Sam gasps, jolting Georgie from her daydream.

'Oh.' She turns to Georgie, eyes wide and shocked. Terrified. 'Oh, oh, oh.'

Georgie looks where Sam is looking.

And then she can't help it. She screams, spilling her glass of vintage bubbly. A scream that goes on and on.

CHAPTER 8

Six months previously
Sam

The day after her outing with Suraj and her discovery that Rohan Garvi had signed his new book with her old name, Sam forces herself into work mode.

She opens the shop and goes about her morning routine in a daze: stock-taking, sorting through the plastic bags of donations left outside the shop overnight and arranging the display.

Needless to say, she couldn't sleep after seeing that name.

It was still playing on her mind as she walked to work. She felt stalked every step of the way, jumping at every small thing — a cyclist on the pavement, squirrels rustling in the bushes, even a cat that whizzed across her path, a prickly mass of outraged fur.

Get a grip, she tells herself.

But she can't.

She's shaken.

Does Rohan Garvi know who she used to be?

Don't be silly. He made a mistake. There must have been someone called Maisy and he gave Sam the book he signed for her by mistake.

Sam racked her brain in the wakeful, nightmarish hours of the night trying to recall if he'd signed the copy in front of her. But it was all a blur. She'd been groggy from fainting and dizzy with nerves at the thought of going out with Suraj Sharma. She remembered the author handing her the book after the event, just as they were leaving, Rohan for home and Suraj taking Sam for coffee. She was so flustered that she hadn't opened the book, just thanked Rohan and slipped it into her bag.

He made a mistake, she told herself, over and over. *There's even now someone called Maisy opening a book written out to Sam.*

But try as she might, she couldn't quite convince herself of it.

That name . . .

She tore out the page and burned it — she who always used bookmarks, who thought folding a page to mark a place was desecrating the book.

And there was that push as Sam was entering the bookshop. She *didn't* imagine it. Was it just an impatient fan, or something more sinister?

Does someone know her real identity?

How?

She covered her tracks well.

Or so she thought . . .

She'd thought only Georgie knew the truth about their shared past. She'd wanted to call Georgie the moment she saw her old name in Garvi's new book, but it was too late at night by then.

She waited until 8 a.m., when she knew Georgie opened her salon, and called her.

Her sister did not pick up.

A moment later, Georgie messaged: *I can't talk. On my way to the hospital.*

Is everything all right? Sam messaged back.

Of course it isn't. Do you even have to ask? The pain is bad again.

I'm sorry, Sam replied.

And she was. But it wasn't enough, of course. And then, because she couldn't help it: *Have you told anyone?*

About what?

Our past.

Why would I do that?

That terse message, so very Georgie, made Sam smile despite her panic.

Three wavering dots indicated that Georgie was typing. Then, *Why do you ask?*

No reason. Take care. If I can do anything, please say.

You've done enough.

Sam shivers. Feels eyes on her back.

Only Mr Venables.

She checks the clock.

It's on the dot of ten.

Instead of his usual morose demeanour, Mr Venables is sprightly, regarding her with avid eyes.

'Top of the morning to you, young lady.' Eyebrows raised, mischievous twinkly gaze harking back to his younger days when he must have been quite the catch. 'You've been out and about, painting the town red, I see. And about time, I say.'

Ah, Sam thinks, her face suffusing with a telltale blush. Her outing with Suraj. In all the palaver since, it slipped to the back of her mind. But how does Mr Venables know? Does he have psychic powers?

The answer is much more mundane. Mr Venables spreads out the newspaper tucked under his arm with the panache of a magician conjuring a trick — he always stops off at the newsagent's on the way here. And there Sam is, looking shell-shocked, stumbling into Suraj's arms as he holds the door of the bookshop open for her.

She cringes. Does she really look like that? And what is she doing there, in the paper, for goodness' sake? Surely there's better news to report? God knows, the last thing she wants is to draw attention to herself.

While she stares at the paper, there's the sound of cars pulling up outside.

'Who's that? It's usually quiet this time on a Monday.' Mr Venables is as curious as Sam.

More cars arriving, doors slamming, loud voices, and then faces pressed against the glass of the shop window.

'There she is!'

The door opens and, suddenly, the shop is crowded.

Microphones thrust at her. 'Miss Reeve, how does it feel to be dating one of the most eligible bachelors in the world?'

It's scary, this sudden noise and busyness in the shop. Mr Venables is looking as stunned as Sam herself. The cameras close in, taking shots of her face against the newspaper spread on the counter, open to her two-dimensional image.

She opens her mouth, which is suddenly dry, manages to say, first softly, then louder, so as to be heard above their questions, 'It wasn't a date.'

'Do we have permission to print that?'

'Please. Leave my place of work. And you do not have permission to print anything I say, or the pictures you've just taken.'

She shuts the door and leans against it, closing her eyes. But light flashes against her eyelids — *pop-pop-pop* — as the reporters take pictures of the outside of the shop.

After that it's non-stop. It must be a slow news day. Reporters are laying siege outside the charity shop, chatting to and publishing quotes from starstruck Edie and Edna, twinkling Mr Venables and toffee-nosed Mrs Arbuthnot, since Sam herself won't oblige. She's nonplussed by this interest in her. It was one coffee, a PR exercise, smoothing ruffled feathers on Suraj Sharma's part. Surely it shouldn't warrant this?

But what does she know?

And how on earth did they find out where she worked?

Easily. They're reporters. They dig things up.

She hopes they don't dig too deeply.

She shivers, hugging herself. It's all too much.

Her regulars will not be dissuaded from interacting with the press.

'It's the most exciting thing to happen to us,' Edie giggles, while Edna asks, 'Do you think we look all right for the cameras?'

'Perhaps we should rouge up our cheeks a little more next time,' Edie says.

'There will be no next time,' Sam says firmly, but she's ignored.

'And look even more like common tramps,' Mrs Arbuthnot declares, snorting under her breath.

Edie and Edna glare and stand up to their full height, which barely reaches to Mrs Arbuthnot's severe shoulders, given that her stature is accentuated by heels (a charity shop find that she claims were gifted her by her beloved Gus before he died). 'We heard that. Who do you think you are?'

'I can trace my lineage back to—'

Mrs Arbuthnot stops short when Edie and Edna march off, hand in hand, as summarily as their bad hip (Edna) and dodgy knees (Edie) will allow.

* * *

That evening, following the shock of the reporters arriving at her place of work, and reeling from lack of sleep the previous night, Sam forgets to do her shopping, which she usually does on Sunday but didn't this week because she was going to see Garvi.

And look how that turned out.

She enjoyed her outing with Suraj but for the grief with the paparazzi. How does he deal with it day in and day out?

And there was the matter of the name. Garvi even got the spelling right — Maisy not Maisie . . .

And the push.

Fixating. Again. It was busy. Someone was impatient, that's all.

But the feeling of being watched, the malevolence . . .

All imagined. Not everything is about you.

She takes the back route home, arguing with herself in her mind as she slips out the side door of the shop, through the alleyway and down the backstreets.

As soon as she gets indoors, she has a shower and changes into her PJs. It's that sort of day. She spent the working day waiting for it to end so she could make her escape, although she'd never seen the regulars so excited.

Mr Venables, Mrs Arbuthnot, Edie and Edna have never, in all of Sam's years at the charity shop, agreed on anything, but this they did. 'Good on you, girl.'

'It was fun while it lasted,' she said, thinking that *fun* wasn't exactly correct. *Overwhelming* was more like it.

'How do you know you won't be seeing him again?' Edie asked. 'If he has any sense, he'll keep a tight hold of you.' Edna agreed, and they giggled like ten-year-olds.

'Ha.' Sam laughed. 'I wish.' *If he ever finds out who I am and what I've done, he'll run a mile, if he hasn't already.*

All she wants now is to sit in her armchair with her book, a couple of slices of hot buttered toast and tea.

But she's out of milk.

And so, as she's done a hundred times before, she pulls on a dressing gown, the pink (faded to grey) one with the bunny ears, over her old but comfy PJs with the ducks on them. Mr Gupta's corner shop is just across the road and he serves her with his usual gentle smile whether she's in her pyjamas or the white shirt and black trousers she wears to work.

She opens her door and is assaulted by flashes going off in her face.

She was pretty sure she escaped them when she fled for home — so how on earth did they found out where she lives?

And if they can find this out so quickly, what else will they find?

CHAPTER 9

Sam

Naturally, the picture in the newspapers the next day is extremely unflattering, seeing as she was caught unawares. Sam in her fraying old PJs and dressing gown, looking shocked, skin grey and eyes like a rabbit caught in headlights, the floppy bunny ears very obligingly complementing the look.

Edie and Edna are once again in rare agreement with Mrs Arbuthnot. 'What on earth were you thinking, girl?'

'I wasn't.'

'Exactly.'

That's it. Goodbye, Mr Sharma.

And the thought is something of a relief, even though she liked Suraj. He was surprisingly down to earth given his celebrity.

She enjoyed their time in that coffee shop, emptied summarily just for them.

But all the while — especially when they left the coffee shop and were ambushed by paparazzi once more, when he offered to drop her off home and she refused, not wanting them to find out where she lived (ha!) — she knew this was an interlude.

And thank goodness for that.

And now, with the image of her in PJs and dressing gown in all the newspapers, she's made sure of it. Which is all well and good. She isn't comfortable being in the limelight. Not since . . .

She shudders, thinking of her name (as was) splashed across the newspapers during that dark time.

Don't go there.

But her mind centres on that page in Rohan Garvi's new book, ashes now, made out to 'Maisy'.

A mistake. Stop dwelling on it. It's over. Done and dusted. Forgotten. You can go back to anonymity.

And just as she thinks that, her phone dings with a message. She shivers. *Stop. Don't regress. You've been doing so well.*

She'd been this way just after prison. Afraid of everything. *You've come a long way since then.*

And yet, she hesitates to check her phone, heart thrumming too hard, beating against the prison bars of her ribcage.

Very few people know her number and she wants to keep it that way — although she *did* share it with Suraj. He'd asked for it and she could hardly refuse a mega-billionaire, especially after he'd been so civil. But he's the last person she's expecting to message.

To her surprise — and pleasure — it's her sister.

I saw the photo of you out with Suraj Sharma of all people. What was he doing with you?

Sam smiles. She and her sister are barely in touch, but this is twice in two days. And this message — it is *so* Georgie.

A PR exercise, after I fainted in the bookshop, she texts back.

You haven't changed, Georgie types. *You used to faint at the drop of a hat, always scaring us all.*

Tears prick Sam's eyes. Her sister hasn't forgotten *everything*, then. There's still hope for them, perhaps. Emboldened, she messages, *How did it go at the hospital?*

Georgie comes back immediately with, *I don't want to talk about it.*

I understand, Sam types. *But please tell me, the pain, is it better? Manageable?*

I have learned to live with it. Some days are worse than others.

My fault, Sam thinks, a salty lump in her throat. It hurts, oh how it hurts. Her sister has learned to live with pain. Because of her.

This . . . going out with celebrities, Georgie types. *Is it wise, given — you know. I'm just saying, don't make a habit of it.*

And Sam laughs, salty chuckles. *As if. I don't think there's any danger of Suraj Sharma asking me out again — have you seen the papers this morning?*

She waits but there's no reply. Georgie has said all she's going to say and Sam probably won't hear from her again until Christmas.

And then her phone rings.

She picks it up gratefully, smiling in anticipation of hearing her sister, and is surprised when a male voice says, 'Hello, Sam.'

It takes her a moment to place it. And when she does, all she can say is, 'Oh, hello. I wasn't expecting you to call.'

'Why?' Suraj sounds puzzled. 'I like you.'

Did he just say he likes *me?*

'I thought we had fun,' he's saying.

She finds her voice. 'We did. But . . . have you seen the papers today?'

'Ah!' He chuckles, rich and infectious.

She finds herself smiling.

'I think you look cute.'

'Oh, really,' she says wryly.

'Truly. I love those bunny ears.'

She laughs. 'You're joking.'

'I'm really not. Can I see you this evening?'

She's blindsided. She wasn't expecting this at all.

Say no. It's a bad idea. You saw what Georgie said and you agree with her. You hate the paparazzi intruding into your life. You have secrets you want to hide.

But... this is Suraj Sharma, and he wants to see me! And perhaps she can find out from him why Rohan Garvi signed her book with that name.

That was a simple mistake, an oversight. Stop this now. Say no.

But the truth is, she's flattered. Wowed. She's been living like a monk, suppressing joy, fun. Keeping her head down. Existing from day to day. Not living.

And now he, this super-celebrity, is showing an interest in *her*.

When he took her out for coffee, it was an obligation, but he must have liked *something* about her to want to see her again. It's wonderful, exhilarating. After what happened, she said goodbye to romance, to dating, to going out with people her own age, to fun.

She's sorely tempted.

What harm can there be in seeing him again, just once?

You want to hide, remember, to not draw attention to yourself. What is this you're doing if not just that? What if your secret comes out?

'Sam?' Suraj asks. 'You there?'

His voice, that smile in it. She pushes the sensible guidance of her conscience to the back of her mind, like she did that horrible evening when everything changed and the girl she was before died, and this shell of a person she is today emerged from the ruins. 'Come over,' she says. 'I'll wear the robe with the bunny ears.'

He's still laughing when she clicks off.

But Sam is not laughing. *Oh God, what have I just done?*

CHAPTER 10

One day before the wedding

The scream rends the plush calm, the purring quiet that is a luxury only available to the moneyed few, the VVIP members of the wedding party housed in the most exclusive lodge of the seven-star resort.

The scream is loud, vulgar, shattering the smug silence into a million shards, causing the guests in the lodge to startle awake in indignant, uncomprehending outrage.

Who is making this godawful row, disrupting the rest they have paid so much for?

They expect silence for their money, peace at this time of night. How *dare* it be broken?

It sounds worse than a thousand keening foxes.

And why, for God's sake, is it *still* going on?

They pull off their eye masks, necessary even though the lighting in their rooms is set to 'soothing', a dimness just sufficient to allow for uninterrupted, deep and dreamless slumber.

Those among them who are playing away furtively slip into their own suites and quickly rumple the covers to make the beds look slept in.

The rudely awakened guests stumble shoeless into the luxuriously carpeted corridors, the discreet lighting bathing them in a golden glow, a balm to the senses — fat lot of help it is now, what with the infernal howling assaulting their ears. They're in various stages of undress, scowling and blinking blearily, some mumbling, others shouting. But their voiced discontent does nothing to drown out the scream, which goes on and on.

Where is it coming from?
No! It isn't . . .
It can't be, can it?
But look . . .
Yes, it is . . .
Oh.

The door of the suite in question is wide open, and the sight which greets them . . . Their mouths fall open.

Oh.

How could this happen?
In a place that has the world's best security system.
Supposedly.

For Christ's sake, doesn't exclusivity mean they're cushioned from such . . . *common*, *despicable* crimes, they grumble, forgetting that they, in the course of amassing their millions, haven't shied away from committing similar crimes themselves.

But their money is supposed to allow them to forget this unpalatable fact. They've paid not to have to have it thrust in their faces like this.

This is not on.
There will be complaints.
They deserve better.

CHAPTER 11

Four months previously
Sam

MURDERER! the message screams, all in caps.

Sam recoils.

How do they know?

Then she reads on: *You killed my dreams. I wanted Suraj. How dare you have him?*

And her heartbeat gradually returns to normal.

Suraj and Sam have been on several dates.

Sam still hasn't got used to the paparazzi. She hates being in the limelight.

Everything she does, what she wears, how she looks, is commented on, dissected in cruel, microscopic detail.

'I love how you are shocked by it, how you dislike being in the public eye.' Suraj laughs, kissing her. 'All my previous girlfriends have played up to it, thrilled to be under the spotlight. I love how unassuming you are.'

'I hate it.' She shivers. 'The constant gawking, the comments. Don't they have anything better to do?' And all the time at the back of her mind is the thought: *What if they find out?*

The quiet life that she'd carved out for herself, while it was without any adventure, held no surprises either. Now, she cannot relax.

'Well, you'd better get used to it. It's not going to stop anytime soon.' Suraj's eyes narrow. 'You're not even on social media. It's almost as if you have something to hide.'

The phrase 'her heart stopped beating' had always annoyed her when she read it in books. Come on. How can someone's heart stop beating, for Christ's sake?

But now she understands.

She makes herself meet Suraj's eyes.

He's smiling affectionately at her, but there's a question in his eyes. 'Do you?'

'Of course not, don't be silly.' She holds his gaze.

But she doesn't fool him, for he kisses her nose and says, 'I wonder . . . Well, whatever it is, I'll find out.'

And her heart stops again.

'There's nothing to find out.'

'We'll see about that.'

'You don't believe me?'

'Shouldn't I believe you?'

He's looking at her, assessing her. Why is he being like this all of a sudden?

His phone rings and as he picks up, she remembers to breathe, even as her mind is scrambling to figure out what she should say if he continues this line of conversation.

But when he puts the phone down, he's his usual self, pulling her to him, kissing her, interrogation forgotten.

She's off the hook. For now.

* * *

Georgie hasn't messaged or texted since the photo of Sam's first outing with Suraj appeared in the papers — but Sam hears Georgie's words of caution every time her conscience harangues her, which is nearly every day.

But, she thinks after every date, it will end now, Suraj's honeymoon period, the novelty of dating an 'ordinary' girl. For she's only just beginning to realise the scale of his wealth, and she cannot get her head around it.

He mentioned his 'pad' in Regent's Park, so she googled it to see how far it was from her flat, and her eyes nearly popped out of her head.

'It's worth more than a hundred million pounds!' she whispered.

He shrugged. 'We have four of those.'

'What? In . . . in London?'

'Around the Regent's Park area. Then a few more in and around Mayfair, Hampstead, Knightsbridge. And several around the country, and of course many more abroad. In just about every part of the world.'

And when she just stared at him, speechless, he laughed and kissed her nose. 'How clueless you are! It's so sweet. The girls I've dated before had all these facts at their fingertips. They knew exactly how much I'm worth.'

'I don't want to know,' she whispered, overwhelmed, still unable to comprehend the price of this one 'pad'. And he had more of them, all over the world.

'That's what I love about you,' he said.

So she's waiting for him to get bored so she can go back to being anonymous.

But he asks her out again. And again. Each time, she hesitates, Georgie's warning ringing in her ears: *Is it wise?*

But . . . she likes Suraj. She's flattered that he wants her. With him, she is discovering, once again, a little of the girl she once was, and it's nice.

He is nice.

Despite his upbringing, he's down to earth. Sure, he likes flashy things, the newest model Rolls or Bugatti, the made-to-order clothes, but he also likes to relax in front of the TV on her sagging sofa, eating takeaway and watching mindless sitcoms.

He says it's something he's never experienced before. 'It's eye-opening,' he says, eyes glowing, 'a slice of normal life.'

And it warms her heart, even as she keeps deliberating whether to end it, even as she worries, constantly, that her secret is about to be exposed.

After all, one day soon he'll come to his senses and this will be over. Whatever this is.

The newspapers report that he's a player. They say he's an inveterate womaniser, and hurl questions at her. 'Miss Reeve, don't you mind that he's been seen with other women?'

It's inevitable, to be expected. Women of all ages throw themselves at him. She doesn't know what he sees in her, why he keeps coming back. She tells herself she might as well enjoy it while it lasts.

She's never got used to the paparazzi — impossible — but at least she's learned not to let them upset her. Her secret seems safe — for now.

And now, this message. It's a troll, of course.

Suraj warned her that she would get these. She's not on social media and her phone number is private, so she receives these messages via her work email, which they've somehow got access to.

She also gets letters at the charity shop. Hateful, vile letters accusing her of being a tramp, a slut, of having no shame. And others, like this one, charging her with shattering the writer's dreams, stealing their man. Thankfully none have come to her home address — yet.

The first time she got one of these messages, she was shocked. Hurt. More than a little upset by this vitriol directed at her.

'Don't take it personally,' Suraj said. 'You'll get hate mail too. A hazard of dating me, I'm afraid.'

'Yet another one,' she said and he laughed.

'I hope you don't have any skeletons in your closet,' he said easily.

'Why do you say that?' she asked, trying to hide her fear, aiming for nonchalance and falling short.

He looked at her quizzically. 'Do you?'

'No.' She managed to match his gaze with a steady one of her own, or at least she hoped she did.

He shrugged. 'Well then, there's nothing to worry about. They can't dig up any dirt on you.'

She inhaled deeply.

'And if you do have something you're hiding, tell me now or for ever keep your peace.'

Her breath caught. She looked up at him.

He was scrutinising her.

What did he know? *Did* he know?

Then he smiled.

'I'm joking, Sam. You should see your face.' And he kissed her. Then, pulling away, 'But seriously, is there anything you want to tell me?' He waited, looking deep into her eyes.

She managed to hold his gaze. 'No.' *Liar.*

'Then we're good.'

And the moment passed, her heart settled.

She tried asking him about Rohan Garvi.

'He's based in India. But, like my parents, he summers here and spends the winters in India. He's more my father's friend than mine really. A distant relative, I think. Something like that, anyway.' And, looking curiously at her, 'Why do you ask?'

'He signed my book to someone else.'

'Don't worry about it. I'll ask him for a new copy.'

'No, it's—'

'He does it all the time. He's so absent-minded. He calls me by my father's name. I have no idea how he concentrates enough to write a book.' He laughed, a little unkindly. 'Perhaps that's why he only manages one every few years.'

So there it was. Absent-mindedness on Rohan's part. And yet the niggle remained, a part of her not wholly convinced.

CHAPTER 12

Sam

For their tenth date, Sam insists on taking charge.

'I'm taking you to my favourite place.'

He beams.

'On one condition.'

He raises an eyebrow.

'You have to come in disguise.'

He laughs. Then, when he sees she's serious, he asks, 'Why?'

'I don't want the cameras ruining my favourite place.'

'I'm intrigued. My security detail won't be very pleased though.'

'I'll take good care of you.'

'I'm sure they'll devise a way of protecting me without making themselves obvious.'

'So that's a yes?'

He grins. 'It's a yes.'

She asks him to meet her at the railway station. She gets there the back way, giving the reporters camped in front of her flat the slip. She's even put on a disguise — a wig with a hat, scarf and sunglasses.

It takes her a few moments to recognise Suraj — she only does so when he comes up to her and nudges her. 'Do I pass muster?'

She beams. He's wearing a baseball cap that overshadows his face, cheap sunglasses and a fake beard and moustache.

'What about your security detail?' she asks and he indicates with a nod a couple of tall men loitering in the background. One is apparently absorbed in his phone, the other reading a newspaper, the two of them looking for all the world like ordinary commuters.

'This is fun,' he says, just as the train pulls in.

And it is. The thrill of being incognito, getting one up on the paparazzi.

'Where are we going, then?' he asks.

'Ah, you wait and see,' she says with a smile, fingers crossed, hoping he likes it.

* * *

They're strolling barefoot along the beach, side by side, their feet sinking, wet sand between their toes, ankles tickled by little frothy wavelets. The two rather disgruntled bodyguards are plodding along behind them at a discreet distance — far enough away not to be noticed, near enough to swoop in and save Suraj if the need should arise.

The other beachgoers walk past without a second glance, and it's a novel, refreshing experience not to be pinned by avid gazes, assaulted by cameras and mobile phones.

Sam turns to look at the horizon. 'When I look at the sea and think of the depth, the volume, the endless rhythm of the tides, I feel reassured. It has been here for centuries, through wars, plagues and famines, and will remain long after we are gone. It puts our puny lives with their petty sorrows and tragedies into perspective.'

She came here after she got out of prison. She was flailing then. Her sister wanted nothing to do with her and she felt lost and alone. The sea gave her solace. Every time she was turned down by one of the many jobs she applied for, she came back. Then she found work at the charity shop and stopped coming so often, but the sea remained close to her heart. What is she doing, bringing him here, to her private place?

He stops in his tracks. 'You sound so sad. Is it the loss of your parents? You never talk about them.'

Guilt, shame at her deception, clogs her throat, and she can only nod.

He takes her hand. 'It's all right. I'm here.'

And she's glad of it, though she knows she doesn't deserve it. His sympathy, his love, are all based on a lie.

They eat fish and chips off newspaper, followed by a Mr Whippy each. He offers her his Flake. It's the best day, she thinks, her moment of guilt and sorrow forgotten.

They walk back along the shoreline.

The wind has picked up, whipping her hair into her eyes and dislodging her wig. Sand stings her face. She must look a fright.

A bottle washes up at his feet.

She laughs. 'Ooh, look, it might have a message.'

He beams at her. 'I love your laugh.'

She glows.

He picks up the bottle, makes a face at the seaweedy gunk inside.

'What's the message say, then?'

He gets down on one knee. 'This. Will you marry me, Samantha, my love?'

She is stunned.

Oh Lord, she wasn't expecting this.

'Well? Come on. The sand is ruining my nice custom-made jeans.'

She chuckles shakily. 'I thought you were in disguise.'

'These jeans are made to look battered and worn, but they fit like a dream and cost the absolute earth, I'll have you know. Anyway, why are we talking about my jeans? Well,

Miss Sam, what's it to be? Don't keep a man in suspense like this.'

No! her conscience screams.

It's not wise! Georgie shouts in her head.

But . . . he's still kneeling on the sand, the waves lapping at him, the wind tossing a lock of hair into his eyes. He's smiling up at her, this man who could have anyone in the world but has chosen her.

And that's when she feels it again. A prickle at the back of her neck. The ominous sensation of danger. She wants to run. Escape. It happened in prison, when she was hemmed in by walls and locks, and again on that day at the bookshop when she was surrounded by crowds.

But why here, her happy place, nothing but open space around her? Just the two of them, the security guards a few paces away, on the empty beach.

Seagulls whirl. The salty brine of the air, the grumble and roar of the sea, turn suddenly angry.

Her throat has closed up. She feels claustrophobic. She's choking with . . . fear. The steady thrum of a warning steals her breath.

'Sam?'

Breathe.

She looks into his warm eyes, finds an anchor in their liquid depths, digs up her voice from where it's hiding.

'Yes?' Her hesitation makes it sound like a question, but he doesn't notice.

He laughs, stands up, gathers her into his arms, wheels her around.

'Here.' He bends down, picks up a strand of seaweed and ties it around her finger. 'Proper ring coming soon.'

He kisses her.

Overwhelmed by panic and trepidation, she sways on her feet, and a black cloak descends.

* * *

'Sam? Sam, love.'

She comes to in Suraj's arms.

'S . . . Sorry.'

He chuckles. 'Well, granted I haven't proposed to a woman before, but to have her literally swoon . . . how romantic!'

She laughs, a tad shakily, while the seaweed ring, drying, starts to peel from her finger.

Later that evening, after he's gone home, she finds it in her bag.

Along with sand, and more sand, a flyer advertising a Punch and Judy show next weekend — why on earth does she have that? — oh, and the newspaper the fish and chips came in.

She saved it, a memento of the day he proposed.

It's greasy and smells of vinegar. She smooths it out, turns it round — and drops it as if it has scalded her hands.

TEENAGE GIRL SENTENCED TO PRISON, the headline reads. *Maisy Evans, seventeen* . . .

Her crime, right there, served to her with her fish and chips.

Just a coincidence?

Or something more sinister?

Is that why she felt so claustrophobic? Why she fainted when Suraj proposed?

Is someone doing this on purpose?

If so, who?

And why now, after all this time?

* * *

The diamond Suraj gets her is huge, ostentatious, not Sam's style at all.

She pretends she's pleased. That she loves it.

But whenever she looks at her finger (too small for it, she secretly thinks), she cringes. She much preferred the ring made of seaweed.

She's on high alert all the time, unable to forget that piece of newspaper the fish and chips came in.

It's too much of a coincidence, surely? Why would they have a newspaper several years old?

She's tried and tried to recall who else was there when they were getting their fish and chips, but there were too many people milling about, a queue, the shop doing brisk business.

The shop has been on the pier for years. She's bought fish and chips there in the past, which is why she took Suraj there. Nothing like this has ever happened before, not that she's ever noticed what her fish and chips were served in.

Naturally, she burned the paper, but it's always on her mind — chilling, ominous.

News of her engagement has leaked out. It's all over the news. There is outrage on social media — one of the most eligible bachelors in the world snagged by an absolute nobody.

Her regulars are thrilled for her. Edie and Edna clap with delight and exclaim in awe when they see the ring.

Mr Venables beams. 'Attagirl.'

Mrs Arbuthnot sniffs. 'I had one just like that, you know. Mine was a teeny bit bigger, mind.'

'In her dreams,' Edie and Edna say in unison, just loud enough for Mrs Arbuthnot to hear.

Mrs Arbuthnot pretends she doesn't.

Surprisingly, Edie and Edna are on social media ('It's common,' Mrs Arbuthnot snorts in disgust), and inform Sam delightedly that she's 'trending'. 'Well . . . it's actually your diamond that is.'

Georgie phones. An unexpected side effect of her relationship with Suraj is that she and her sister have communicated more in the last few weeks than in all the years since the incident.

'What are you *doing*?'

'I don't know.'

Georgie is the only person she can be completely honest with.

'Is it wise?' Georgie asks again.

'I don't know.'

'Think long and hard.'

'I've already said yes.'

'Do you want to marry *him* or is it his mo—?'

'It has nothing to do with that. I couldn't care less about his wealth.'

'Ha,' Georgie mocks.

She no longer knows me, Sam thinks. It hurts that her sister, like the rest of the world — with the possible exception of her regulars at the shop — thinks she's nothing but a gold-digger.

'Have you told him?'

She closes her eyes. She knows exactly what Georgie means.

'No.'

'If it gets out, and it will—'

'How? The records are sealed.' But even as she speaks, she wonders if they really are as watertight as all that. She thinks of the newspaper and its headlines announcing the fact of her crime that somehow ended up in her bag. Rohan signing the book to Maisy . . .

That was a mistake. Don't make more of this than it is.

'You think that will deter them? If you think the media are being too intrusive now, wait till the wedding. Some nosy reporter will go digging into your past, and boom! I'm surprised they haven't already f—'

'Don't, Georgie.'

'He won't want to marry you when he finds out.'

'Which is why I haven't told him.'

'Your funeral,' her sister says and cuts the call.

Your funeral. She shivers.

Her head is so full with anxiety about her secret getting out that when her phone pings with a text message from a withheld number, she immediately thinks it's someone who has discovered her secret.

Her number is private and very few people know it. So how did this person discover it?

Stop catastrophising. It's just spam.

Nevertheless, her fingers shake as she opens the message. She's fully expecting it to say something along the lines of, *Maisy, we've found you out.*

So, at first she cannot make sense of it.

Yes, it's a warning, just not the one she was expecting.

How well do you know the man you've pledged to marry? Just who is behind the persona he projects?

She's just finished reading it for the third or fourth time when another text appears, also from a withheld number.

He's keeping secrets from you.

She has never considered the fact that Suraj might be hiding things too.

CHAPTER 13

The day of the wedding
The resort employee

Oh god, oh god, oh god.

What should she do?

Suppose she pretends she was somewhere else. That she didn't enter the room.

Didn't see what she saw.

Didn't hear what she heard.

Didn't do what she did.

Lalita is supposed to be invisible — what was she *thinking*?

She *wasn't* thinking.

How could she have been such a *fool*?

She should have stayed well away. She shouldn't have got herself involved.

But after she heard . . . she couldn't stay away.

And now? How can she stay invisible?

But she *must*.

For the sake of her children in India, whom she hasn't seen for years.

The money she sends puts them through school, so they can get good jobs, so they will grow up to be like the people she works for, not like her, Lalita, cleaning up other people's messes, taking their insults, enduring their indifference, swallowing their slurs.

Diya is running all over the place nowadays, getting in trouble, Ma writes. Her letters take an age to reach Lalita, since her mother has to find someone to post them for her. Diya was a babe in arms when she left.

Raj is now in Standard Three at the English-medium school. The money Lalita sends pays the fees. Lalita wants them to be able to read and write and converse fluently in English.

Raj was just about to start kindergarten at the local missionary free school when Lalita left.

How he held onto Lalita's sari. How he cried! Lalita hadn't told him she was leaving, but young as he was, somehow he guessed.

He sobbed and sobbed and it broke her heart afresh. Seeing him crying, Diya started as well, though, of course, she didn't understand what was happening.

Lalita's husband died young, too young. He was a fisherman and his boat overturned, the cruel sea taking him to itself, leaving his young family with nowhere to turn.

Lalita's in-laws blamed her for his death. They said she was cursed, that she'd brought bad luck upon the family, depriving them of their only son. They cast her out.

Lalita had to support her children somehow. Her ma had only just retired, having spent her whole life working as a maidservant. She was ready to start working again, for Lalita and her grandchildren's sake, despite her bad back and her dodgy knees.

'No,' Lalita said.

Her friend Janaki knew someone who knew someone who, for a sum of money, could smuggle Lalita into England. She was prepared to do anything to support her kids and prevent her mother having to go back to work. Even if it meant working illegally, in a country halfway across the world, separated from everyone she loved, even if it meant not seeing her children until they were grown.

Lalita sold her jewellery — the *mangalsutra* her husband had tied around her neck on their wedding day, a symbol of his marital commitment and cementing her status as a married woman, along with the gold bangles that Ma had slogged her whole life to give Lalita at her wedding. With that money, and some of the blood money from her husband's death, Lalita bought her place here, one of the many illegals working at this world-renowned resort for what the other maids call a pittance. But for Lalita, it's everything.

They give the employees free board (a small closet with bunk beds, three to a room, communal washrooms down the corridor) and food (measly rations that are never enough) in return for toiling fifteen to eighteen hours every day for half the legal minimum wage.

But Lalita will not complain.

The money keeps her children clothed and fed. It sends them to the English-medium school, where they mix with the rich kids, and have the same opportunities as them.

But now this has happened.

Should Lalita go to the police, and lose this chance to support her children?

What's the alternative?

Does she keep quiet for the sake of her children's livelihood, their future, and carry the burden of her guilt for the rest of her life?

CHAPTER 14

One month previously
Sam

Someone is following her, and it's not paparazzi. They've long since given up stalking her when she's at work or out on her own.

She speeds up and the steps behind her do the same — boots thudding on the rain-slicked pavement. A man?

She left work later than usual, having stayed behind to finish up the stock-taking and accounts. Suraj is coming to her place later. They seem to be spending every night together now.

'Want to move in with me?' he asked when he gave her the diamond, their engagement now official.

She was stumped. She hadn't considered this. The panic clutching at her chest told her she wasn't ready.

Will you ever be? her conscience asked. *Especially when you're keeping such a huge thing from him.*

Suraj chuckled. 'The look on your face! Anyone would think I'd asked you to commit murder.'

Her heart thumped. *Why did he say that?*

But he was looking at her with affection. Love.

Stop thinking the worst. If you're so worried about being found out, why not confess?

She swallowed. 'I'd rather continue living here, if you don't mind. It'll make the wedding more special.'

He smiled. 'I don't mind at all. In fact, I think it's wonderful. I love you for it, and for being different from everyone else.'

You'd hate me if you knew why.

She's continued to receive those texts urging her to break up with him, telling her she doesn't really know him. *What are you keeping from me?* she thought.

'I'm also glad for another reason. I've quite grown to like this flat, even if it is smaller than the smallest bedroom in my apartment.'

'Hey, watch it,' she said, smiling sweetly. *Relieved.*

'*You* watch it. I might just move in here with you instead.' And he laughed, pulling her to him.

In fact, that's pretty much what's happened.

And she's got so used to having him around that the flat feels empty without him, which is why, knowing he wouldn't be home until later, she stayed on at the shop. It looks out onto their small high street, the posse of teenagers mucking about by the KFC giving the illusion of company.

She's walking home through the backstreets — the quickest route, as she wants to get home before Suraj. It's dark and chilly. It rained earlier.

She shivers, more to do with the footsteps behind her than the cold.

'What do you want?' She turns around. Nobody. But . . . was that a shadow darting behind the lamp post? The air is misty, the light dim.

She runs. The footsteps run with her.

Her chest closes up with panic. She feels that chill creeping at the back of her neck, the choking sensation stealing the breath from her.

I can't have a panic attack now.
Breathe. Deep breaths.
She slows down.
The steps slow down too.
She turns round. Struggling for breath, she manages, 'Show yourself.'
A hand clamps her arm, a voice hisses in her ear. Breath hot, sour and spicy. Alcohol and chilli. 'You're getting too big for your boots. He won't be able to protect you, you know. No one will.'
The point of a blade tickles like a kiss on her neck.
She's unable to scream.
Unable to breathe.
When he suddenly lets go, she collapses onto the rain-spattered pavement.

* * *

When she finally gets home, Suraj is there, pacing anxiously.
'Sam, what happened? Look at the state of you.'
He gathers her in his arms. 'You weren't answering your phone. I was so worried,' he whispers into her hair.
She can barely speak. She'd lain on the pavement until her breath returned, and then walked home. Heart in her mouth, listening for footsteps . . . that hand, coming out of nowhere, gripping her arm, peppery breath in her ear.
Suraj holds her, whispering soothingly, until she calms down and is able to recount what happened.
He listens quietly, a muscle in his jaw working. Softly, but with a dangerous glint in his eyes, he says, 'My security team will find this person. They'll get what's coming to them.'
'Thank you,' she says.
'Sam,' Suraj says gently, 'don't you think you should stop working now?'
He's repeated this same question a number of times since they got engaged.

'No,' she says again. 'I want to keep working till we are married.'

'I don't understand why you're so attached to it,' he says, his lips thinning with displeasure. He's not used to people contradicting him.

She can't tell him why — that this job was the only thing that got her through the lonely days that followed her release from prison. That it gave her a reason to go on. She's found friends through it. It's given her some semblance of a life.

'All right then, if you insist, but from now on, one of my men will accompany you to work and back,' Suraj says.

She nods, relieved. She's never imagined having a bodyguard, let alone being grateful for it. But after what happened, she'll gladly accept the offer. She doesn't want to go through that again. Prison was bad enough.

* * *

That night she wakes, gasping, from a nightmare.

Suraj holds her, reassures her until she's able to breathe again.

'Are you okay now?'

'Yes,' she lies.

She cannot sleep. In the nightmare, she heard that voice again, felt the hot breath on her neck. Whispering, 'I know what you did.'

Did he really say that? She cannot remember.

She must back out of this wedding. It's the only thing to do. But so much money has been spent, the arrangements have moved ahead, so fast she's in a whirl, carried along in the current. The invitations have been sent, the wedding dress made, the fitting booked.

The wedding is to take place at a seven-star resort in Cornwall. Sam has never been to any place with more than a three-star rating, so this alone will be an experience.

'Suppose we have a destination wedding,' Suraj suggested. 'They're all the rage these days. And I know just the place.'

Overwhelmed by it all, the proposal and the speed of everything that followed, she'd have said yes if he'd suggested they fly to the moon.

How to stop it all now?

Besides, Suraj makes her feel safe.

But . . . those messages. Can she really trust him?

Was the sender just another troll?

How did they get her number?

The texts still arrive with alarming regularity.

Do you know who you're marrying?
He's not as charming as you think.
He's a liar. A cheat. In fact, he's cheating on you right now.

She doesn't know whether there's any truth to the messages. The texts about him cheating on her strike a little too close to the bone — the paparazzi asking, 'Does it worry you that he plays away?'

She doesn't know what he does on the nights when he doesn't stay at her flat. She's not going to ask. He's entitled to his secrets — after all, she has a secret of her own.

And what if he flat out asks her about it? What will she say then?

'I hate people who lie,' Suraj declares. They're discussing politics and politicians. She enjoys their conversations. She hadn't realised how much she missed exchanging views with people her own age.

'Even lying by omission?' she asks, thinking of her own situation.

'Especially that,' he says. 'Why? Is that what you're doing?' He twinkles mischievously at her.

I think we're both lying to each other. You're keeping things from me and I'm keeping something from you.

'Of course not,' she manages, even as her conscience screams, *Tell him! You must tell him before this goes any further.*

'Trust is very important in a relationship, whether political or personal.' He takes her hands in his. 'I trust you implicitly.'

But he notices the colour rising to her face.

'I hope it's not misplaced.'

There's something in his voice — something insinuating — that makes her look up sharply.

But he's smiling tenderly at her.

Tell him, her conscience continues to urge.

She ignores it, returning the smile. 'You can trust me. But the question is, can I trust you, Mr Playboy? The reporters all keep asking me what I have to say about the rumours about you playing away.'

'Ah now, that'd be telling, wouldn't it?' He laughs, dodging her question just as she dodged his.

So here she is, still engaged to Suraj, their wedding day inexorably drawing closer. Her secret, the thing she is keeping from him, hanging over her like a noose, waiting for her to step into it.

Each day that passes, she expects to be found out, and the fairy tale to end.

As the clock ticks, here she is, wedding finalised, venue booked, invites printed, ready to send. No other girl he's dated has ever got this far.

You fool, her conscience chides. *The longer this goes on the harder you'll fall, the more you'll lose. Isn't it better to get it over with now? Is this any way to live, being on high alert all the time?*

'My mother's in England. She's currently staying at our house in Surrey as it's too hot in India. She wants to meet you,' Suraj suddenly declares.

'Oh?' Sam's mind is whirring nineteen to the dozen. Why now? Neither of his parents had seemed inclined to meet her when their engagement was announced, nor even when the wedding date was agreed, the wedding venue booked.

When Sam asked why, Suraj merely shrugged. 'My family's like that. Pa's too busy supposedly working, Ma's too busy beautifying herself.'

Does Suraj's mother know something? Has she found out that 'Sam' is a fake?

CHAPTER 15

Now
The resort employee

'Now, Miss . . .'

'Mrs Anand,' Lalita says, tasting dread and sorrow as she pronounces her long-dead husband's name. She took his first name when she married him, as custom dictated.

What would you think if you knew, Anand? You would never have imagined that your wife would one day be questioned by white policemen in a country thousands of miles from home on the other side of the world, bringing disgrace on your name. Perhaps your parents were right and I am bad luck. I wish you were here to help me, Anand. But of course, if you were alive, I wouldn't be here, in this position. Oh, Anand, what have I done?

It's always the way, she thinks, fear making her teeth chatter. *The rich pay expensive lawyers to shield them from questions. Whereas I . . .*

Lalita has been assigned a lawyer — much good he is. He's sitting beside her, twirling his pen, bored. He nodded at her when he arrived, his gaze elsewhere.

'Sir, I . . . What do I do?' she asked him, out of her mind with terror.

He sighed. 'Just tell them what you know,' and returned to staring at the wall, at the floor, anywhere but at her. They were seated in the cramped, windowless office (the guests have the best of everything, and the management has to make do) that has been allotted to the police for their investigation.

'Mrs Anand,' the older of the two policemen begins. His hard brown eyes have no mercy in them. 'It has come to our attention that you do not have leave to remain in this country, let alone work here.'

'Please. My children depend on me.' She hears herself whining, like the beggars crying for alms at the temple where Ma used to take her to pray for a good husband.

The detective folds his arms, pitiless eyes fastened on hers. 'You tell us the truth, Mrs Anand, and we'll see what we can do.'

CHAPTER 16

One month previously
Sam

They're driving to Surrey to meet Suraj's mother.

'My parents live in England during the summer and spend their winters in India — it's marginally cooler over there then. Not that the weather matters to them — Ma spends her days in an air-conditioned cocoon, my father's never around.' Bitterness seeps into Suraj's voice when he speaks of his father, billionaire Dheeraj Sharma, one of the richest men in the world, the man the media have dubbed 'the Steel King'.

Sam tells herself to expect Suraj's mother, the renowned socialite, and one of the ten most beautiful women in the world, to be cool with her. She's known to be icy and unapproachable. Sam looked her up, and soon realised it was a mistake to have done so. Aru is reputedly as hard as the diamonds she favours. Sam is fascinated and terrified at the thought of the woman who is soon to be her mother-in-law. It will take a lot to impress Aru — she has impossibly high standards, from the clothes and jewels she wears to the products she endorses.

Suraj says, 'You'll get on well with her, she's like you.'

This takes Sam aback. 'Really?'

They're in his Bugatti with the top down, the wind whipping her hair against her face. Lord knows what the perfectly turned-out Aru will think of knotty-haired Sam.

After what happened she no longer drives and she's an anxious passenger. Whenever possible she avoids travelling by car. Combined with her apprehension at the prospect of meeting Aru, she's an absolute wreck.

'Yes, you're both up front, nothing to hide,' Suraj is saying.

Nothing to hide . . . She cringes. In her lap, her hands curl into fists.

'What you see is what you get,' he adds.

Is he kidding? But no, he sounds sincere.

Tell him, her conscience screams.

His mother is expecting me. I can't tell him now.

Then when? At the altar?

'Will your father be there?' she asks. 'At the wedding?'

Suraj makes a face. 'He's *never* there. I'll be very surprised if he makes it.' He laughs, a short, sharp, mirthless bark.

She guesses he's masking the hurt he feels at the lack of interest his father shows in his only son.

'Supposedly, he's always working. But the newspapers tell a different story. I feel sorry for my mother.'

She touches his arm. 'I'm sorry. I feel for you.'

He pulls it away sharply. 'Don't. I'm fine.'

He's silent for the rest of the journey.

They never mention his father again.

***

The drive leading to Suraj's parents' palatial Jacobean mansion seems endless. The magnificent house towers above the immaculately maintained grounds with their sweeping manicured lawns. The sheer size of it is overwhelming.

On the steps leading up to an impressive front door, an actual butler is waiting to gravely usher them inside.

Following him through the hall, Sam has an impression of chandeliers, antiques, plush carpets and priceless paintings, impossibly high, carved and frescoed ceilings, majestically curving staircases leading to the upper floors and vast, echoing space. An atmosphere of hushed reverence prevails. Suddenly, Aru is there before them, cool and impeccable. An ice goddess as imposing as her house, she's at one with her surroundings.

Until she met Suraj, Sam is ashamed to admit that she thought of all South Asians as being small, cuddly and warm, an impression formed out of Indian restaurants and Mr Gupta at the shop across the road from her flat. Once, in another life, Sam had visited an Indian friend's home. This friend had a big family, full of women who bustled around always cooking, eating and laughing, talking non-stop as they introduced Sam to such delicacies as samosas and jalebis, chaat and tandoori chicken, biryani and chicken mughlai, and tarka dhal and salmon tikka. So much food. Such rotund, jolly people.

Suraj's mother is as far from that family as it is possible to get. Tall and thin and elegant, she gazes down upon her visitor. There is no welcoming smile. Aru inclines her head, cold eyes taking in the messed-up hair, the inappropriate clothes. Sam half raises her hand to shake Aru's but then drops it. Something in Aru's bearing says, *Stay away. Look, but don't touch.* Like the precious, expensive collectibles in her home, she seems delicate and brittle, as if at the merest touch she might break into a thousand glittering shards.

Sam agonised over what to wear for this meeting, and now she can see it's all wrong.

Suraj was no help. He just smiled. 'Oh, anything will do. She's easy-going, my ma.'

When Sam pressed, he grew impatient. 'Oh, I don't know. A dress or a smart top with a skirt. Trousers will also do nicely. Anything, really. Don't fuss.'

The way Suraj spoke of his mother made Sam think that perhaps Aru's reputation for being remote and inaccessible was assumed for the public gaze, and that in private she was like Mrs Joshi, Deepika's mum.

Along with everyone else, Sam stopped seeing her friend Deepika after what happened. She misses Mrs Joshi, and the way she always plied her with food. 'Are you not eating?' Mrs Joshi would cluck. 'You need fattening up, my girl.'

'I can get you something to wear if you like,' Suraj said.

'Oh no. I'm fine,' Sam replied.

She refuses to accept the gifts Suraj offers, not wanting to take advantage of his wealth before they're married. *If they marry.*

She insists on splitting the bill whenever they go out, which makes him laugh, but he lets her. It eats into her savings (Suraj only ever goes to the best places) and it hurts to see them dwindling before her eyes, the years of frugal living resulting in a nice little nest egg spent on fine dining that always leaves her hungry.

And what if there is no marriage? What if Suraj finds out her secret and breaks off their engagement?

She'd be left with nothing — all those years of hard work, for what?

It doesn't matter. At least I'll have had the experience, enjoyed something other than my quiet life. It's worth it for that. I can always make more money working in the shop if it all goes pear-shaped.

If you even have a job, her conscience counters. *When it all comes out, do you think anyone will trust you? Who will want to give you a job, the woman who deceived a multi-billionaire, lied to him?*

She shushes her inner counsel, unable to bear the thought of what might happen, how this is going to end.

Then why do it at all? When you know it will be nothing but a disaster and no savings to show for it either? This is exactly like before, when you jumped headlong into actions you'll regret for the rest of your life.

Stop! she pleads. *Just stop.*

'You never wear anything I give you, anyway,' Suraj said, an edge to his voice.

The clothes he'd presented her with, thrust on her so she had to accept them, never fit properly. They were either too tight or too loose, emphasising all the bits of her that she didn't want emphasised.

The first time he gave her a dress, it was a size eight, whereas she was a size twelve on a good day.

She debated whether to tell him, but when she saw the price tag, she decided she had to. It made her feel faint. *That much for a dress!* 'Could you see if you can exchange or return it?'

He laughed. 'All my previous girlfriends have been a size eight or less. Give it to someone. Or sell it in your shop.'

She tried (and failed) not to feel inadequate.

The next time he bought her something — a kaftan — it was a size sixteen.

'I'm a size twelve,' she said stiffly. Why did he keep getting her clothes the wrong size? What was he implying?

It's a simple oversight. You're insecure, that's all. Let it go.

But she couldn't. She held it up against herself. 'This makes me look like a tent.'

'Doesn't everyone above a size ten?' he asked.

His response shocked her. 'What are you saying?'

His phone rang and he walked away. 'I need to take this.'

She blinked back the tears that stung her eyes. *He didn't mean it*, she told herself. She'd misunderstood. If he didn't find size twelve women attractive, what was he doing with her? He could be brusque, she reminded herself, but he was also kind. She loved him. Why else subject herself to all this? Why go ahead with the wedding when she risked being found out and exposed?

That morning's text message rang in her head — she still gets them every day without fail. *He's not who you think he is.*

After trying on her entire wardrobe and discarding most of it, Sam settled on a pair of trousers she'd got in a Zara sale and an understated yet elegant designer top she'd bought herself in the charity shop. At least she's comfortable in them.

It was the exact wrong thing to wear.

Suraj's beautiful ice sculpture of a mother is in a flowing white dress, looking more like a new bride than Sam herself.

Suraj breezily makes the introductions, before squeezing Sam's arm. 'Right, I'll let you two get to know each other, then.'

And off he disappears into the depths of this great palace of a house, blithely unaware of Sam's silent plea: *Don't leave me alone with her!*

The next twenty minutes or so, until Suraj returns, are among the most excruciating of Sam's life.

Without a word, Aru sits down regally on a straight-backed chair that looks like an antique and waves Sam to the seat opposite.

She crosses her legs, steeples her fingers and regards Sam coolly.

It feels like Suraj's mother is minutely examining each hair on her head, appraising her features, taking stock of her figure. Her fleshy thighs. The clothes that don't suit the occasion, the top that Sam is sure Aru knows is pre-loved. The high-street trousers digging into the protruding belly — she's been so nervous about this meeting that she's been eating non-stop these last two days, resulting in a food baby. Whenever she's stressed or anxious, Sam turns to food for comfort.

Aru's gaze lingers on the engagement ring. Ostentatious and loud, it's the most expensive thing Sam is wearing. It jars. It isn't her style. She dresses to blend in with her surroundings, not to stand out.

So what on earth is she doing with Suraj? She hasn't the faintest idea.

What she does know is that this woman in front of her is thinking the exact same thing.

She can read Aru's thoughts as clearly as if she's speaking them aloud: *What is this girl, ordinary in every way, doing with my Eton- and Oxbridge-educated, film-star-handsome son?*

Yet even as Sam squirms under Aru's scrutiny, she also feels *seen*, as if Aru's gaze has pierced her disappointing exterior and has pared her down to her truest self. Under that gaze, all her flaws are laid bare, along with everything she's hiding — including her terrible, explosive secret.

And, weirdly, it's freeing.

A bevy of staff arrive with tea on a silver service, complete with matching tea cosy and elaborately patterned china that wouldn't have looked out of place at Buckingham palace. Sam fancies it might even cost more than the royal tea service.

Her once-upon-a-time friend Deepika's ma would boil tea leaves on the hob, with cardamom pods and cinnamon bark and chunky knobs of ginger and vast amounts of sugar and milk, all mixed together.

It was thick and sweet, like drinking pudding. Sam would sometimes find cardamom leaves or a sliver of ginger in it. Mrs Joshi would serve it with homemade samosas. 'I made them less spicy, just for you,' she beamed the first time Sam tried them. Even so, first Sam's ears and then her whole face turned red.

'You still find it spicy,' Mrs Joshi clucked. 'Here, have a gulab jamun. That will help.'

She thrust the syrupy golden-red globule at Sam, dripping nectar, which exploded into gooey sweetness in her mouth. And, as promised, it did help ease the fiery zing of chilli, brilliantly so.

Aru (or her maid) has provided a selection of different teas — black or green, Darjeeling, Ceylon, Lapsang Souchong, Moroccan mint, Mulberry, Jasmine, Earl Grey and countless other exotic varieties to choose from.

Another maid wheels a four-tier stand towards them, bearing a vast array of sandwiches, miniature cakes, puddings and quiches, scones and vol au vents. Another tray holds cream, jam, milk, squares of butter and brown and white sugar.

Aru waves the help away. 'Which tea would you like?' She raises an eyebrow, cold eyes boring into Sam's like flint. Her voice is clipped, cultured.

Sam clears her dry throat. 'Lapsang Souchong, please.' She's always liked the name, so she might as well try it.

With a regal nod, Aru pours the tea, and Sam feels disproportionately pleased that she's chosen the same tea as her hostess.

'Help yourself to milk and sugar. Or honey, if you prefer.' Her accent is cut-glass British, with only the merest hint of another tongue, which adds a slight softness to her otherwise icy tone.

Sam notes that Aru is drinking hers black, no sugar. She briefly considers following suit but she needs a bit of sweetness to take the edge off this cold lady and her vast house — heated to just the right temperature, but which nevertheless makes her shiver.

Almost defiantly, she helps herself to two cubes of white sugar, and if her hand trembles a little, sending the spoon clattering against the china and causing Aru to shut her eyes briefly, well, that's just too bad.

She takes a sip of her tea and looks up at Aru, sees she is watching her.

There's something in her eyes . . .

It's gone before Sam can quite take it in. A spark of animation. A brief glimpse of something other than impassive frostiness.

Does she know?

'Sandwich? Cake?' Aru asks.

'No, thank you.' She doesn't think she can possibly eat anything while this woman is examining her every move.

Ten minutes of silence follows, punctured only by the delicate chink of porcelain and the indelicate scrutiny.

At last Suraj arrives, breaking the silence, filling it with bonhomie. He plants a kiss on his mother's cheek. 'I'm sure you two got on brilliantly. See you soon, Ma.'

Sam exhales in abject relief. 'It was lovely to meet you,' she gushes.

Aru lifts her left eyebrow just a fraction, as if to say, *Oh really?*

Does Aru have a sense of humour?

Sam is still nonplussed when she steps outside the mansion, breathing in huge gulps of fresh air. It's nippy, but this cold has never felt more welcome.

* * *

'She's wonderful, isn't she, my ma?' Suraj says on the drive back.

'Yes,' Sam lies.

She's anything but. The whole experience was excruciating, and very, very strange.

Suraj beams. 'I knew you would get along splendidly.'

She looks at him, driving his Bugatti as carelessly as if it was a battered old Ford, his hair ruffling in the breeze. She wonders if he's playing some game with her. She's pretty sure his mother was.

Why can't she ask him? Why can't she speak freely with him? Is this how their married life is going to be — if they get married, that is — with her keeping things from him, and, if the texts she receives daily are to be believed, he from her? Some game.

He *appears* genuine. His smile is so warm.

Did he really not see it? Did he not pick up on how unfriendly his mother was towards his fiancée? Didn't he sense the atmosphere in the room, so icy it could freeze water?

She doesn't get this man. And she doesn't get his family either. Absent father, cold mother and — deliberately? — obtuse son. He's so caring at times and so utterly thoughtless at others.

Not that your family is much better. A sister who doesn't want anything to do with you. Parents who—

She shivers, hugging her coat to her, hair whipping around her face, getting into her mouth. It smells of doubt, tastes of that palatial house, frosty and unwelcoming, without a trace of warmth despite the heating. Even the chilly outdoors is an improvement.

What is Sam marrying into?

CHAPTER 17

Now
The resort employee

In her mouth, the taste of dread, a bitter cocktail of fear and shame. Closing her eyes, Lalita sees the sharp outline of the grey cliffs where the ruthless wind batters the trees and sends the waves crashing against the rocks below. A lone seagull hovers above, its harsh cry a premonition, a warning of what is to come.

Lalita shivers, hugging herself.

'Let's start at the beginning, shall we?' the detective says, hard eyes regarding her. No sympathy there.

Beside Lalita, her lawyer drops his pen and stoops to pick it up, squirms in his chair.

'You were assigned to clean the suites of the wedding party. You must have seen *something*. Tell me, Mrs Anand, did you notice anything out of the ordinary in the days leading up to the crime?'

Lalita clears her throat. 'Well, there were the notes.'

Her lawyer sits up straighter.

The younger detective's eyes shine with curiosity.

The detective asking the questions, however, remains impassive. She cannot guess his thoughts. 'Notes?'

'The bride.' Lalita pictures Sam's face, her eyes wide, fearful. 'She was receiving threatening notes.'

CHAPTER 18

Two weeks previously
Sam

When the postcard arrives she's ready, or so Sam thinks.

After all, this is what she's been waiting for — the hammer to fall. Someone to connect the dots.

She hears the letterbox rattle and collects the post from the mat.

Thinking nothing of it, she switches on the kettle and absently flicks through the mail.

Bill. Flyer. Bill. Final demand for payment.

Suraj has offered time and again to pay her bills, but she always refuses. She'll pay her own way, at least until they're married.

Yet another bill. Bank statement. *Hey ho.* She tosses each one aside as she fetches her mug, puts the teabag in.

Her heart stops. *What's this?*
A postcard?
A picture of the town where ...
No. It can't be.
Another weird coincidence. That's all.

Be still, my heart.
It's okay. It's all right.

She looks at the postmark. The card was posted there too, in the town she's tried so hard to forget. This is no coincidence. Someone knows exactly what they're doing.

The diamond on her finger catches the light, glints at her, mocking.

Wait. It's all right. It's just a postcard. What harm can that do?

She thought she was ready.

But she isn't, of course.

Her heart beating in her throat, her hands clumsy, shaking, she turns the postcard over and nearly drops it.

She reads the five words printed on it in bold. Letters the vivid crimson of a fresh wound.

I KNOW WHAT YOU DID.

The postcard falls from her hand.

She thought she'd covered her tracks.

She thought nobody other than Georgie knew who she really was.

But ever since Rohan Garvi signed her book with her old name, she's been uneasy.

For the thousandth time, that was a mistake.

But why *that* name?

And the fish and chip newspaper with details of her crime . . .

And that man who followed her, and held a knife to her throat. Did he really whisper, 'I know what you did'?

He didn't. You dreamed it.

At least since the bodyguard started accompanying her to work, she hasn't been followed. But Suraj's security detail haven't been able to find whoever it was — and not for want of trying. He's covered his tracks well.

The thought of him being at large is terrifying.

And now this.

Could it be Georgie?

Oh, come on. They might not be close, but Georgie is her sister. She has her best interests at heart. Doesn't she?

What am I thinking? Sam chides herself. *Of course it isn't Georgie. She'd just tell me what she thought, straight out. Georgie doesn't play games.*

And in any case, why now?

No, this is someone else. Someone who knows the terrible act she perpetrated.

The act nobody knows about.

But it seems somebody does. And they're going to be her undoing.

She hears Georgie's words again. *If it gets out, and it will... Some nosy reporter will go digging into your past, and boom!*

Fool. Thinking she could date someone so high-profile and get away with it.

Oh God. Oh dear Lord. Sam feels a panic attack coming on — she had plenty of those after it happened.

Breathe.

This is worse than the social media trolling, the hateful emails and the letters sent to the charity shop. This is personal. This gets to the heart of the matter. The postcard showing the town where it happened, even posted from there. *I know what you did.* It seems that they do.

But who? Is it Aru? She recalls that awkward encounter, the strange look in the woman's eyes as they drank their tea. The feeling she had then that Aru knew. But if so, wouldn't she just tell Suraj?

She was convicted while still a juvenile, so her record is sealed. But she started her sentence just as she turned eighteen and so the newspapers had free rein. Perhaps that's how this person found out?

But she and Georgie changed their names, the colour and style of their hair. Their clothes. They look nothing like the girls they were before. They moved away, made new lives for themselves. Maybe it was naive of her, but Sam believed that all trace of the person she once was was gone for ever.

It bound Sam and her sister together, but those bonds stifled whatever love they'd had for each other. Georgie might hate her for what she did — Sam hated herself for it — but Georgie wouldn't tell. Never. In any case, she asked Georgie about it when she discovered that Rohan Garvi had signed his book to Maisy, and her sister said she hadn't told a soul.

Nevertheless, she picks up the phone and calls her.

Her sister's phone rings out, and she's asked to leave a message after the tone. 'Um . . .' Sam begins, but loses steam.

She cuts the call, thinks what to say and rings again.

Her sister picks up. 'What is it?'

So Georgie had seen her name and hadn't wanted to answer, until she called again. Now she's brusque, impatient.

It hurts that it has come to this, her sister avoiding having to speak to her, and when they do speak, nothing is said.

But today, before she loses courage, Sam gets straight to the point. 'Have you told anyone?'

'Told anyone what?'

'You know,' Sam says. 'About . . . our past.'

A long silence. Sam bites her nails, paces the room.

'Of course not,' Georgie snaps. 'This is the second time you've asked me that recently, and the answer's still no. Do you think I *want* it to come out? To be subjected to all that abuse and vitriol all over again?'

Sam hurts afresh for Georgie, for what she's had to endure because of her. In prison, Sam was insulted, slurred and worse, but she deserved it. Georgie didn't. She was forced to bear the brunt of it alone, until they both took on new identities and started new lives.

No wonder her sister doesn't want to talk to her.

No, Georgie hasn't told anyone.

A dark cloud of dread settles over her. If not Georgie, then who? How does the sender of this postcard know?

'Why are you asking?' Georgie asks. 'Has something happened?'

'No,' Sam says, too fast.

'Sam, what aren't you telling me?'

'Nothing. It's all okay. Bye now.'

'Wait, Sa—'

She cuts the call, unable to speak, even though, more than anything, she wants to tell her sister.

Deep breaths.
And again.

When she gets her breath back, Sam considers what to do next.

She has two choices, and neither of them appeal.

All this is happening because she's marrying Suraj — the most eligible bachelor in the world.

So, she tells him what she did, or—

No. She cannot tell him.

Then there's only one thing for it.

Her heart aches, but she hardens it. It's the only course of action left.

In her heart of hearts, she's always known it. She just allowed herself to be swept up in the fantasy. She let down her guard, gave herself permission to dream, as if she were just like anyone else, even though she isn't. Why not, though, if nobody knew?

But someone does.

So, before they tell Suraj, she must act.

Since she hasn't the courage to tell him outright, her only other option is to call off the wedding.

She'll go back to being Sam Nobody. After that, if her secret comes out, that's all right — she alone will suffer the consequences. She'll make sure Georgie isn't involved. When they were assuming their new identities, they selected different names — Georgie's suggestion. It had hurt Sam at the time — she saw it as a severing of ties, a refusal to be associated with her — but now she's glad of it. Sam will change her name again and start over, somewhere new, preferably on the other side of the world.

If she'd been brave enough to tell Suraj, he'd have called off the wedding anyway, so she might as well get in there first.

She switches on the gas, holds the postcard to the flame, watches the edges curl until it burns her fingers.

It's for the best.

CHAPTER 19

Now
The resort employee

'Did Ms Reeve know who was sending the notes?' the flint-eyed detective asks.

Lalita gulps. 'I don't know, sir.'

This is a lie, and she's sure the detective knows it. 'You tell us the truth, Mrs Anand, and we'll see what we can do about the fact that you've been breaking the law and staying in the country illegally.'

'I don't know anything, sir.'

'Is "I don't know" all you have to say, Mrs Anand?' the detective snaps. 'At this rate, we'll not be able to arrive at an agreement regarding your papers or lack thereof. You know what that means, don't you?'

Next to her, the lawyer clears his throat but says nothing.

'Please, sir,' Lalita begs, tasting salt. 'My children.'

'Someone died, Mrs Anand. Do you understand that?'

'Yes, sir.'

'Well then, please help us get to the bottom of this. So far you've told us that the bride was receiving threatening notes.

Was there anything else you noticed in the lead-up to the crime? Anything suspicious?'

'Well, there was the incident on the day of the Mehendi . . .'

CHAPTER 20

Two weeks previously
Sam

'My mother wants to see you again,' Suraj announces.

'What?' Sam is surprised. Stunned actually. Is this because Aru knows who she is and wants to confront her?

Sam has spent the entire time since the postcard arrived readying herself for the moment when she would call off the wedding. Now, she's so taken aback by this that she forgets her resolve. 'I thought she hated me.'

Suraj looks quizzically at her, eyebrows raised. He smiles. 'Well, let's just say you're a bit different from the other women I've taken home to meet my mother.'

'You bet I am,' she quips. 'I'm unique.'

Now's the time to tell him the wedding's off, her conscience advises.

'That you are.' Suraj gathers her in his arms and kisses her. 'And in any case, since I've chosen you to be my wife, my ma probably wants to get to know you better.'

What are you doing? her inner voice shouts. *Pull away. Tell him it's over.*

Too late. He has taken her hand and is leading her to the bed . . .

All right, she tells her conscience. *Just one last time.*

You're crazy.

When it's over, they lie side by side, gazing up at the ceiling.

Tell him now.

The plaster is cracked and bubbling. The ceiling needs painting, she thinks. Look at those cobwebs.

Stop procrastinating.

She takes a deep breath. 'Suraj,' she says, the ceiling beginning to blur before her eyes. The diamond on her finger glints accusingly. She takes the ring off. 'It's over. I'm so sorry. I'm calling off the wedding.'

Silence.

She waits.

And waits.

She turns her head, cautiously.

He's fast asleep, snoring gently.

She kisses his cheek, puts the ring back on and lays her head on his chest.

I'll tell him tomorrow.

CHAPTER 21

One week previously
Sam

They're watching TV. There's an item on the news about prison reform.

Staring at the screen, Sam feels claustrophobic. She needs air.

Tell him now.

She opens her mouth.

'I don't believe in reforming prisoners,' he says.

'You don't?' Her voice is too shrill.

'No, I don't. Criminals don't change. Whatever they may say, inside they're the same as they always were. They should be hanged, the lot of them.'

She cannot speak.

'Where are you going?'

'I need the loo.' Blinded by tears, she makes her way to the toilet.

She closes the lid and sits down heavily, grappling with her conscience. She's in there so long he knocks on the door.

'Sam? Are you all right?'

'I ate something that didn't agree with me.'

'Oh, poor you. D'you need anything?'

'No, I'm okay, thanks.'

Tell him now, her conscience urges, and this time it prevails.

But when she finally emerges, he brings her tea, puts her to bed and tucks her in. How kind he is.

And it's so nice. Nobody has fussed over her like this since it all happened.

You are a fool! her conscience cries.

* * *

They're on their way to see Suraj's mum.

Suraj is beaming. 'This is the first time she's asked to meet one of my girlfriends again. Though you're not just any girlfriend, are you? You'll soon be my wife.'

Tell him that you're not going to be his wife.

Since that terrible postcard, she's received a couple more notes. *I know what you did. And soon the world will know too.*

Is Suraj's mum sending them? But it's not her style, Sam thinks. Aru would be straight, not furtive like this. In any case, if it *is* her, Sam will know soon enough.

She *must* end it before Suraj finds out from someone else, before everyone knows what she did. She hasn't been sleeping. She's been comfort-eating. She looks terrible. The threats have been taking their toll.

Now is the time, her conscience nags.

Sam takes a breath, but she can't get the words out.

What's wrong with you? her conscience chides.

Images of the notes rise before her eyes: *I KNOW WHAT YOU DID*, in bold letters the colour of fresh blood.

She swallows, fighting back nausea.

'Are you okay?' Suraj says.

She smiles. 'Yes, fine.'

He beams at her, swings the car round a corner too fast. She grips the seat.

'She'll love you in that dress,' he says.

It's too tight, her breasts and stomach straining against the fabric. And the colour!

But she had to wear the thing. Suraj had given it to her the previous day. *'It's for tomorrow, it's my ma's favourite colour.'*

It's bright yellow, making her look sallow and washed out.

'Maybe you should cut down on dessert until the wedding,' Suraj says with a grin.

She's too dispirited to think up a retort.

He kisses her, pinching her stomach. 'Never mind. I love you just as you are.'

But she's self-conscious, awkward in the uncomfortable dress.

She won't even think about what they're saying on social media — paparazzi ambushed them as they were coming out of her flat.

Anyway, Edie and Edna keep her informed, so she hears whether she wants to or not. Their handle on social media is @TheMissesCrump. 'Since you started dating Suraj, our following is through the roof, thanks to all the interviews we've been giving on your behalf!' they told her delightedly.

Mrs Arbuthnot snorted in disgust. 'Social media! At their age! Common, that's what it is.'

Sam checks her phone, and sure enough there's a text from them. *Nice dress, my dear. But not quite your style, is it? And not your colour either, we're sorry to say.*

It's Edie and Edna's way of tactfully telling her that her dress has caused quite a storm on social media, and not a good one.

She's invited Edie, Edna and the other shop regulars — her only friends — to the wedding, but they've all said no. This is surprising, especially since they've all, in their different ways, basked in the limelight, more than willing to speak to the press when Sam herself has refused. She thought Mrs Arbuthnot, at least, would want to be there, to mingle with 'her kind', as Sam put it when she asked.

Mrs Arbuthnot shook her head. 'Oh no, dear. They're not my kind. They're new money. Cheap and vulgar.'

Nevertheless, she thought they'd enjoy the chance of a free couple of days at the world-famous resort in Cornwall where Suraj had decided to hold the wedding. He'd booked the entire resort, all several hundred acres of it, for their exclusive use.

But her friends weren't to be tempted. 'Sorry, dear. My knees,' Edie said.

'My hip,' Edna added.

'But you'll be driven there in a limo. And you won't have to lift a finger while you're there, you'll be waited on hand and foot. You'll want for nothing, I promise.'

Both averted their eyes. 'Sorry, dear, we would have loved to, but . . .'

She got the same response from Mrs Arbuthnot and Mr Venables. She finds it disheartening. Her only friends, and they refuse to come to her wedding.

Suraj shrugged when she told him. 'It happens. They're jealous, that's what it is.'

'Not my friends. They're happy for me.'

Although, having said that, Sam couldn't help but notice that their enthusiasm for the forthcoming marriage had cooled somewhat of late.

Suraj snorted. 'If they were happy for you, they'd want to celebrate with you, wouldn't they?'

Seeing her face fall, he drew her close. 'Sorry, babe. Anyway, who needs friends when you have me?'

She smiled, while inside she felt like crying. But, she consoled herself, at least Georgie will be there. Her sister had replied to Sam's invitation with a terse 'Yes.' It was enough. Sam had resolved to try harder with her sister when they met, use the wedding as an opportunity to bridge the distance between them.

After the notes started arriving and Sam decided to call the whole thing off, she thought it a good thing her friends had said no. Perhaps they sensed something — they're all very wise, each in their own way.

They were so enthusiastic about the wedding when she first got engaged. But recently, especially since she gave them the invitations, they haven't seemed so keen.

'Are you sure you want to go ahead, dear?' they ask. 'Don't be swept away by his wealth and celebrity. Do what you think best. After all, it's your future that's at stake.'

Why are they saying that? Do they sense her doubts?

'How well do you know him, dear?' they query.

Which is exactly what the daily texts from that withheld number repeat. Surely, her friends aren't sending them?

'It's just that it seems to be happening very quickly, that's all,' they say thoughtfully, and smile gently at her. 'We know it's not about the money in your case, dear. You're a good person. We hope he knows how lucky he is.'

Oh, my friends. If only you knew what I'm hiding. You wouldn't think I'm so good then.

Was the dress that bad? she texts Edie and Edna. *It was a gift from Suraj. I felt I should wear it.*

There's a long pause. Sam sees the three dots, which means that Edie — who professes to have better eyesight — is typing. She pictures Edna peering over her shoulder and adding her two pennies' worth.

Sam smiles. Now Edie will be getting annoyed, and she'll ask Edna to stop.

'But you spelt "their" wrong,' Edna will say.

'That correcting thing will take care of that,' Edie will tut.

'But it hasn't — look.'

'Listen, I'm the one typing.'

'I would if you let me—'

'Oh, sure. And your messages would be so littered with spelling errors that even the auto-whatsit wouldn't be able to help.'

Sam smiles again. No wonder the message is taking so long.

'What are you grinning at?' Suraj asks.

'Nothing.'

'Nothing?' He raises an eyebrow playfully.

'Edie and Edna are trying to message me and I'm imagining them arguing with each other.'

'Oh, them.' Suraj's lip curls. 'Your so-called friends who won't even come to your wedding.'

'They can't. Edie's got sore knees, and Edna's hip—'

'You're making excuses for them.'

'I—'

'Give me your phone.'

'Why?'

'Forget about your friends. Let's enjoy today.'

'But . . .' Edie is still texting, the three dots still on her screen.

'No buts.' He beams at her. Suddenly, he reaches out and snatches the phone from her hand.

Shocked, she can do nothing but watch him type, one hand on the wheel.

'Suraj, what are you *doing*? That's dangerous. And anyway, you can't answer my messages for me — I didn't give you my permission to do such a thing.'

'You're to be my wife, I don't need your permission,' he says, still typing.

'Yes, you do.' Her voice is shrill. She's very close to tears. Angry tears. How *dare* he?

She's about to say, *We're not getting married, I don't want to!* when their car swerves into the opposite lane. A lorry is heading straight for them.

'Suraj! Look out!'

With seconds to spare, he manages to avoid hitting the oncoming lorry, which blasts its horn.

Her heart still pounding, she scrabbles for the phone, which has fallen under her seat.

Fuck off, Suraj has typed. *If you won't attend my wedding, I want nothing to do with you.*

Her heart sinks, then she's racked with anger. The three dots have disappeared. Edie and Edna have gone.

'Why did you do that?' Her voice is trembling with fury.

'Chill, babe,' Suraj says, his flippant tone making her even more furious. 'It was a joke.'

'You call snatching *my* phone, sending *that* message to *my* friends a *joke*?'

He laughs.

She realises that, as far as he's concerned, it *is* a joke. She's sick with rage.

'Why are you so het up?' he says. 'In any case, we're here.' The gates of his parents' mansion swing open and they wind their way up the endless drive, through the lush, manicured gardens.

How could she have thought they were compatible, she and this man? A man who treats people and their emotions like toys to be played with.

'You had no right.' It's all she can manage, although she wants to say more. Far, far more.

'I'm soon to be your husband, I have every right. And what I said is true. They're supposed to be your friends, but they won't even come to your wedding.'

'That's not the point. And they're still my friends. Whether or not they attend my wedding, that doesn't change.' She's so angry with him that she's shaking. As always happens when she's overcome by emotion, tears catch her unawares, stealing the words as she tastes salt on her lips.

She'll have to sort things out with Edie and Edna later, text them to say it was a mistake. They'll understand and forgive her. But can she forgive Suraj? When he took her phone, he crossed a line.

She's never seen this side of him before, and she doesn't like it — no, she *hates* it. How dare he treat her like a possession, invade her personal space and her privacy in this way, whether they are to be married or — most likely now — not.

I'll get this meeting with his mother over and call off the wedding, she thinks, lurching forward as he pulls up with a screech of brakes. At the front door, the butler is waiting to conduct them inside.

I hate him right now. I hate, hate, hate him.

'At least you're loyal, and that's a good thing,' Suraj says patronisingly, taking her arm.

Every part of her wants to flinch away from his touch, but the butler is holding the door open for them, so all she can do is grit her teeth and endure it.

'Don't you see, my love? You're too good for those people, your supposed friends.'

She opens her mouth to retort, but his mother is coming towards them, offering her cheek to be kissed.

'What's this about friends?' she says to Suraj.

'Her friends, Ma. They're time-servers. I'm trying to make her see it.'

Aru doesn't reply. Her cold gaze runs over Sam, taking in the too-tight dress, the bulging stomach, the pinched flesh.

She's wearing a flowing kaftan in a green that brings out the hazel orange glints in her lovely, frosty eyes.

Sam waits for her to say something cutting, but . . . what is this?

A miracle has occurred. Suraj's mother is smiling at Sam.

The surprise of it causes all Sam's anger to evaporate.

CHAPTER 22

Sam

'We'll sit in the library. It has a view of the garden. I've instructed Maria to serve us tea in there,' Aru calls over her shoulder, expecting Sam to follow. 'Suraj, are you joining us?'

Behind her wafts the delicate scent of roses and jasmine, a tropical bower on a summer's evening. Aru is light on her feet, swaying gently like a dancer.

Sam feels gauche and uncoordinated as she trudges in her wake.

'No, Ma,' Suraj says. 'I'll let you girls chat. I'll be in the study. I need to catch up on a few things.'

Just as well. Sam can't bear the sight of Suraj right now.

This time around, Aru is marginally warmer.

She doesn't know who I really am, what I've done. She's not the note writer.

'Did Suraj give you that dress?' Aru asks as soon as they're seated.

'Yes,' Sam says, aware of the fabric straining now she's sitting down.

'My son doesn't have the best taste in clothes,' Aru says dryly.

103

Sam is resisting the urge to pull the dress down over her knees. By now it has ridden up almost to the top of her thighs. 'It doesn't suit me, I know.'

'I didn't say that.' Aru raises an eyebrow.

'But you implied it.' If she's going to break up with Suraj, she might as well be honest with this woman. After all, she'll never see her again.

Both of Aru's eyebrows shoot up. 'You have a big chip on your shoulder.'

Sam shrugs. 'Well, it's my shoulder.'

The eyebrows are still raised, but the lips quirk upward. 'Do you like the ring he gave you?'

I've burned my bridges now anyway, so I might as well tell her the truth. Sam swallows. 'To be perfectly honest, no.' Voicing what's been on her mind since Suraj slipped the ring on her finger is liberating. 'It's not to my taste at all.'

This time, Aru really smiles at her. 'You *are* honest. It makes a refreshing change from the others.'

'Have there been many others?' Sam asks.

'Yes. He changes them like women change dresses. So it came as a surprise when he proposed to you. Why you, I wonder?' She regards Sam quizzically.

'I was hoping you'd be able to tell me that.'

Aru shrugs. 'I have no idea. But I know why you said yes.'

'You think it's his money, I suppose.'

'Obviously.'

All her anger at Suraj resurfaces, ambushing her afresh. How dare he? How dare this woman? What right do they have?

She gets to her feet. 'Just because you're rich doesn't mean you can insult people, you ought to show more respect.'

'Sit down. There's no need for—'

'Don't patronise me.'

'All right then, if it isn't money, you tell me. Why *are* you marrying my son?' Her tone is calm. 'I'm genuinely curious. Surely you must see what it's like. Every single person we encounter fawns over us because of our wealth, tells us what we want to hear. What else was I to assume?' Aru is matter-of-fact.

Placated, Sam nods. 'Okay, I can see why you'd think that. But, I . . . I genuinely like your son. At least, I . . .'

'Go on,' his mother says.

'Well, he behaved badly just now in the car. He snatched my phone out of my hand and sent a rude text to my friends.'

'Ah.'

Maria arrives with the tea. 'Please,' Aru says, 'will you take tea with me?'

Despite herself, Sam is touched by her almost humble tone. She nods in assent.

'Lapsang Souchong?' Aru asks, and Sam is surprised and pleased that she remembers.

'Help yourself to milk and sugar.'

Sam eschews the milk but stirs in two cubes of sugar.

Aru regards her over the rim of her cup. 'So . . . what's next?'

Sam thinks of Suraj, his passionate kisses, the way he falls asleep on her bed and gently snores, which he denies vehemently. The way he cuddles with her on her sofa watching reruns of *Friends*, asking her which character most resembles him. The personality quizzes they do together, the jokes they share.

Her conscience prods at her. *Careful. You're breaking up with him right after this meeting.*

He was heavy-handed because he doesn't know any different. He's always had his own way, always had people bending over backwards to do his bidding.

Stop making excuses for him.

'I . . .' She hesitates. How to answer?

'I think you should break up with him.'

'Pardon?'

Suraj's mother is starting to sound like her conscience.

I'm damned if I'll do it just because you say so, she thinks, looking directly at the woman sitting regally opposite her, sipping tea from a cup that probably cost more than the contents of

Sam's entire flat. *I'll do what I want*, she thinks, recalling how Suraj reaches for her in his sleep, how anxious he looks if he doesn't find her, his face settling back into a restful smile when he feels her spooning him.

To hell with whoever's sending me those notes. I will not be cowed into ending it.

Pushed into a corner, Sam finds that the girl she was is still there. The girl who stood firm, until a single impulsive act sent her scurrying away from life and she began doing the safe thing, careful of every move.

Not anymore.

Now she sends a silent challenge to the note writer. *Come for me. I'm ready.*

'Thanks for your advice,' she tells Aru. 'I'll bear it in mind.'

CHAPTER 23

Aru

When Sam and Suraj have left, Aru sits alone in the vast library, staring unseeing at the floor-to-ceiling bookshelves, at the expensive first editions. Never read, they gather no dust, thanks to the attentions of the battalion of helpers who care nothing for the wealth of knowledge the expensive leather bindings contain.

Her hand tightens around her cup, so hard that it shatters, shards of porcelain digging into her palms, drawing blood. Her maids dance around her, fussing over the wounds with horrified exclamations.

She waves them away like so many flies.

I messed up.

She goes to her room and orders the shades to be drawn. She lies down in the dark.

You handled that wrong, didn't you? How could you have been so stupid?

The cuts on her hands sting, and she berates herself, while in her head, she hears the familiar laugh. Mocking, sneering at her. *You klutz. Useless bitch. When will you learn? You can't do anything right.*

You can take the girl out of the street but you can never take the street out of the girl. A mere stone can never be a diamond, no matter how hard you polish.

CHAPTER 24

Now
The resort employee

'So, from what you're telling us, I gather there were several unusual occurrences in the lead-up to the wedding.'

'Yes, sir,' Lalita says.

'But you have no idea who was behind them?'

'No, sir,' she lies.

But the detective isn't fooled. He sees right through her. 'All right, Mrs Anand. Here's what I'd like to know. What were you doing at the crime scene?'

CHAPTER 25

One week previously
Sam

Sam and Suraj drive away from the house, Sam having decided, thanks to Aru's high-handedness, not to call off the wedding after all. She will not be scared off by the threatening notes, or warned off by Suraj's mother.

Nevertheless, it didn't put right what Suraj had done, and she says so. A huge row ensues.

'I know you're used to getting your own way all the time, but that doesn't mean you have the right to take *my* phone and insult *my* friends.'

Suraj says nothing.

There is a long silence after she finishes venting her anger. 'Well? Don't you have anything to say?'

'I'll crash at mine tonight. I've stuff to be getting on with.'

It's only as she's putting the kettle on in her empty flat — quiet without him, suddenly lonely — that she realises he hasn't apologised.

Why aren't you calling it off? her conscience screams while she sits on the sofa with her tea — good old Typhoo from

Mr Gupta's, no Lapsang nonsense for her. She misses Suraj. The TV is off, and the empty space beside her feels vast. How is it that, despite being so angry with him, she still wants to marry him? She'd been content with her life before he came swanning in and turned it around. She'd been happy to blend into the background, happy that her only acquaintances were older people, that she didn't go on dates and shied away from men. Her life had settled into a comfortable groove — running the charity shop, coming home and immersing herself in a book. Now she's lonely without him.

So, basically you're bringing trouble down on your head, marrying him just to escape loneliness. Ha! Have you forgotten that you chose this life precisely because you wanted to be left alone after prison? Well, don't say you weren't warned.

She debates whether to message Edie and Edna, but leaves it, deciding the apology is better made face to face.

As soon as they enter the shop — she was terrified that they wouldn't come at all — she reaches out to them and takes their hands in hers.

'I'm so sorry. I don't know what came over me. I'm nervous about the wedding, but that's no excuse. I understand that you can't come to the wedding, and honestly, regardless of what I said in that horrid text message, I don't hold it against you. I'm so very sorry. Please forgive me.'

They're gracious. Both gather her in their thin, birdlike arms, and tell her she has nothing to worry about.

'If you think you can get rid of us that easily, my dear, you'd better think again,' they cluck.

'Forget about the message, dear. We all have our off days,' Edie says.

Edna looks closely at Sam. 'Are you sure it was *you* who sent it, dear?'

'Yes.' She looks down at her scuffed trainers, unable to meet their kind gazes.

'It's just that you don't usually swear,' Edie says.

'Never, in fact,' Edna adds.

'I was anxious about meeting Suraj's mother and I took it out on you,' Sam mutters.

'All right, dear.'

Sam can see they aren't convinced.

Edie says gently, 'My dear, if you're not sure about it, or you're having second thoughts, it's not too late to back out, you know.'

They've all, each in their individual way, told her the same thing recently.

Mrs Arbuthnot was first. 'I wouldn't trust anyone with that amount of money, dear. Tread carefully, now. Don't go ahead with it if you're in doubt.'

Mr Venables sidled up to her. 'I know what my Maud would have advised. She would have told you to ask yourself if you're happy, if you feel comfortable about taking the plunge.'

'If there's even a tiny niggle at the back of your head, you shouldn't go ahead,' Edna said.

What do they know? What are her friends trying to tell her?

And now, Suraj. 'I believe in absolute honesty in a couple.'

That's rich, coming from him. There has to be some truth in the daily texts this person with the withheld number, who has somehow got hold of hers, is sending.

They're in bed, having just made love.

'It's the most important thing in a relationship, don't you agree?' The light from the street lamp that insists on piercing the slightest gap in her curtains streaks Suraj's face, making his eyes glitter. 'Without trust, there's nothing.'

Why does he keep harping on about this?

She's been running her fingers over his body, tracing love messages. She pauses, nonplussed. Is this a threat? What does he know?

'Carry on, it was nice. Why have you stopped?' he asks.

She does as he asks, hoping he doesn't notice the tremor in her hands.

'That's what I love about you,' he says.

'Hmmm?'

'You're honest. Upfront. I can trust you.'

He doesn't know.

But she thinks of the texts that keep coming. Her friends at the shop.

All of them asking the same thing. *How well do you really know him?*

Suraj keeps asking her to give up working.

When she says no, he's displeased.

He can be controlling. He sulks if he doesn't get his way.

He has secrets too. Is all this talk about trust and honesty intended to cover them up?

But how can she ask him what he's keeping from her when she won't come clean about what she's hiding from him?

He turns his head towards her, his dark eyes boring into hers as if to dredge the truth from her.

She manages to meet his gaze without flinching. Not a peep out of her conscience — it's given up, left her to it.

Is this what their marriage is going to be like, each keeping secrets from the other, their relationship built on a foundation of lies?

She hears Georgie's voice. *Your funeral.*

Sam shivers beneath the covers.

What she's hiding sits like a leaden weight in her stomach. Georgie knows. The note writer knows.

Suraj must *not* know. At all costs.

PART TWO

CHAPTER 26

Three days before the wedding
The sister of the bride

Suraj's car — and what a car it is too, a chauffeur-driven limousine, the real deal — pulls up outside the door of Georgie's block of flats. She's ready and waiting. So are all the neighbours, from the looks of it, a group of them outside the building, others at their windows, having a good old nose.

There's barely enough space for the limousine, what with the gawpers and the paparazzi. Where did they spring from all of a sudden? It doesn't help that it's bin collection day either, but the driver manages it, just, the sleek car as out of place here as a wolf cub among a litter of kittens.

Clutching her (knock-off) Prada bag, Georgie steps outside and is immediately dazzled by the flash of the cameras. This is how celebrities must feel. Thank goodness she did her face extra carefully. But then she always does. Running a hair and make-up business — which she started from scratch, and is rightly very proud of — she knows she's her own best advertisement.

Georgie will look good in the photographs, even when she's taken unawares, as now. Unlike her sister, who should be used to it by now but who still appears caught out, stunned, gobsmacked by the attention.

When will she learn? Even though she's been with Suraj for months now, her sister still doesn't wear make-up. Why not? She used to.

Georgie remembers how, as teenagers, they would do each other's faces, taking hours over it, never venturing outside until they were satisfied with their looks. They both looked like horrors, to tell the truth — they've come a long way since then. Now Georgie has learned to apply it tastefully, while Sam doesn't bother with it at all.

Georgie would understand it if her sister could get away with it, if she had chiselled cheekbones and full lips. But Sam has thin lips that cry out for liner and lipstick, and an almost sallow complexion that begs for a touch of colour. She has a round face that just looks chubby whenever she puts on weight. She always was a stress eater.

She's piled on the pounds recently, although why, when she's bagged the most eligible bachelor on earth, Georgie has no idea. Georgie will have her work cut out preparing her for the wedding. It'll be a brilliant advertisement for her business, what with all the movers and shakers who'll be there.

This is Georgie's chance, her opportunity to shine. The only problem is the poor material she has to work with. Sam's hair, for a start. Hair that hasn't been cut in God knows how long — how is she to make something from it that will launch her into the big time?

She takes a deep breath and smiles for the cameras. God knows where they've materialised from, thrusting their microphones at her. She would swear the street was empty five minutes ago. Now it's chock-a-block, and — oh dear — the bin lorry has just turned up.

Georgie keeps her cool, beaming at the cameras, making sure to give them her good side. She pats her sleek, glossy mane — one of the girls at the salon did it for her yesterday. Yes, it's in place, highlighting her firm jawline, which, even if she says so herself, is one of her best features.

'How do you feel about your sister marrying the most sought-after bachelor in the world?'

'Are you looking forward to being the bridesmaid?'

And then a question that jolts Georgie from her complacency. It comes from someone nearby, so close that she can feel the speaker's breath on her cheek.

'What does it feel like to have your sister marrying him, when it should be you?'

Georgie swings around, startled.

But the cameras are flashing, blinding her, and she cannot see the speaker.

Georgie keeps smiling, her jaws aching with the effort.

The chauffeur, who has been waiting patiently, opens the car door for her. The bin lorry is honking loudly, its path blocked by the limousine.

Georgie is about to step inside when she hears the voice again, smooth as velvet in her ear. 'I know what you did.'

She dives into the limo.

CHAPTER 27

The sister of the bride

It's Georgie's first time in a limo, and this is not your average one, either. You wouldn't find kids riding to their proms in this. This one is sleek. This one has seats that fold themselves around your body. It has champagne.

Suraj Sharma is charming and affable, radiating that special charisma that only movie stars and celebrities project. He places a hand on Georgie's knee and offers her a glass of bubbly — a Dom Pérignon, no less.

'Pleased to meet you, Georgie. I'm so glad you're joining us,' Suraj says.

Georgie basks in the radiance of his smile, her racing heart slowing to its normal pace.

Carefully, the chauffeur navigates the car out of her street, between bin lorries, paparazzi vans and huddles of gawpers.

Georgie has been so looking forward to this, but any pleasure she might have had in the ride has gone, taken by the voice whispering in her ear, *I know what you did.*

As she fell into the car, Georgie tried to catch a glimpse of the owner of that voice. It had been so close she'd felt their breath on her neck, yet she couldn't tell if the speaker was a man or a woman.

I know what you did.

And — just as the door closed — a warning. *And soon the world will know too.*

Georgie takes a sip of her champagne but she hardly tastes it.

Before she knows it, her glass is empty and her attentive host takes the bottle from the bucket of ice and tops it up, right to the brim.

'Caviar?' he asks, handing her a platter.

Georgie suppresses a shudder. 'No, thanks.'

She hasn't eaten since yesterday afternoon — the outfit she's chosen to wear today, an off-the-shoulder chiffon jumpsuit, is just the right mix of casual and chic, perfect for journeying to the resort, but just a little too snug. She tells herself she'll be drunk if she doesn't take it slow. She should eat something to soak up the booze, but right now all she wants is alcohol to calm her fear.

'Are you okay, Georgie?'

Georgie starts. She hadn't even noticed her sister, who isn't exactly small — she's always struggled with her weight, even as a teen.

Georgie's sister looks worn out. There are dark circles under her eyes, as if she hasn't slept. Given that she's about to be married to the most eligible bachelor in the world she should be glowing, looking a million dollars — *Listen to me*, Georgie thinks. *I'm even thinking like a tabloid.*

Sam is holding a glass of champagne, but from the looks of it she hasn't touched it, while Georgie is on her third glass now. A bit of nervousness is understandable, but this . . .

Sam is worried it will all come out.

And, now, Georgie is too.

I know what you did.

'Yes,' Georgie snaps. 'I'm fine.' Sam always provokes this reaction in her. It's that hangdog look she wears, Spaniel eyes, large with worry, always eager to please.

This is all Sam's fault. If it wasn't for this stupid wedding, they'd have been all right. Nobody would be digging into their past. Georgie's secret would be safe.

Sam looks hurt. She bites her lower lip, like she used to as a child.

Georgie doesn't want to look at her, or at Suraj, who is watching them speculatively. What is he thinking?

She leans her head back against the plush upholstery and closes her eyes.

She's jittery, all over the place, unable to relax despite the champagne. Despite the fact that she's travelling in a luxury limo with one of the richest men in the world. She's been counting the days to this moment. Now it's all spoiled. She opens her eyes and catches Suraj watching her, and forces herself to smile. Meanwhile, her eyes are stinging, her legs shaking.

To give herself something to do, she scrolls through her social media.

The photos are up already. For a change it's Georgie who's trending and not her sister: #bridesmaid #sisterofthebride.

#sisterofthebride. How demeaning. She's Georgie, self-made, successful businesswoman, founder of a thriving hair and beauty enterprise. She's made the most of this wedding, blogging endlessly about her plans for the bride's hair and make-up, and has no doubt that she'll soon be make-up artist to the stars. She'll be a household name, booked up years in advance. She'll launch her own range of cosmetics, a wellness brand. She's a firm believer in positive thinking. After all, hasn't she built her business from nothing?

But now she can't seem to think straight, can't get that ominous whisper out of her head.

Ah, the pictures. Those will comfort her at least.

But far from helping, they make Georgie's heart sink further.

The photo trending on social media shows Georgie looking startled, mouth open. Caught at the very moment she'd turned to look for the person who'd whispered in her ear.

She's wearing that 'deer caught in headlights' look, poised to run, rather than just poised.

Georgie would rather die than admit that she and Sam look anything like each other, but no one seeing that picture could deny they're sisters.

CHAPTER 28

Now
The resort employee

'I'd like to know what you were doing at the crime scene,' the lead detective says.

'I . . . My cleaning trolley. I went to retrieve it.' Lalita cannot seem to raise her voice above a small, trembly whisper.

He grunts. 'It would seem that, illegal or not, the management is lucky to have such an employee as you, willing to go to such lengths, as far as the cliff edge even, just to find a cleaning trolley.'

'Sir?'

'Sarcasm, Mrs Anand. Never mind. Tell me this, if you will. Why was blood matching that of the victim found in the bed in one of the suites you were assigned to clean?'

CHAPTER 29

Three days before the wedding
The bride-to-be

Georgie intercepts Sam on the way to the loo. Well, 'loo' doesn't quite describe the suite of luxurious rooms, comprising a washroom with sinks and a sofa, a shower and, finally, the actual toilet stall, twice the size of the bathroom in Sam's flat. And all this in the Sharma family's private jet! No matter how much time Sam spends with Suraj, the extent of his wealth never fails to amaze her.

For Christ's sake, who needs a suite of rooms just to go to the lavatory, private jet or not?

It looks like Sam does, for when she comes out of the loo, Georgie is there, waiting for her, pacing up and down in the washroom.

She looks agitated. She can barely stand — she drank too much in the limo on an empty stomach, and it went straight to her head. She's always been this way, forgetting to eat when she's drinking. This sudden reminder of the past makes Sam feel immeasurably sad. They're so distant from each other now.

'We need to talk,' Georgie hisses, or rather slurs, staggering and nearly falling as the jet takes a plunge. Batting away Sam's outstretched hand, she slumps onto the sofa.

'What's happened?' Sam asks. Her sister spent the entire journey in the limo ignoring her, refusing to even look at her.

'You tell me.' Georgie glares at Sam.

'Um . . .'

Georgie tuts impatiently. 'Has anyone contacted you, saying they know about what you did?'

Her words send a shiver through Sam. She checks the door to make sure it's locked. It is. Trying to appear calm, she plonks herself down next to her sister — glad now of the huge private bathroom. She takes a breath, clears her dry throat. 'Why do you ask that?' When it comes, her voice is only a little shaky.

'Because you called me out of the blue asking if I'd told anyone.' Georgie scrunches up her face as if she's trying to rid herself of a bad memory. She used to do that as a child when she had nightmares, and despite everything that's going on, how scared Sam is, her heart aches with love for her sister. 'Someone came up to me just as I was getting into the limo. They said they knew what you'd done.'

'Oh.' Sam chokes. She can't breathe. Head between her knees, she gasps, counts down slowly. Breathe. Breathe.

'They said that soon the world will know,' Georgie is saying. 'You know me, I don't scare easily, but that—' she shudders — 'was scary.'

'Did you see who—' Sam manages.

'No. There was such a crowd.'

Sam realises now why Georgie was drinking glass after glass of champagne in the limo, downing it like water.

Georgie grasps Sam's arm, her manicured nails piercing the flesh. Her breath is sour from the drink. 'It's your mess, you deal with it. I'm tired of keeping your secret.'

Sam is on her way to her wedding in a world-renowned seven-star resort. She should be happy. Instead, she's terrified.

'If you hadn't decided to marry him, this wouldn't have happened,' George is saying.

Her sister is right.

Where is the resolve she found, to go ahead with the wedding despite the ominous warnings in the postcard and those notes?

Georgie is the only person from the bride's side to attend the wedding.

And even she is no longer on my side.

Georgie and Sam aren't close, but Sam always believed that if push came to shove, she would be able to rely on her sister.

It seems she was wrong.

And her determination to marry Suraj, and to hell with the note sender, has disappeared. Now she's certain of nothing.

All she feels is fear. Blinded, she cannot see a way forward.

'Sort it out,' Georgie hisses. Unsteadily, she gets to her feet and sways to the door.

She fumbles with the lock, and when she finally opens it, she recoils, staggering back against Sam.

Standing in the doorway is Aru, one hand raised as if to knock. If she heard what they said, her expression doesn't show it.

Having been conveyed to the heliport in a limo even sleeker than theirs, they had found Suraj's mother waiting for them. She'd led the way into the plane, where they were plied with more champagne — which Sam refused — and canapés, which she'd eaten with relish.

Suraj had nodded towards his mother, who'd taken a seat across the aisle some distance from them. 'I did offer to pick her up, but she said she didn't want to be crowded.'

Sam had repressed a smile at this. Crowded? *There was so much space in that car that Georgie didn't even see me when she got in.*

His father would be joining them later, according to Suraj.

'Just before the ceremony most likely — if he makes it at all, that is. Probably some business deal will prevent him attending his only son's wedding,' Suraj had said bitterly.

Seeing his hurt, Sam had softened towards him, like she always does in the end.

Her feelings towards him swing back and forth between anger — when he gives her clothes that don't fit, when he comments on her weight — and tenderness — when he does something nice, like washing the dishes (a novelty for him). And especially when he talks about his father.

Her emotions are on a roller-coaster. What a relief it would be to call the whole thing off and sink back into anonymity, safe from the threats.

And yet. And yet he's cruel because he's been given everything except love. She can give him that. They're both broken, both hiding secrets, perhaps they can heal each other...

Georgie says, 'Oh, hello there,' and stumbles past Aru.

Aru recoils ever so slightly and raises an eyebrow.

How much did she overhear?

CHAPTER 30

The mother of the groom

Those two are up to something.

Aru is watching the sisters, observing the way they interact. There's obviously no parents on the scene, so you would think they'd be close, thick as thieves. They're certainly acting like thieves, yet they don't seem to be close.

Aru notices the way Georgie throws her arm around her sister when she's introduced to Aru. She sees Sam flinch, covering it up with a smile that is less than convincing.

She follows them to the washroom, where they've been closeted for the past ten minutes, whispering furiously.

She tries the door and finds it locked, confirming her suspicions.

With a quick glance at Suraj, who is fast asleep, she listens at the door.

She can't hear much of their conversation — just enough to know that something is definitely up. Sam, for a start, looks nothing like a blushing bride. In fact, she looks terrible.

She catches Aru's eye and flushes guiltily.

Who is this woman her son is marrying?

She's hiding something, but what?

Aru intends to make it her business to find out.

CHAPTER 31

The resort employee

There's excitement in the resort like never before.

Everyone here is infected with it, from the cleaning staff to the management.

The cleaning staff have been busier than ever — cleaning, scrubbing, polishing, until every room is pristine.

They've hosted VVIP guests here before, of course — it's the only sort they get. But these guests are something special. For a start, they've booked the entire resort, something that never happens. And as the date of their arrival draws closer, everyone is on tenterhooks.

'Remember, these are not just any guests,' they're told, yet again. 'If they're happy, our resort will go from being "one of the best in the world" to "the very best". They could have chosen anywhere in the world to hold this wedding, but they're coming here. Let's give them an experience they'll never forget.'

Lalita can't help feeling excited too — like a little child in anticipation of their birthday. With a pang, she thinks of her little boy, how his eyes would widen as his father neared home.

Her husband always stopped off at Duja's shack on the way home — not, like the other men, to buy the arrack Duja sold illicitly at the back entrance, but for the boiled sweets or the plastic tubes of frozen sugar water that his 'legal' business comprised.

When his father was due home, Lalita's son would be out in the courtyard, peering anxiously down the lane, and when he spotted him approaching through the paddy fields, he would yell, 'Baba!' and run to him, throwing himself into his father's arms.

His father would lift him up and twirl him round and around. Lalita would laugh at the sight of them, feeling their little girl dance inside her belly.

'Stop, Baba, stop!' Their boy would laugh so much he was almost in tears. 'Did you get me anything?'

And her husband would set their son down and hit his forehead with the palm of his hand. 'Oh, I forgot. What a silly Baba I am. Will you forgive me?'

Their son's face would fall but he would nod, tucking his small soft hand in his father's callused one.

'Oh, wait. What's this?' Lalita's husband would exclaim, patting his lungi. Just as father and son reached the washing line, where she was busy hanging the washing out to dry, Raj's eyes would light up again.

'You got something, you did,' he'd yell, jumping up and down, clapping his hands excitedly, raising the dust into a gritty orange mirage. And above him in the mango trees, the bulbuls would chitter and the crows would chastise and the parrots would screech at this boy who dared disturb their peace.

And from the folds of his lungi, Anand, harbinger of joy, true to his name, would produce the sweet, and their son would laugh, and there, tented amid the billowing washing, fragrant air caressing their cheeks, Lalita's husband would gather her in his arms and kiss first her cheeks and then her stomach where their daughter nestled.

Remembering those precious times brings her both pain and comfort. Here, in this cold and alien land, memories are all she has.

Each night as Lalita settles wearily into her bunk, bone tired after a long day's work, she tries to picture their beloved, longed-for faces. Some days their features are clear, while on others, however hard she tries, she cannot summon them. Her husband is for ever young — she's older than him now. Unlike hers, his hair will not turn grey.

Lalita's children, however, will have grown older — the picture of them she carries in her head is years out of date. Her son's round face must be angular now, he must look more like his father. And her daughter? Who does Diya look like?

In her letters, Ma says she's the image of Lalita herself when she was a child. *Your daughter is exactly like you, both in looks and behaviour. She's a stubborn little thing,* she writes, *just like you were. I sometimes forget and call her by your name and she looks puzzled. 'That's not my name,' she says firmly, hands on hips.*

When Lalita left home, Diya had only just started speaking. As well as 'Mama,' she kept saying 'Baba,' and Raj would correct her. 'Not "Baba". Baba is gone. He's not coming back.'

'Your boy is gentle, so patient with his sister, but she . . . A little shrew Diya is, just like you were at that age.'

Lalita has no picture of her daughter or her son. And, oh, how that hurts. She yearns to hold them in her arms again, longs to heft their warm weight, to take in that smell they had, of mud and mischief and innocence.

Each member of staff has been issued with a walkie-talkie; they are constantly at the beck and call of the management. Until now, it has mostly been used to dump more work on Lalita just as her shift is ending. Now it crackles with an announcement. 'They're nearly here. Get ready.'

The other staff perk up, dust off their uniforms, stand up straighter as they go about their jobs, casting envious glances her way.

Lalita, by virtue of hours of uncomplaining hard work, carrying out her tasks efficiently and with her head down, so unobtrusive that the guests don't even see her, has been assigned to clean the suites of the most important members of the bridal party — the groom, his mother, the bride and her sister.

The accommodation consists of a number of self-contained 'lodges' dotted around the property, each one allowing the occupants complete privacy. Aside from being responsible for the cleaning and maintenance of these, she'll cater to the guests' every whim.

Normally, Lalita has nothing to do with the people who stay here. They come and go, faceless entities without interest for her. But this time she's caught up in the general excitement. In her case this has a particular edge because, like her, Suraj Sharma and his mother are from India.

Of course, the resort has hosted Indian guests before, and they've been just as obnoxious and spoilt as the others, if not more. She doesn't really expect anything different from these people. She'll most likely be run ragged by their demands and long for them to depart.

But there has been a lot of talk about these guests, said to be the richest people in the world. The son, by all accounts, is *the* most eligible bachelor, and has chosen a very ordinary woman to be his wife. Now this *is* interesting. Why would someone who could have his pick of the most beautiful and privileged women in the world — actresses, models, celebrities — choose such a woman?

Naturally, Lalita wants to see him, but she's especially interested to see the woman he's chosen.

Perhaps it's because Lalita herself married for love, against her mother's wishes, sending their entire community into shock. Where Lalita comes from, marriages are arranged. Her mother had wanted her to marry someone from town. Lalita was, everyone agreed, the most beautiful girl in the village. Her mother had had high hopes for her, that her beauty would land her a husband from a higher caste, an office worker perhaps.

And dutiful daughter that she was, Lalita was all set to go along with her mother's wishes. But then she met Anand, and all her mother's plans came to nothing.

Lalita was in the habit of taking long walks along the shoreline, searching for treasure washed up by the sea, especially following a storm.

That morning, she had seen something glinting on the beach and made a beeline for it. Like the magpies, which she rather likes, Lalita had gone to swoop and pick up the shiny object, when, suddenly, a large hand had reached forward and snatched it.

Bare feet. Hairy legs. Lalita's eyes had travelled up to a pair of brown eyes that held glints of amber. With a broad smile that lit up his face, he'd held it out to her. 'Is this what you were aiming for?'

It was a hairpin with a shiny clasp. Just Lalita's kind of treasure.

He'd bent down and washed the pin in the sea lapping around their feet.

'Here, let me put it on for you.'

He'd just come off his boat, having been out fishing all night, he told Lalita later. He'd dragged it up the sand and left it there. 'I took one look at this vision of loveliness coming towards me and I completely forgot about my catch. I forgot everything but you.'

Unable to speak, Lalita had stood with her hands at her sides while he gently took up the curl of hair that had escaped her plait and fixed it in place with the pin. It was the first time a man had touched her.

'Perfect,' he'd said. He'd smiled again, his face alight.

He later told her that he'd never behaved like that with a woman before. 'Not even those I know well. The other fishermen laugh at me for my shyness.'

Lalita had laughed. 'I'm glad you were bold with me.'

'Good. Then I will be bold again.' And he'd kissed her.

Lalita's mother was not happy.

'A fisherman! He's not even good looking. You could do a lot better for yourself. What do you see in him?'

Lalita couldn't explain. She had no words for what she'd experienced that morning. Only that she'd fallen under a spell.

They'd been fated to meet on that magical morning, as the tide lazily rolled out and the sun rose above the horizon, streaking the sky with crimson and gold, and the seagulls cawed above the gently washing waves. Anand was her destiny.

Perhaps it was the same for this rich man, this Suraj Sharma. He'd seen that girl and fallen in love with her, despite her lower class and his family's displeasure.

CHAPTER 32

The resort employee

A tremor of excitement rumbles through the resort like an impending earthquake. 'They're here!'

Lalita has finished cleaning and prepping the rooms — they're as ready as they'll ever be. She steps back to watch them arrive, a break from the endless routine that, for once, the boss has allowed.

'Since you've been working so hard, you can take a half hour off when they arrive.'

It comes at a cost, of course. She'll have to make up the time later.

'If you're planning to watch, please do so discreetly. There's to be no gawping, understand? God knows they get enough of that in their day-to-day lives. They're coming here to relax, to unwind in private. Or that's what they think.' The manager winks at Lalita, who is taken aback by this rare glimpse of humour.

Lalita realises that her boss, who she sometimes thinks of as some kind of machine, is excited too. It's a thrilling moment for him as well. Who knew it? The man is human after all.

The wedding party arrives in a cavalcade of limousines.

Working here, Lalita has learned that there are limos and there are *limos*. These are in a class of their own. They even bear a crest, the monogram of the Sharma empire.

A chauffeur, whose uniform (not a crease to be seen) also sports the Sharma logo, jumps out of the first one and helps a woman out.

She's every inch a lady: A green dress that sets off her dark skin perfectly. An emerald necklace — each individual jewel, of which there are at least a dozen, as large as a child's fist. Standing tall in impossibly high black heels and a coat, simple yet elegant, worn like a cape about her shoulders. A small black hat completes the ensemble. Her demeanour is regal. She acknowledges the chauffeur with a minuscule incline of her head but does not look at him.

This must be the mother of the groom, the wife of the man paying for exclusive use of this resort for his son's wedding. He wants a 'no-holds-barred celebration, a wedding that will be talked about for decades to come,' he reportedly said when he booked the resort. Lalita has learned this from the resort's gossip channel, which runs as efficiently as the 'official' services in the seven-star resort.

Mr Sharma Senior is footing the bill, but he isn't part of the arriving cavalcade. He won't be here until just before the wedding ceremony, and conjecture has it that he'll be landing in his private jet. According to the gossip channel, this aircraft is more exclusive and luxurious than any belonging to the oil-rich sheikhs, and more secure.

'But it's true,' said the maids, whispering in a huddle. 'He's worth more than the US president, *and* he's party to more secrets.'

'Ah.'

'And he has no qualms about making use of that information to get what he wants. How do you think he made all his money?'

Lalita took it all with a pinch of salt. Ever since word got out that the resort had been booked for this wedding, the rumours have been swirling like the mist that covers the cliffs on icy winter mornings.

Nevertheless, looking at this man's wife, now following an obsequious maitre d' to the best lodge in the resort, Lalita can't help experiencing a stab of envy.

What wouldn't she give for even a tiny amount of that self-assurance, that poise.

She's bred to it, of course, Lalita thinks. It's imbibed with her mother's milk. And who is she, Lalita? Just a maid — voiceless, invisible. Illegal.

But I am here, working so that my children's children, perhaps, will be at home with these people — or at least won't feel so out of place as me.

The next limo pulls up.

The chauffeur opens the door.

Inside there is what appears to be a scuffle, and then . . .

Lalita sees a stiletto, followed by a leg trying and failing to find purchase on the gravel.

The chauffeur, eyes averted, offers his arm.

A manicured hand grasps it, none too gently by the looks of it because the chauffeur almost stumbles.

'Whoopsies,' says a voice.

Not well bred.

When Lalita first arrived in this country, everyone sounded the same. They all seemed to speak too fast, in tones that were clipped and staccato, like sharp stones. It was yet another wall that she had to penetrate. Now, she can discern which class they belong to from a single word.

Now she can distinguish between the upper class and the *nouveaux riches*. She's learned a lot from her fellow staff, people from all over the world, all of whom speak, like her, in halting, broken English. They help one another to navigate this alien world, all of them desperate to earn enough money so that they may one day go back home.

She sees the same faraway glint in all of their eyes. Guesses their thoughts when they watch one of their own welcomed as a guest at the resort.

Those darker-skinned guests receive the same service as the upper-class English — after all, money has no colour — yet there is a subtle difference in the way they're treated, both by the staff and their fellow guests. Lalita can now detect the slight difference in tone, the averted eyes that say, *You don't belong, and however hard you try, however much money you have, you never will.*

This woman is white, but she, too, doesn't belong. She's fashionably thin and expensively, though flashily, dressed in her scarlet one-piece. Unlike the older woman, this one is loud, just like her clothes. Her make-up, though expertly applied, is beginning to cake. Lalita suddenly realises that the woman is drunk.

Swaying slightly, she stands, taking in her surroundings — the 'rustic' buildings designed to blend in with the landscape, the infinity pools and personal spas, the majestic cliffs and the silver waves below.

Lalita is so engrossed in observing the woman that she hasn't seen a second one emerge from the car.

'Oh there you are, Sam. You took your time.'

Beside her companion, this one looks pale and drab. Lalita can see the dark circles under her eyes.

This is the bride?

She doesn't look happy. Why? After all, she's marrying the most talked-about and pursued man in the world.

She could be anyone, Lalita thinks. *Even one of us.*

The other maids, who have talked of nothing but the wedding since the resort was booked, told Lalita that the bride-to-be was nothing to write home about. But Lalita put it down to envy.

But now . . . She doesn't want to judge, but looking at the woman, now smiling wanly at her sister, Lalita is forced to agree with the others.

Lalita is intrigued. And this makes her even more curious to see the man of the hour.

There's an impatient rap coming from inside the vehicle, and the chauffeur snaps to attention, gently disentangling himself from his drunken charge. She lurches unsteadily and her sister steps forward to support her, nodding quietly at the chauffeur, whose master is drumming ever more impatiently on the limo door.

Lalita takes note of this small, kind action. The bride-to-be's sister is leaning heavily against her, humming out of tune.

The chauffeur hurries round to open the door for the man who is now banging on the side of the car as if it's an old Ford rather than an expensive limo. Lalita watches, already predisposed to dislike him.

While his fiancée got out by herself, without any fuss, this man is bent on making an entrance.

It's the entitlement that grates on Lalita.

Why this show of temper? It's not as if the limo has child locks fitted on it.

The thought of child locks makes Lalita smile. In her village, on the rare occasion whenever a car came by, all the children, including Lalita's boy, would collect by the side of the lane to wave at it.

She pushes the memory away, as she always does, for it hurts too much, the ache to see her children overpowering. Usually, she buries herself in her work, which is why she's so good at it, scrubbing her thoughts away, along with the filth her guests leave behind — they turn the best resort in the world into a pigsty. This is even better, the perfect distraction.

The man of the moment descends, majestically, from the car. One polished boot after the other.

Lalita cannot even begin to imagine how much those boots cost — it would probably cover both her children's school fees for at least a year. Those of her roommates who can read English pounce on the gossip magazines the guests leave behind and amaze Lalita with the price of outfits like the ones this man wears. And the watch! Lalita, her mother and her children could have lived comfortably for the rest of their lives on what that watch must have cost. And according to the others, he has thousands of them!

Lost in a daydream, Lalita nearly misses the grand entrance. The world's most eligible bachelor is clad in a tailor-made suit that fits him like a glove. He's about as tall as Lalita but muscular, without, as far as she can see, an ounce of fat on him. He works at it, so her roommates say, employing several personal trainers. He stands very straight, pushing his shoulders back, muscles rippling underneath.

He has a fashionable beard. *Maybe he has a personal groomer too*, Lalita thinks. *The things I've learned here. And how cynical I've become.*

There is something about him that seems familiar, and it's not that his face is all over the press. He looks . . . sinister. The sight of him makes her uneasy.

Now you're being fanciful, she tells herself. *He's handsome enough, but there's almost an air of evil about him . . .*

You're letting your imagination run away with you.

I expect he's just not my type. It's a phrase the younger maids use about the men they fancy.

Listen to me. Not my type, indeed. Anything else, milady? The chuckle dies in her throat as she follows his gaze.

He's staring intently at his bride-to-be and her sister, who is still leaning heavily against her. And the expression on his face makes the hairs at the back of Lalita's neck stand to attention, her skin start to prickle.

One of Lalita's roommates, Ola, who speaks the best English, teaches her and their other roommate, Magda, various sayings while they get themselves ready for bed.

One expression made them fall about laughing: 'If looks could kill.'

'Looks can kill? Oh, come on,' Magda said, scrunching up her nose. 'This language, it's mad. Crazy.'

Lalita isn't laughing now.

She understands exactly what it means.

The look on his face is murderous.

What Lalita cannot tell is whether it's directed at his fiancée or at her sister. What could either of them have done to merit such a glance?

CHAPTER 33

Now
The resort employee

'Mrs Anand? The blood on the bed,' the detective prompts. 'I'm waiting.'

'Sir, the rooms I clean, well, I have often found blood and worse.'

The detective's eyes narrow. 'Mrs Anand, you are being deliberately obtuse. Let me spell it out for you. There was blood belonging to the victim on the bed. A substantial amount, enough to cause concern. The bed was stripped and remade with fresh sheets, but the victim's blood had seeped through to the mattress.'

Lalita closes her eyes, trying to rid herself of the image. It's no good.

'Did you strip the bed and remake it with clean sheets, Mrs Anand?'

Lalita swallows. Her throat is dry and her voice, when it comes, is a hoarse whisper. 'No, sir. As I said, I couldn't find the trolley. I went to look for it.'

She sees the cliffs, the sheer drop, the arms flailing, seeking, uselessly, for purchase . . .

CHAPTER 34

Three days before the wedding
The mother of the groom

Phone in hand, Aru stands in front of the mirror, regarding herself critically while she presses redial.

Why the hell isn't he picking up?

It's the middle of the night in India, but this is what she pays him for — the plastic surgeon is supposed to be available to her twenty-four hours a day.

Pick up, she thinks savagely, remembering nevertheless to smile. It won't do to get frown lines this close to the wedding. Not that she has any — he is good — but it's no excuse for not picking up the phone.

Then she does frown. How dare that itty-bitty sister of the bride say to her, 'I can do your make-up and hair, make you look half your age.'

My age, indeed. Aru knows she looks barely older than the girl, who has attempted to hide her poor complexion under a cake of make-up. Her own skin is a lot smoother. Well, that girl will get her comeuppance. Nobody, but nobody, insults the most photographed socialite in India — one of the top ten beauties in the world, according to *People* magazine — and gets away with it.

The girl had shrivelled under her gaze. 'I . . . I was only trying to help.'

Aru had replied in a tone that could shatter crystal, 'I don't need help, especially from you.'

The phone rings out.

She throws it on the bed.

Her plastic surgeon will pay for this.

Even as she thinks this, her phone starts ringing.

He's calling back.

No, she will not pick up. Why should she? She's not at anyone's beck and call.

His next salary will suffer a significant cut.

That should teach him.

A timid knock at the door.

'Come in,' she calls.

It's the tea she ordered.

'Lapsang Souchong?'

'Yes, ma'am.'

'And the cucumber slices?'

'Here, ma'am.'

'Well, pour the tea, then,' Aru snaps. What is she waiting for, for God's sake?

'Yes, ma'am.'

The girl's hand trembles. She sets the cup down with a rattle.

Aru will be complaining about that. And she won't be leaving a tip either. They're paying the earth for these rooms. The very least they can do is provide competent staff.

She takes the cup from the girl's hand — at least she hasn't spilled any.

She sips very slowly.

Breathe in. Pause. And out. Like her guru instructs.

Ah. Calm.

The knot between her shoulders begins to ease.

143

She places the cucumber slices on her eyes.

There is another knock, the door opens and Suraj pops his head in. 'Ma!'

She smiles. 'Suraj, my boy. Come, sit beside me.'

He does as she bids.

'How are you, *beta*?'

'All right.'

'Excited about the wedding?' She removes the cucumber slices and opens her eyes, smiling at her son. 'Fancy you being old enough to get married. My *chota beta*.'

'Ma!' Suraj sounds embarrassed, but he's smiling.

'I will ask you one last time—'

He sighs. 'Do you have to?'

There's a knock at the door, which they both ignore.

'Suraj, *beta*, there are so many girls from our community, girls from the right class. Acceptable girls, all lining up to marry you, and you—'

'Ma, we've been through this so many times.'

'There's still time to change your mind. What is it about this Sam person? Go on, I'm listening.'

'Ma—'

'It's certainly not her looks.'

Just as Aru speaks, the door opens.

Sam stands in the doorway. Her pale eyes — everything about the girl is pale, so . . . colourless — widen. She puts her hand to her mouth. She turns.

'Sam!' Suraj cries.

Sam flees from the room.

'Where are you going, *beta*?'

'Ma, she's upset.'

'So?'

'Ma, enough. Why must you insist on making mischief? You knew she'd be coming now, didn't you?'

Aru looks at the ceiling. 'Come to think of it, I might have invited her . . .'

'Ma.' Suraj takes her hands in his. 'I *am* going to marry her. So, please, will you just try? For my sake?'

She sighs. 'All right, I'll try. Although I don't see—'

'I'll hold you to it. This is the last time we're having this discussion, all right?' Suraj plants a kiss on her cheek. 'See you later.'

Her tea has gone cold, the cucumber slices dry.

Aru tuts in exasperation and rings for the maid.

CHAPTER 35

The sister of the bride

Patience.

Georgie is exasperated. Ready to scream.

All this luxury, anything she wants, at the snap of her fingers. People at her beck and call, night and day.

'A bottle of Dom Pérignon, please.'

'Of course, ma'am. Would ma'am like caviar with it? Ceviche?'

Georgie could get used to this.

Yet even as she luxuriates, almost lost among the eiderdown pillows in the most comfortable bed she's ever slept in, even as she sips her champagne, she cannot banish the thought from her mind: *In a couple of days I'll be leaving all this behind.*

Unlike her sister. After the wedding, this will be her life. It's not fair.

Georgie has never pretended to be anything other than what she is, whereas Sam — who's spent time in prison, for God's sake — lies through her teeth and gets all this.

She doesn't deserve it. *Georgie* does.

She hears that voice in her ear again, whispering suggestively, *'How does it feel for your sister to be marrying him when it should be you?'*

It should be me.

The old envy resurfaces, and Georgie is aware that she's whining like she used to as a child.

'Why her? Why not me? I was good, yet Santa got her the better present. It's not fair.'

'But you asked for that,' her mum would say.

Well, maybe she had, but as soon as Georgie saw what Sam had been given, her own present lost its shine.

Well, here's the truth, Mum. Now you try to defend her. See if you can.

Suraj was mine first. Mine.

And just like always, she gets what's rightfully mine, the richest man in the world.

And she's acting like it's all some kind of burden. You'd think she's carrying the weight of the whole world on her shoulders.

What's that about?

So what if she's getting threats, if someone has discovered what she did. *It's not my problem, is it?*

They'd threatened Georgie too, and she must admit that it shook her, briefly. But they'd made a mistake.

And if it all comes out — no, *when* it all comes out, for it's only a matter of time — she'll get her present.

Patience, that's all she needs.

CHAPTER 36

The mother of the groom

The clock is ticking, counting the hours until the wedding, and Aru is again in front of the mirror.

She seems to spend her life examining herself for telltale signs of approaching old age, afraid of not meeting Dheeraj's exacting standards. So far, she's succeeded, thanks to the best plastic surgeon in the world. But for how long? And if what that girl, Georgie, said is anything to go by, Aru is failing anyway. Dheeraj will be here soon — he's promised not to miss his only son's wedding.

She's happiest when Dheeraj is away. It suits them both. She can let things slide a little and he can do as he likes.

Part of her wishes he won't make it, but for her son's sake she hopes he will.

Suraj looks up to his father. He pretends not to care whether Dheeraj comes or not, but Aru knows he does, very much.

And if and when Dheeraj does turn up . . .

She shivers. She should be used to it by now.

In any case, there's still time to call the whole thing off.

Oh really? The voice in her head sounds a lot like Dheeraj. *You're clutching at straws, aren't you?*

Aru has sensed the tension between the two sisters. Something is going on there — bad blood, secrets. She must find out what's behind it, and make use of it.

No woman will ever be a match for her son, least of all quiet, unassuming Sam.

Yes, she invited Sam to her room — sent a maid with a bottle of bubbly and a message: *Meet me in my suite at 4 p.m. There's something I'd like to discuss with you* — knowing full well that Suraj would be coming to see her at the same time.

Her son has his faults, but poor timekeeping isn't one of them. Apparently Sam, too, is punctual.

She pronounced those wounding words just as Sam opened the door. Maybe they've done the trick.

She's ascertained that Sam isn't marrying Suraj for his money. She seems genuinely unaffected by the glitter, the ostentation of all that wealth. She shies away from the limelight instead of seeking it out like the others.

What's more, the girl hasn't even moved in with him. It seems she hasn't taken a penny from him, insisting on paying her way when they go out. Ever since Suraj announced the engagement, Aru has hired someone she trusts to keep a discreet eye on the girl. And Sam openly admitted to her that she's uncomfortable with the ring Suraj gave her.

So, if it's not money, what is it? She doesn't even appear particularly happy about the forthcoming wedding. From her expression, she might be going to her doom.

What is it about her? She's unattractive, overweight and dull. Yet on two occasions she's stood up to Aru, which none of the others ever did. For all her meekness, she has backbone. Perhaps this is what attracts Suraj.

Sam's sister, on the other hand . . . No surprises there.

Anyone can see she's out of her depth, and envious of Sam.

If Aru wasn't so committed to putting an end to this marriage, she might even have grown to like Sam.

In her head, her husband sneers. *Ha, but would she like you? Nobody likes you. They only put up with you because of me. Look at you, you're nothing without me. Even your famous beauty is fading. You're starting to look old.*

Aru glares at her reflection.

The mirror, reflecting the vast, empty room, which could easily accommodate three of the huts she grew up in, seems to mock her. *You have everything money could buy. But are you happy?*

Turning away from the mirror, she rings for the maid.

It's time for her skincare routine.

You can't hold it off for ever, you know. Gravity and the years will win in the end.

For once, she welcomes the maid's tentative knock at the door, though her husband's hostile laughter still rings in her ears. Dheeraj, hounding her, even in his absence.

CHAPTER 37

Two days before the wedding
The resort employee

Lalita dreams of home.

It's early morning. She and Raj are standing on the beach, waiting for Anand's boat to come in.

The saffron sun stretches slowly out, spreading its light across the frisky waves, turning them from silver-grey to crimson. The feel of wet sand between their toes. The familiar smell of fish, stranded kelp and seaweed. Seagulls caw, waiting for the catch.

The fisherwomen yawn, ready with their baskets, wiping the sleep from their eyes.

Raj's hand in hers is sticky with the mango she gave him to keep his hunger at bay.

'Look! Baba!' He points at the horizon, while in her stomach, the baby kicks as if she, too, is delighted.

'It's a girl,' her mother pronounced. 'The way she sits lower down in your belly. Definitely a girl.' She beamed at Lalita. 'One of each. You're blessed.'

A seagull shrieks overhead and, suddenly, the sun has disappeared, swallowed up by a shelf of ominous dark clouds that have appeared from nowhere.

Despite the warmth, Lalita shivers. Meanwhile, the fisherwomen still chatter, the seagulls still cry.

A boat. Tiny, it bobs on a froth-capped monster of a wave. A speck in the vast sweep of the ocean.

'Baba!' Her son jumps excitedly up and down.

She looks at the impressions his tiny bare feet have left in the wet sand, and a wave of fiercely protective love sweeps through her. The kind of love only a mother knows.

His bony little body. Her son.

And out there, the miniature boat carrying her husband is tossed about beneath the looming storm clouds, risking his life to earn their livelihood.

Be safe, she prays. She draws her son towards her, while her other hand rests on the child within her belly.

They look so small, her family, before the vast ocean and the glowering sky, as now, the thunder booms and a silver trident of lightning pierces the heavens.

It's all so precarious . . .

Lalita wakes with a start, the taste of salt on her tongue.

She's been crying again.

Beside her, in the room no bigger than a closet, her companions, two other maids, snore on.

Go back to sleep, she tells herself. God knows they get little enough time to rest, and here she is, squandering these few precious hours.

But try as she might, she's unable to.

The ache for her family is too great. It's unbearable to dream about them and then wake with her arms empty.

Her dream is always the same: that morning when the storm broke just as her husband's boat came in, the squawks of the fisherwomen rushing to haggle over his catch.

Anand pulled the nets in, while the sky split open and the monsoon pelted down. Drenched, he beamed at his wife and son racing towards him.

Taking his son in his arms, his eyes met Lalita's. *I will love you later.*

And he did, gently kissing her eyes, her lips, her throat, her belly, while their baby danced happily inside her womb.

He had come back.

But one day, he didn't.

Giving up on sleep, she quietly gets to her feet and pads out of the room.

She stands at the door and shivers, hugging herself.

She can never get used to how cold it is here, even in summer. Now there is a chill in the air, and a scent of pine. Below the cliffs, the sea is a dull charcoal mass with, here and there, a twinkle of silver.

All is silent. Nothing moves. In this seven-star resort, driving is prohibited after dark.

The rich can arrange it this way.

She thought England would be different.

But, like everywhere in the world, the rich can do what they like with their money, down to dictating how and when people may come and go.

Let them throw their money around, she's not complaining. Thanks to their extravagance, she's sending money home, supporting her family.

Lalita hears a noise.

It seems to be coming from the guests' accommodation.

It sounds like a door opening.

The staff quarters are a squat building near enough to where the guests are housed for them to attend to their wants, but far enough away that the guests are not confronted with the fact that the miserable creatures actually have lives.

Lalita squints into the dark.

There. Something moving in the most exclusive lodge in the resort, where the guests Lalita has been assigned to are staying. All the doors in each of the private suites in this lodge open onto a corridor that leads down to the pool and lawns.

They should all be asleep at this hour. Anyway, it's none of her business what they get up to.

But she's curious.

Her instincts tell her to go back to bed — they haven't called, have they? She ignores them and tiptoes towards the sound. Years of running back and forth at all hours means she knows the way by heart, can navigate it in the dark — she knows exactly where to step and what to avoid. It sounds like they're attempting to be quiet and not making a very good job of it.

A crash.

'Shit,' one whispers, followed by a muffled giggle.

It sounds like there are two of them — a man and a woman?

A wet sound, the two of them kissing.

Nearer now, she sees a silhouette, which splits into two. One moves away and opens a door — she can see them framed in the dim light within, but she can't make out which of the guests it is. They wave, and the pair disappear inside.

Silence again.

Lalita has seen any number of illicit affairs among the guests in her charge, yet this comes as a surprise — after all, they're here for a wedding.

She can guess who it was, because she knows who's occupying the rooms whose doors have just shut.

And that is a surprise. She'll confirm it later this morning when she cleans those rooms. Experience has told her that there is always something that gives lovers away.

All is quiet now. So why is the hair at the back of her neck still standing to attention?

Why that ominous feeling of something being amiss?

Lalita peers into the darkness. A flicker, so slight she almost missed it.

Another silhouette.

There. Tucked away beneath that awning.

A third figure, watching.

They remain standing, motionless, until the first creamy brushstrokes of light herald the dawning of a new day.

The figure is gone.

Lalita is determined to get to the bottom of this mystery, mostly to take her mind off the children she misses so badly. Anything, even the games of the super-rich, is a welcome diversion from the endless, unbearable ache of separation. She's now been apart from her daughter for longer than she was with her, more than half her daughter's life.

She shakes her head, turns and trudges wearily back to begin another day.

CHAPTER 38

The bride-to-be

Murderer!

Sam finds the note tucked under her door, lying there like a snake waiting to strike.

She drops it as if it has bitten her. It lies at her feet, the words, written in blood-red ink, screaming at her.

Despite her anxiety, Sam slept well for once, the carefully designed ambience having done its work. Suraj had said they should stick to their own rooms in the lead-up to the wedding.

'Regardless of the image she likes to project, my ma is very traditional — she wouldn't approve of us sleeping together before we are married,' he'd said, looking sheepish.

It came as a relief. She couldn't stop thinking about what Georgie had told her, that she'd been approached and threatened by someone who could only be the note writer. Sam no longer knew why she persisted in going ahead with the wedding. She tried to tell herself it was pride — no one was going to tell *her* what to do, neither Suraj's mother nor the writer of those notes. But deep down she knew it was just the opposite — cowardice. She'd had any number of opportunities to end it with Suraj, but instead she kept hoping it would all somehow go away. After all, she reasoned, the note writer hadn't made a move, so the notes were probably just empty threats intended to scare her. Nevertheless, each time a new note arrived, she was overcome with panic.

When the gates of the resort finally closed behind them, she heaved a sigh of relief. At least there would be no more notes — not with the security measures in place here. The entire resort had been reserved for their exclusive use, and no one else could get in.

Still, she couldn't relax. And now she had the additional worry of Georgie. If her sister were to be hurt — again — because of her, she wouldn't be able to bear it. Did the note writer know this? Was this why they'd approached Georgie?

How did they know so much about her?

The thoughts kept going round and around in Sam's head.

Relieved to be alone at last, she went into her room and flopped down on the bed, only to be summoned by Aru. Sam was tempted not to go, but she couldn't refuse her future mother-in-law, especially since she suspected that Aru had overheard at least some of her conversation with Georgie in the jet.

Wearily, she brushed her hair, put some colour on her lips and dragged herself over to Aru's room.

Getting no response to her knock, she hesitated outside for a moment or two, and then went in.

Just in time to overhear Aru's last-ditch attempt to break her and Suraj up.

It was the last straw.

She turned on her heel and went back to her room. Almost immediately, Suraj appeared to smooth things over. He kissed her, told her he couldn't wait to see her wearing the lehenga his family had presented her with — such a great honour.

Break it off now! her conscience screamed. *It's the perfect opportunity, and the best outcome all round.*

But she was too exhausted to summon her resolve.

Too exhausted. Huh. Another excuse.

True.

She lay down on the bed, fully prepared for another sleepless night.

To her surprise, she fell asleep as soon as her head hit the pillow.

And woke up to find the note.

At least Suraj hadn't been there. What would she have said to him? How could she possibly explain it?

It sat there by the door, a blot on the plush cream carpet, its bold, crimson letters proclaiming, *Murderer*.

She cradles her head in her hands now, longing to go back to the days when she was just plain Sam from Essex, who'd put her dark past behind her. If only she'd never met Suraj, the most eligible bachelor in the world, heir to countless millions.

How she misses being able to just wear what she liked with no one commenting on it and pulling it apart. When she could throw on a dressing gown over her PJs and run out to the corner shop for milk for her cornflakes, and no one batting an eyelid.

Sam stares at the note. What to do? In a few hours the Mehendi ceremony will take place, signalling the start of the wedding festivities.

Is it too late to confide in Georgie?

Apart from the odd obligatory word, they haven't spoken since that brief exchange in the jet.

Sam recalls her sister's bitter words: *'It's your mess, you deal with it.'*

She looks at the note.

It has to be someone here, one of the wedding party, who slipped it under her door.

Georgie is the only other person, as far as Sam can see, who knows the truth. Surely, it's not . . .

What is she thinking, doubting her own sister?

But how well does she *really* know her? Before this, she hadn't seen her in years.

And how would anyone else know? Her juvenile records are sealed. She's changed her name, her appearance, moved away and made a new life. So how come the notes were delivered to her home address?

How has the note writer found her here, at this exclusive and supposedly secure resort? How is that possible, if not . . . ?

She turns towards the floor-to-ceiling windows of the ostentatious room. Outside, the wind rages. It's the middle of summer, supposedly, but Cornwall never got the memo. She watches the waves, whipped into a frenzy beneath cliffs that jut into the sky, where dark clouds scowl upon what should be the most joyful time of her life.

So much for her fairy-tale wedding.

If the truth comes out, the consequences will be shattering, bad enough even for Sam Nobody from Essex.

But as the bride of Suraj . . . the whole world will be watching.

She'd been delusional in thinking that it wouldn't get out. Kidding herself that she could become another person. She'd paid her dues, lived a quiet life since the incident. But it wasn't enough, was it?

Who did she think she was, acting as though she hadn't done what she had? How dared she?

How dare you? one of the first notes had asked.

Not only had she dared, she'd allowed herself to think that by marrying Suraj she could wipe the slate clean. She'd been swept along in the belief that where Suraj Sharma was concerned, there were no obstacles that couldn't be waved away by the magic wand of his billions.

The truth is she never wanted to tell him. She doesn't want it to be over. She might not enjoy being under the spotlight, but she does like *his* attention. He makes her feel seen, desired, the person she would have been had she not done that terrible thing. In his eyes, she is good, and she wants to remain that way.

And now it's too late to back out.

Now, the only option is to keep her past hidden. At all costs, her secret must not come out.

If she is to do that, she'll have to resurrect Maisy. Maisy the Strong, who, like a phoenix, will rise from the ashes and set her world to rights.

Georgie's words ring in her ears. *It's your mess. You deal with it.*
All right, I will.

CHAPTER 39

Now
The resort employee

'So, from what you're telling us, there were a number of odd goings-on in the lead-up to the wedding. Am I right?'

'Yes, sir,' Lalita says.

'But you have no idea who was behind them?'

'No, sir.'

'But you must have wondered, surely? Why were they targeting Miss Reeve?'

'Well, sir, I think it was because she wasn't who she said she was.'

CHAPTER 40

Two days before the wedding
The bride-to-be

Sam should be getting up, preparing herself to face the first of her wedding festivities, the Mehendi ceremony, in which her hands and feet will be painted by the best henna artist in India. She's arriving this afternoon, flown in by private helicopter, alongside some of the world's top entertainers, who are to perform for the wedding party.

There is the usual knot in her chest, a combination of sheer terror and the thrill of being an imposter.

Georgie will be here later to do Sam's hair and make-up. Sam is both looking forward to and dreading being alone with her sister. Can she trust her?

Sam decides that she has no option but to trust Georgie. Her sister — her sole guest at this lavish wedding — is all she has.

Should she tell her about the note?

No. What's the point of worrying her too?

Sam formulates a plan of action.

She must find the note writer before they ruin her life. Before Suraj or, worse, his mother finds out about her past.

The postcard and notes have all been written by the same person, sent to her home address and slipped under the door of her room here. She's sure of this, for she recognises the style. She thought it was a stranger, but when they started arriving here she had second thoughts. It has to be one of the few people who are already here, since the majority of the guests are arriving this evening. The notes are from someone who knows her well. Too well.

Outside, the blustery wind makes the trees dance. The waves crash against the rocks, sending up a furious spray of foam.

So far, the note writer has made no move, apparently content with verbal threats. She hopes it will remain that way until after the marriage. Once the ceremony is out of the way, she'll tell Suraj everything. The thought of it turns her stomach, but she can't spend the rest of her life with a sword hanging over her head.

What will Suraj do when he learns the truth? Divorce her? He loves her, but how much? She has no choice but to wait and see.

Unless . . .

If she can find out who is sending the notes and is able to silence them, she won't have to do anything at all. She can go on as she is, with Suraj and his family none the wiser. She's been punished for what she did, has paid her debt to society. Isn't that enough?

The note writer has to be somebody in the wedding party, which narrows the field to Suraj, his mother and Georgie. But Suraj or his mother would have confronted her with it. It can't be Georgie, for she was threatened too. She could have been lying, but she looked so shaken when she told Sam about the threat. In any case, Sam refuses to believe it's her sister. Which means it has to be one of the staff.

This makes her feel better. A staff member will be easier to deal with.

But . . .

They've all been thoroughly vetted by Suraj's security detail. None of them have a criminal record, none have anything against the Sharma family, or are connected with their business interests.

But what if one of them harbours a grudge against *her*? Suraj's security detail won't have checked for that.

If the note writer *is* one of the staff, which one is it, and how to find them?

Restless, the silken sheets bunched in her fists, Sam ponders her dilemma. She feels like she did in prison, as if ants are crawling over her body. Skin prickling, forever on high alert, never knowing what would come next.

Before Suraj, she hadn't thought about prison in years. With time, she'd succeeded in banishing the memory of it to a small dark recess in her mind. If it ever surfaced, she told herself another person had done that terrible thing, not her. Someone who was dead now, gone, along with her parents . . .

Don't go there . . .

But her mind goes there anyway.

The notes are right. I am a murderer. The worst kind. One who killed her own parents and nearly killed her sister, maimed another innocent soul who happened to be in the wrong place at the wrong time.

Her mind will not shut out the guilt and shame. It's always with her.

I must resurrect that murderer, the ruthless monster who killed her parents and injured two others. I must find out who is behind this and stop them. If I can wipe out my family, I can do this.

She opens her eyes and her gaze travels the luxurious room and its elegant furnishings. It lands on her bedside table and the leaflet from housekeeping which promises, *If you require assistance, press zero, and someone will come to attend to your needs.*

Sam does require assistance. She needs someone to be her eyes and ears.

Of course! The person assigned to take care of the wedding party, whose job gives her access to all their rooms.

Sam was introduced to her yesterday — a small woman, too shy to make eye contact. Sam cannot remember her name but she's certain they've never met, have never even crossed paths with each other. She would know — she has an uncanny knack for remembering faces. So it can't be this woman who is posting the notes. *But she can keep an eye out for me.*

Sam takes a deep breath. *Okay, so this is my plan of action. I befriend the woman. Take her into my confidence — paying her if necessary — and get her to help me find the person who's hellbent on destroying my life.*

When I've discovered who they are, I'll find out what they know. Are they just some chancer, hoping to blackmail the wife of the richest man in the world? What evidence do they have?

So far they haven't revealed much, if anything.

They might just be fishing.

I have to know what they know. Only then can I decide on my next steps.

CHAPTER 41

The resort employee

'Hello there. I'm sorry but I've forgotten your name.'

Startled, Lalita nearly drops the bundle of towels she's just collected from the bathroom — a room so vast it takes her at least an hour to clean. So huge, in fact, that it could easily accommodate two of the huts from Lalita's village. Almost her entire village would fit into the suite itself, and this isn't the biggest one.

That particular honour is reserved for the mother of the groom, who, within the space of an hour has somehow managed to occupy the entire suite, her clothes and make-up strewn everywhere.

Lalita can't stop comparing this cold, alien place with home. No matter how many years she's been away, the little village by the sea will always be home. The sea that gave her so much, before it took everything away. Running after the car. The petrol fumes, the grit thrown in her face, his smirking face a blur in the dust churned up by the wheels. The tears, blinding her . . .

Lalita shakes herself.

No time to think about that now.

Lalita turns her thoughts to the present. How messy she is, the mother of the groom. They all are — and why not, when they have someone to clean up after them? Not the bride, though. She keeps her room tidy, appearing to take up as little space as she possibly can.

Interesting that the bride and her sister have suites of the same size. She would have expected the bride to have a bigger one. But what does she know? Working here has taught her that she'll never understand the rich, how they think or why they all seem so unhappy, despite their wealth. She's watched them drowning their sorrows.

And the waste! Perfectly good food left to be thrown away, meals ordered and then discarded on a whim. The employees aren't permitted to take the leftovers — it all goes straight in the bin. 'You're not authorised,' say management.

Lalita's heart weeps at the sight of it. What wouldn't her children give for a small portion of the food that goes to waste here. How they would marvel at the delicacies she sees being discarded. How can people buy things they don't need, only to throw them away untouched?

When she first started working here, Lalita had been tempted to pocket some of the leftovers — after all, she wasn't stealing, was she, if nobody wanted it? But the other maids warned her that she would face instant dismissal. And Lalita can't afford to lose her job — it's her family's lifeline.

'Hello there?'

Lalita had been taking her time in the bathroom, afraid to come out. It's strictly against the rules to clean a room while a guest is present. Lalita had knocked but, receiving no response, had assumed the suite to be empty.

She's curious about this woman, who is nothing like the rich socialites who usually stay at the resort. They're loud, while this woman is quiet. They're glamorous. She's not. She doesn't even wear make-up. They're dangerously thin, starving themselves until they're flat as the fish her son likes so much.

How he would eat, separating the bones from the flesh with such care. Relishing every bite. She and her husband would smile, their eyes bright with pride. *Look at our son, how grown up he is . . .*

She closes her eyes for a moment and forces herself back to the present. This woman doesn't starve herself. The meal she ordered last night has been eaten, all of it.

She always seems to be trying to take up as little space as possible, to cause the minimum amount of fuss. So, why is she marrying this man, subjecting herself to the public gaze when she's clearly uncomfortable with it? Doesn't she see that he's not right for her, that he—

It's not my business.

'Hello?'

Lalita has no option but to come out of hiding. 'I—I'm sorry, ma'am. I did knock.'

The woman waves it away. 'Oh, don't worry about it. What's your name?'

This is the first time one of the guests has noticed her. She prides herself on being as inconspicuous as possible — a little like this woman, in fact.

Does she, too, have something to hide? Lalita wonders. *And if so, what? Why draw attention to yourself by marrying one of the most influential men in the world?*

Lalita supposes it's the novelty of being singled out by this sought-after man.

Or is she hiding in plain sight?

She's waiting for a reply, and when she finally dares to look at her, Lalita realises that, actually, she is attractive. Her eyes are her best feature. Wide, full of curiosity, they are the pale grey of the sea at dawn.

Lalita has never been asked for her name before. All the guests see the resort workers as interchangeable, invisible presences that pander to their whims before melting away again.

Lalita is tongue-tied, unable to respond. She clears her throat. 'Lalita.'

'Lolita?'

'Lalita,' she says louder.

'Ah, Lalita. A beautiful name.' The woman pauses, twisting the sheets in her hands. 'Look, this might sound odd, but . . .'

Lalita waits, while the woman seems to search for words.

'Lalita, I have a proposition for you . . .'

CHAPTER 42

Now
The resort employee

'So, Mrs Anand,' the detective says. 'You think Miss Reeve was being targeted because she was — well, an imposter.'

'Imposter?'

'Not who she pretended to be.' The detective steeples his fingers and looks at Lalita, his gaze boring into her. 'Do you happen to know who she really was, and why she was lying about it?'

'No, sir,' Lalita lies.

CHAPTER 43

Two days before the wedding
The resort employee

'Prop—Proposition, ma'am?' Lalita asks uncertainly.

It's a new word for her, one Ola hasn't taught her. Lalita likes the sound of it.

'Please, call me Sam,' the woman says.

A boy's name? At least it's easy to remember.

But the habit of deference has been drilled into her over the years and she can't say it.

'Believe me, I'm no different from you,' the woman — Sam — says.

Lalita, who had been warming to her, closes her mind again. *You're nothing like me. You don't know a thing about me or where I'm from.*

She doesn't want to engage in conversation with this woman – it's not allowed anyway. Her manager would be displeased if he knew she was fraternising with the guests when she should be getting on with her job. She wants to leave but there's the matter of her cleaning trolley, which she's left in the bathroom. She can't be seen leaving without it. The cameras will show that, and management will wonder what she's been doing in there if she hasn't been cleaning. She might get a warning. She can't afford to lose this job. Where else will she find a place willing to employ an illegal?

As if she's read her mind, Sam says, 'I'm sorry.'

Lalita looks up at her. No guest has *ever* apologised to her, even when they were in the wrong.

'That was patronising of me,' Sam is saying. 'I know nothing about you and your circumstances. What I meant is that I . . . I'm not like the Sharma family.'

You certainly are not, Lalita thinks, wondering just what this woman wants with her.

'I . . . I got a note this morning, a threatening message. It was pushed under the door.' Sam's eyes are bright with tears.

Lalita is taken aback — both by what Sam has said, and why she's confiding in *her*.

'It must be someone at the resort. I just . . .' Sam is unable to continue, bunching the sheets in upset.

Those sheets. It will be a devil of a job to iron out the creases.

Lalita thinks of what she saw this morning, what is going on right under this woman's nose. *That* is bad enough on its own, but then to post threatening messages . . . Someone really has it in for this woman. She recalls the figure watching from the shadows. Did they approach Sam's door? No, she doesn't think so.

'I've been observing you since I arrived,' Sam says.

Lalita is jolted out of her musing. She doesn't understand what this woman means. This is getting a bit creepy. But the woman sounds desperate. That note. She must be feeling watched, hounded. Poor woman. It must be frightening to think that one of her party, someone close to her, is threatening her.

'You're best placed to know what goes on around here . . .'

Now Lalita understands what this woman wants. She wants Lalita to spy for her.

'Please, could you keep an eye out for me? See who's doing this?' She looks at Lalita, her huge eyes beseeching.

I shouldn't get involved. I'm working here illegally. I have a lot at stake.

As if she's reading Lalita's mind again, Sam says, 'I'll make sure you don't get into trouble.'

Lalita hesitates, remembering what she saw in those moments before dawn. Should she tell this woman? But why hurt her? She's anxious enough as it is.

Lalita recalls something else from those moments. That prickle of unease, a sensation that she was in the presence of something, someone evil. Who was it? Did they post the note?

Still, Lalita hesitates. Why involve herself in these rich people's messy affairs?

'Please?'

Something about this woman's pleading tone suddenly reminds Lalita of her son. He used to sound just like that when he wanted something.

She nods. 'Okay.'

CHAPTER 44

Now
The resort employee

'So, Mrs Anand, you say you have no idea how the victim's blood ended up on the bed.'

Wishing the detective wouldn't keep coming back to this, she says, 'No, sir.'

'And did you *find* the cleaning trolley, Mrs Anand?'

'No, sir.'

'You went to all that trouble and still didn't find it.'

'No, sir.'

'Do you think that's where the bloodstained sheets are?'

'I don't know, sir.'

'And what about the lamp that went missing from the room? Where might that be, Mrs Anand?'

'I don't know, sir.'

'You didn't take it?'

'No, sir, I'm not a thief.'

'Yet you've shown you're not above breaking the law since you're staying in this country illegally. Well?'

Lalita swallows. 'I didn't steal the lamp, sir, or the sheets. You can check with my manager. In all the time I've been working here, I haven't taken a thing that wasn't mine.'

'Mrs Anand, every minute you've spent working here you've been breaking the law.'

'Sir, I—' If only her voice would stop shaking.

She glances at her lawyer, who just sits there, doing nothing. Every so often he gives a loud sigh.

'I'm not lying, sir,' Lalita lies.

CHAPTER 45

Two days before the wedding
The mother of the groom

Aru is getting ready for the Mehendi ceremony when there is an urgent knocking at the door.

It can't be Dheeraj. Predictably, there has been no word from her husband.

What did she expect? It'll be a surprise if he even turns up for the marriage ceremony.

All his life the only thing he has cared about is work — or rather, making money.

And he didn't really do that. 'How do you think we've amassed all this wealth, eh?' he would bluster. 'Who do you think pays for your lifestyle, the diamonds you like so much, the mansions, the sports cars, the cash you spend. Your pin money would sustain a poor family for a lifetime!' How righteous he sounded, as if the money they had was all due to his hard work, and not inherited from his father. Yes, he invested it wisely, but he didn't work for it.

Aru has stopped asking him to attend important family occasions. She's come to accept that as far as Dheeraj is concerned, his family is way down the list of priorities.

She sighs. No point going over all that again.

The world-famous artistes who will provide the entertainment during the Mehendi ceremony have arrived, along with their entourage. They're setting up for the performance while the resort manager and the event organiser dance around them, getting in everyone's way.

At Dheeraj Sharma's expense, the artistes are being pampered and catered to by the resort staff. One, a boyband heartthrob who a year ago went solo and never looked back, reclines on what appears to be — yes, it is — a golden throne, having his throat massaged.

Amused, Aru watches a woman performer pose dramatically, waiting, Aru supposes, for the cameras to focus on her.

Well, she'll have to wait a little longer.

The select few reporters who are broadcasting the event will only be let in ten minutes before the Mehendi is due to start.

The caterers are setting up in one corner of the lawn, by the pool, which is strung with lights, their reflections sparkling in the turquoise water below.

Even the weather, which had thrown a tantrum this morning, has calmed down and is playing its part. It seems that even the sky dare not disobey the great Dheeraj Sharma.

Nevertheless, there are arrangements in place — weatherproof canopies, the indoor pool and its attendant reception area made ready just in case the weather does indeed turn.

The stage is at the opposite corner, criss-crossed by determined-looking technicians fine-tuning the acoustics.

On the other side of the pool, the shapes of the star mehendi artist and her attendants can be seen moving to and fro in a brightly coloured tent. As Aru watches, the dance troupe arrives, followed by the bhangra cohort carrying their tablas.

The guests arriving for the Mehendi are welcomed with champagne and canapés and ushered towards the luxurious pool house, where more drinks and vol au vents have been laid out, and waiting staff circulate with trays of delicacies.

It all runs as smoothly as a well-oiled machine — fuelled by the Sharma billions. While Aru watches the scene below, the soft tones of a Bach partita fill the room. *So much more appropriate for a woman of my age*, she thinks, and then stops herself. *But I'm not old. I'm not.*

She turns away from the window. Time to dress for the Mehendi. Aru has chosen a white sari with handcrafted beadwork. Each sequin, each tiny mirror, each bead, has been sewn on by hand, a task that must have taken days of painstaking work. It will show off her diamond necklace to perfection.

Aru likes to apply her make-up herself. She knows her skin better than any make-up artist — especially that common woman, the sister of the bride. *She* isn't getting anywhere near her.

The rapping on her door grows more urgent. Aru glances at the clock on her bedside table. No, it's too soon to make her entrance.

Aru is always fashionably late — not *too* late, that would merely be bad manners. But she does like to keep people waiting. She enjoys the gasp when she walks in, the way all conversation stops when they see her.

Bang, bang, bang.

Who on earth is knocking like this? If it's the maid, there'll be hell to pay. No, it can't be her, she's too timid. And in any case, she's been instructed to bring Aru her glass of chilled water with a thin slice of lime (not lemon, mind) in — Aru checks the clock again — exactly fifteen minutes.

Bang, bang, bang.

She hung a 'Do Not Disturb' sign on the door. Are they blind?

She's tempted to ignore them, but what if it's really urgent? Has something happened?

Aru glances out of the window, where the preparations are continuing perfectly calmly.

Bang, bang, bang.

'All right!' Aru snaps. 'I'm coming.'

Whoever it is, they'll pay for interrupting her like this.

She flings open the door to find Georgie, one hand raised to knock again.

She smells of alcohol. Does she never stop?

Georgie, clothed in a garment that looks suspiciously like it's made of nylon — how cheap — and which leaves little to the imagination, is teetering on her heels. The make-up caking her face is already beginning to run.

Aru steps back, afraid that the girl might lurch forward and fall into her arms. 'Well? What is it?'

'My sister,' Georgie says. 'There's been a . . . an incident.'

CHAPTER 46

The mother of the groom

Aru stands at the door to Sam's room and surveys the chaos.

Clothes are strewn across the bed, the floor, the chairs. Make-up is scattered on the rumpled bedclothes, lipstick marking the sheets.

And Sam herself, Aru's prospective daughter-in-law, is a disaster — hair a tangled mess, face pale and blotchy, eyes bloodshot.

'What is going on here? Why aren't you ready? The guests have arrived. You're leaving everyone waiting, especially my son.'

'The . . . the lehenga,' Sam whispers, pointing shakily in the direction of the wardrobe. It runs the entire length of one of the walls, and all the doors are open, clothes spilling out, like dirty secrets from the mouth of a gossip.

'And how am I supposed to find your lehenga in that lot?' Aru demands.

Surely, this girl hasn't sent her sister for that? Who does she think she is?

Sam shakes her head, indicating something lying on the carpet just in front of the wardrobe.

At first Aru thinks it's a rag, and then she sees.

The lehenga Aru and her husband gave Sam to wear for the Mehendi, inlaid with real sapphires, rubies, emeralds, is torn to shreds, the jewels scattered across the carpet like pebbles on a beach.

Painted in white across the red-gold fabric are the words, *You don't deserve him.*

Aru nods at it, and without thinking, responds, 'No, you don't.'

Sam flinches.

By the door, the sister smirks.

No love lost between those two.

Swallowing her words, Aru takes command of the situation. 'Well, what are you going to do? Do you want to go ahead with the Mehendi? I can tell the guests you've been taken ill, and we'll have the celebration without you.'

Sam looks at Aru, her eyes huge, beseeching at first, and then they narrow slightly. The girl's expression hardens. 'No, I won't be scared into hiding.'

Her sister, who was checking her phone, looks up, surprised.

So is Aru. There is more to this girl than she's given her credit for.

'All right then,' she says. 'We don't have much time. Do you have something else you can wear?'

'I—'

'You can wear one of my saris. A good thing about saris is that they're loose — you can make them fit any size.'

Georgie smirks again, catching the reference to Sam's figure.

Aru experiences a stab of pity. *That sister of hers is no support. The poor girl really is alone.*

'I don't suppose you know how to wear a sari?' Aru asks more kindly.

Sam shakes her head.

Aru considers. She may be feeling more sympathetic towards the girl, but she'd really rather not have to help her dress. Ugh.

Who, then?

Her gaze travelling around the disaster of a room, she thinks, *I pity whoever has to clean this up.*

Then it comes to her. The maid. Of course. Not that she'd taken much notice of her, but she thought she might be Tamil. She had that South Indian look about her.

Aru rings for her.

'Do you know how to wear a sari?' Aru asks.

'Yes, ma'am.'

'Good. Get the gold and navy sari from my room, please, and put it on the bride.'

'Yes, ma'am.'

When the maid has left, Aru turns and regards Sam thoughtfully. 'My blouse won't do. Your bust is bigger than mine. Hmm. I suppose you could wear your own top — that's still intact, isn't it, or did the—?'

Sam clears her throat. 'It wasn't touched.'

Aru nods. 'And do something to your hair and face. If you're to wear my sari, you must do it justice.'

Aru glances at Georgie, who is still wearing that irritating smirk. 'And I'd advise you not to let your sister anywhere near you. Do it yourself, or ask the maid to help.'

'Hang on a minute,' Georgie says. 'Why not me? I'm a hair and make-up—'

'You're drunk,' Aru cuts in. 'And if your own make-up is anything to go by, your sister is better off without your help.'

With that, she turns on her heel and sashays out of the room.

CHAPTER 47

Now
The resort employee

'Mrs Anand, this isn't the first time sheets with blood on them have ended up in your cleaning trolley, is it?'

Her manager must have told them.

Lalita swallows, the taste of fear bitter on her tongue.

Do they know?

What do they know?

'Mrs Anand? I'm waiting. What do you have to say for yourself?'

CHAPTER 48

One day before the wedding
The resort employee

On the morning after the Mehendi, Lalita wakes up like she always does, long before dawn. Her heart aches, as ever, heavy with longing, missing her family.

Her thoughts return to the previous day's events. Oh, the games these rich people play. They've too much time and money on their hands and nothing to do with it, so they take their frustrations out on other people, not caring who they affect by their actions, who they harm.

Her husband, for one. The love of her life, lost through having to dance to a wealthy man's tune.

She's sickened by it all. The guests here, their wicked sport, played at other peoples' expense.

You *didn't have to grow up constantly hungry because there wasn't enough to eat.* You *never had to worry about how you were going to survive the coming day. If you had, you wouldn't be so cavalier with the lives of others.*

The last thing Lalita had imagined was that she'd end up here, far from home, catering to a bunch of overindulged fat cats beside a stone-grey sea.

Ola told her once that in America illegal immigrants are called 'aliens'.

Alien. It described her situation perfectly, everything about it.

This sea is alien. It is not her sea. Not the one she grew up by and loved.

The sand is rough and pebbly. The water, even in the height of summer, remains cold, forbidding. Refusing entry.

Warm and caressing, the Arabian sea calls to you, irresistible as a seductress. But as soon as your feet no longer touch sand, it reveals its dark side. Then it's a raging shrew, unleashing whirlpools that suck you into the deep, never letting you go.

Even the rain here is alien. It doesn't soak you like the monsoon rain, instead it's insidious, seeping into your very bones until you're rigid with the bitter chill.

Alien people, sharp-toned. The staccato notes of their language, the sardonic humour it contains. Smiling, they cut you down with a word that bites like the icy wind.

Lalita yearns for the open-hearted warmth of her people, the innocence and uncomplicated joy of her children.

She misses the food. Spices that bring tears to the eyes. Even congee — gruel made from water that rice has been cooked in, with the addition of green chillies and ginger — was tastier than the heavy meals the people eat here. They had congee when there was nothing else. Now she'd give anything for a bowl of it.

She's deeply ashamed of the way she'd scolded her husband when their son cried from hunger and she'd feared her unborn baby might starve. How she wishes she could take back her cruel words.

They'd had congee for supper the evening before she lost him. As always, she'd reproached him for failing to provide for his family. Then, as always, her scolding forgotten, they'd made love in silence, so as not to wake the sleeping children on the floor at their side.

When, afterwards, he got up to go, she'd whispered, 'Come back to me, won't you?'

She could just make out his smile in the dark. 'I always do.'

'Even though I nag you so much?'

'Try and stop me. Even when you're a toothless old crone and still nagging me, I'll come back to you.'

'Go on,' she'd laughed. 'Off you go.'

The last words he'd spoken to her were, 'I'll be back.'

She sighs. Above the horizon, the sky is beginning to turn pale. Soon it will be time to get to work again.

They all complain about the long hours, except Lalita. The mindless toil takes her thoughts off her longing for home. The days pass in a blur, and only when she falls into bed does she see again the faces of her loved ones. Sometimes she wonders what they look like now. Would the endless battles with the sea have engraved lines of hardship and experience on her husband's face? Would his thick, black hair be grey?

To her, he will always be the young boy she fell in love with...

Lalita turns away from the door, suddenly recalling that she has an additional task now. She's promised Sam she'll try to discover the person behind the messages.

She still has her misgivings, but she found herself unable to refuse. Sam looked so frightened, so utterly out of her depth. That vulnerability and desperation awakened a sense of kinship in Lalita, despite the chasm that separated them. Even as she said yes, all her instincts cried out, *Don't get involved in rich people's murky problems. In the end it's you who's going to get hurt.*

It was Sam's utter aloneness that tipped the balance in her favour. She'd fallen victim to a cruel and relentless pursuer, clever enough to have delivered the notes and destroyed the lehenga unseen. Sam has no one but her, Lalita, on her side.

Lalita is in a precarious situation herself, but in Sam she's found someone who treats her on an equal footing. It has restored her self-respect, her dignity. And it has given her a purpose. She's needed again.

Lalita suddenly realises that she would much rather be herself, vulnerable as she is, than be poor, lonely Sam. At least Lalita has people who love her, who think about her — her mother, her children. She had a husband who loved her deeply, whereas Sam . . .

With a shake of her head, Lalita takes up her post and prepares to wait.

She doesn't have to wait long. Just like yesterday, a shadowy figure emerges from a room they have no business to be visiting.

There is the other watcher too, another guest. Like her, they're keeping their gaze fastened on the couple who stand outside a door, kiss and separate. As another dawn bleakly breaks through the clouds, the two of them keep their separate vigils.

What does this other person want? What will they do?

Time for work.

As she turns to go, she sees the shadowy watcher move too. There is something in the way they walk . . .

Suddenly, Lalita knows who it is. Knows which door they will open.

Just as they reach their room, they stop and look back. They can't have seen her, surely?

But if I can see them, then they must be able to see me.

Oh, what have I done?

In the grip of her rising panic, Lalita sees her children's future crumble to ashes.

But wait. As the sky turns paler, Lalita can see the watcher more clearly now. They aren't, after all, looking at her. Their gaze rests on the door to the room one of the illicit lovers has just entered. Now it opens again, and someone makes their way to Sam's room and pushes something under the door. They return to their own room, and the watcher turns away.

But it's not over yet.

Lalita is about to go when the watcher's door opens. She sees this person, too, slip something under Sam's door.

Lalita has seen enough. Poor, poor Sam.

CHAPTER 49

Now
Blog post — Starry-Eyed Gal
Well, Well, Well

Hello there, my lovelies,

I want to thank you all from the bottom of my heart. It's absolutely glorious to see so many new followers! You are all very welcome! I can't help feeling a thrill, even given the tragic circumstances. What a to-do, eh? And it keeps going from bad to worse as new information comes to light.

Now to business. Must we? Sigh! I was so very excited about this wedding. So thrilled, I can't tell you. Suraj Sharma, one of the world's most eligible bachelors, choosing down-to-earth, one-of-us Sam Reeve, had given all of us hope. And now, I must say, just like the rest of you all, I cannot help feeling disillusioned.

For it appears that nothing was as it seemed. There were so many intrigues going on behind the scenes. This just goes to prove, scratch the surface of even the most golden of couples and you will find mud and dirt, just like all the rest of us. Or perhaps even worse than the rest of us. I mean, did you see those photos of Mr Dheeraj Sharma, the groom's august father, gallivanting on a beach in the Dominican Republic with a scantily clad woman young enough to be his daughter? And this on the day of his son's Mehendi ceremony, for which I heard Beyoncé flew in! Mr Dheeraj Sharma reportedly was too busy to attend his only son's pre-wedding celebrations, so what then was he doing on a beach on the other side of the world with a girl at least twenty years his junior?

Well, well, well, just goes to show, doesn't it, that however much you don't like to stereotype the rich, they do seem to live up to and cultivate these horrible reputations. They don't give us an excuse not to, do they?

Now, I promised you updates and here is one. I have it on good authority that a resort employee is 'helping the police with the investigation'. Reports are emerging of a substantial amount of blood found in the bed of one of the key members of the wedding party. So, in addition to whatever happened out there on the cliffs, there was something seriously awry in at least one of the rooms too, it appears. I have also heard from my source that the police are very interested in certain items that have gone missing from the rooms occupied by the wedding party.

Hmm . . . Makes you wonder, doesn't it?

Whatever happened out there on the cliffside that evening, it was definitely foul play, IMHO, for, if not, why else is the resort overrun with police and detectives? Mark my words, my lovelies, despite the rich players being lawyered up to the hilt, there's more to this story than meets the eye, and I will try my hardest to get to the bottom of it.

Hang in here with me, my dearies, and I will update you as and when I have news, that's a promise.

And I, contrary to our politicians and bigwigs, do keep my promises.

As always, please do follow and like and share and keep the comments coming.

You know how much I love hearing from you all.

Back soon, my lovelies.

Keep safe and well.

Cheerio.

CHAPTER 50

One day before the wedding
The bride-to-be

Sam awakens in dread. Her hands, feet and arms are stencilled with intricate designs in vermilion henna, while engraved in her heart are fear and panic — the certainty that worse is to come.

It's the day after her Mehendi ceremony and the endless celebrations that followed, continuing well into the night. Somehow, she managed to get through it.

In the end, thanks to Aru's ministrations and Lalita's help, she was a mere fifteen minutes late, which, according to Aru, was perfectly acceptable.

'As for me,' Aru said airily, 'I'm *always* twenty minutes late. It doesn't do to get there early, it spoils your entrance.'

Aru saved the day, dismissing the sinister implications of the message and the slashed lehenga, and commandeering Lalita to help Sam dress. She even advised Sam on her make-up — despite Georgie's protestations — which was limited to a touch of mascara and a dab of red lipstick.

Once Aru had left Sam's room, Georgie, under the cover of gathering up the jewels from the slashed lehenga that were scattered across the carpet, slipped a few into her pocket. Straightening up, she said, 'I must be going, then. I'd better get ready myself. Once you're dressed, I'll come back to do your hair and make—'

'I can do it myself, Georgie.'

'But my business . . .'

Georgie dug in her heels, stubborn and ready for a fight, like she used to when they were kids. Sam felt sorry for her sister, and her pathetic theft of a few jewels. She was determined to build bridges with her after the wedding was out of the way. 'I promise you'll be doing my make-up and hair for the wedding, Georgie.' *If there even is a wedding.*

'But you promised I'd do it for the Mehendi too,' Georgie said petulantly.

'There isn't time, Georgie. We're already running late.'

'You're just saying that because Aru said you should do it yourself,' Georgie said. 'You're not even married yet, and already you're letting her order you around.'

Lalita interrupted, saying quietly, 'Ma'am, would you mind checking that the jewels are all there?'

Shooting her a grateful look, Sam turned to count the jewels that Lalita had arranged on the dressing table. Georgie turned on her heel and stomped out of the room.

'They're okay?' Lalita asked again as the door slammed behind Georgie, making them both flinch.

Sam realised that Lalita was afraid that she would be held accountable if any of the jewels were found to be missing.

'I'm illegal,' she confessed, anxiously twisting her apron when Sam asked for her help. 'I can't be deported, my children and my mother depend on me.'

'I'll make sure that doesn't happen,' Sam promised.

While Lalita was dressing her in Aru's sari, Sam asked her if she'd managed to get an idea of who might be threatening her.

'Have you seen anything yet? Who do you think might have done this?' she asked, indicating the torn lehenga.

Lalita, her mouth full of pins, was busy arranging the sari in pleats. Her gaze met Sam's in the mirror.

Unable to speak for the pins, Lalita shook her head, keeping her gaze steady.

Whoever it was, they were clever, and they seemed to know everything about her. Again, Sam's thoughts turned to her sister.

If she could steal those jewels, what else might she be capable of?

Lalita put Sam's hair up and, as a finishing touch, threaded a pearl necklace through it — a gift from Suraj — so that it shimmered.

The Mehendi was held beside the infinity pool next to their lodge, one of many dotted about the resort. The venue was tastefully illuminated by lanterns — no harsh electric light to spoil the guests' complexions. Even the weather played its part to perfection. It was a balmy evening, the sky a dreamy blue, with just the hint of a breeze to waft the scent of roses, hawthorn and lavender across the pool. Live music, performed by internationally renowned stars of rock, pop and bhangra, played at just the right volume to allow for conversation.

As the evening progressed, the guests — celebrities all — began to let their hair down. There was dancing, drinking, socialising, swimming, lounging by the pool, in the pool, while the poolside bar did brisk business. Smartly dressed waiters circulated with more drinks in tall glasses and plates of canapés.

Suraj's eyes lit up appreciatively when he saw Sam. 'I was expecting to see you in the lehenga, but you look even better in this.'

He was already quite drunk, and spent the evening partying with the men, while the women had their mehendi done.

The festivities grew louder and rowdier as the drink flowed.

Sam went through the motions, glass in hand, its contents untouched. She hadn't drunk alcohol since . . .

A fixed smile on her face, she observed the partygoers carefully, trying to determine who among them might be the note writer, the shredder of cloth.

She saw Georgie dancing with Suraj, rather close, saw too that Aru was watching them, her eyes narrowed.

Finally, Sam decided she could leave without appearing rude.

Suraj gave her a kiss and indicated a noisy group of young men laughing and gesticulating dangerously close to the edge of the pool. 'I'm going to wait and see them off. They're flying soon. See you later, babe.'

Sam went up to her room and opened the door, dreading what might be waiting for her.

The room had been cleaned, the carpet pristine and unstained. Exhausted, she lay down on the bed and immediately fell asleep . . .

She wakes a couple of hours later, dazzled by the light coming in through the window. She forgot to close the curtains before she went to bed.

Now, the branches of trees send flickering shadows across the window. Outside, a storm has blown up. Sam fancies she can hear the waves crashing against the rocks.

She glances toward the door.

There, on the carpet, a notecard is lying face up. She can read the message from her bed: *In a few hours the world will know what you did.*

Beside it, one of the wedding tokens — a pretty cream gift box bearing the words '*Sam weds Suraj*' along with tomorrow's date.

The inscription has been crossed out. Written above it, the words, *You don't deserve him. Stop it now or there will be worse to come.*

CHAPTER 51

Now
The resort employee

'Mrs Anand, you discovered blood on the sheets in another room, didn't you? When was that?'
'When one of the guests went missing.'
'Went missing?'
'Yes, sir.'
'When, exactly?'
'The night before the wedding.'

CHAPTER 52

The night before the wedding
The mother of the groom

Aru is woken to the sound of someone screaming. To say she's annoyed is an understatement. She's furious. She needs to look her best for the wedding, and now she'll have bags under her eyes, requiring an additional hour with the cucumber slices.

She gets up and goes to the door of her room, just as Suraj emerges from . . . a room that isn't his.

She tuts. The night before his wedding.

What are you up to, eh? She searches his face for the child she never really knew. The boy who never needed her, even then. Suraj has always been his father's son.

He deserves a piece of her mind at the very least.

But he won't get it, never has, even when he was a boy. The heir to the Sharma billions does not get told off, even by his own mother, even when she's trying to teach him some morals.

Anyway, no time for that now, she thinks. She must find out what's going on, try to do some damage control before Dheeraj gets here.

Georgie appears behind her son, in a virtually see-through negligée. Her face is made up, despite the fact that it's the middle of the night. 'Who's making that noise?' she says, looking at Suraj.

'It came from Sam's room.' Aru's hand is already on the door.

She opens it to find the little maid, that South Indian one, just inside, blocking Aru's view of the room.

'Sorry for disturbing.' She's very pale, her eyes huge and bloodshot.

'What's happened?' Aru asks briskly.

'I . . . I was just finishing my chores . . .'

But it's after midnight, Aru thinks, *and then she's on duty at dawn.* She hadn't realised how overworked this slip of a girl is. Aru recalls her own beginnings. *There but for the grace of God . . .*

And then, another sobering thought. *Is my life any better? I'm trapped too — in a different way, but I'm still trapped, just as much as this girl.*

Ruminating again. It's why Aru dislikes being woken at night. At night the thoughts creep up on her, ambushing her. At night she sees the empty shell her life has become.

'I was walking past,' the maid is saying, 'and I heard a noise, so I thought I'd check to see what it was.'

She seems unable to meet Aru's eyes. She's hiding something.

'And?' Aru asks.

The maid steps aside.

Sam's empty bed is unmade. There's blood on the sheets — not much, but enough to cause concern.

On the carpet beside the bed, a gift box, one of the wedding tokens, lies open and upended. There's blood on that too.

Aru reads the words written across it: *You don't deserve him. Stop it now or there will be worse to come.*

Aru suddenly realises that Sam is not in the room.

The bride is missing.

CHAPTER 53

Now
The resort employee

'Coming back to the lamp that went missing from the victim's room.' The detective fastens his gaze on Lalita's face.

'I . . . I don't know where it is, sir.' Lalita tries and fails to stop the horrific images from ambushing her. The blood seeping into the sheets from a head wound. The body unmoving, much too still . . .

'Are you sure, Mrs Anand? I hope you realise the importance of this vital piece of evidence. You see, we believe it was used to perpetrate a violent attack on the victim.'

CHAPTER 54

The day of the wedding
The resort employee

The resort is all geared up for the occasion. Today, the world's most sought-after bachelor is about to wed the girl next door.

It's like a fairy tale. Trouble is, the girl next door is missing.

Apart from Aru, Suraj and Georgie, only Lalita and her manager are aware of the fact of Sam's disappearance. Aru and Suraj are adamant that it must be kept under wraps, and naturally, since they're paying, what they say goes.

Suraj Sharma's security detail is conducting a discreet search of the premises, while Suraj himself appears untroubled by the disaster.

'She'll turn up,' he says nonchalantly. 'It's just pre-wedding nerves. If she hasn't turned up by lunchtime, then we'll worry. But I'm sure she'll be back.'

How can you be so cool? Lalita wonders. *What about the blood on the sheets? Why aren't you worried? What do you know?*

This is supposed to be the happiest day of her life.

Yet Sam has disappeared.

Where is she? Is she hurt? Has she come to harm?

Lalita isn't able to sleep. By the time she gets to bed, it's already light, and then, a couple of hours later, she has to be up again. For once, it isn't her children's faces that come to her in the night but Sam's, pleading with her. *Please help me. I'm going mad. It's my wedding, I should be happy. But someone doesn't want my marriage to go ahead, and I don't know how far they'll go to stop it.*

Poor Sam, having to turn to her, a complete stranger, instead of her family or a friend.

The thing is, Lalita had seen them, those three shadowy forms. Did one of them do it? She doesn't know. She feels responsible somehow, yet what could she have done? These people are powerful. They hold all the strings. An illegal immigrant — an alien — all Lalita can do is keep her head down, swallow what she knows, get on with her job.

Since she discovered the bloodstained wedding token in Sam's room, Sam herself nowhere to be found, and she let out that scream, Lalita has been trying to make herself even more inconspicuous than usual.

In any case, once the guests came and saw what had happened, Lalita was forgotten about.

She should never have screamed like that and drawn attention to herself.

The manager told her off but he was half-hearted about it. Thankfully, he didn't cut her pay or issue a warning. He was too shaken by what had happened, too concerned about the damage to the resort's reputation.

'Just do your job,' he said tightly.

In other words, stay out of sight.

Which she was more than happy to do. Except where Sam was concerned. Something about that young woman — her vulnerability, her very ordinariness — spoke to Lalita. She could see that Sam was out of her depth, didn't belong.

And Lalita understood that oh so well.

Lalita suspects Aru has seen through her story. That woman misses nothing.

The truth is, she hadn't heard any noise. After she'd discovered who was posting the notes — two different people, both of whom bore malice toward Sam — Lalita had debated with herself whether to tell Sam or not. In the end, she'd decided that she must. She'd been about to do just that, late as it was. After all, Sam had told her to knock any time. *'I'm a light sleeper, I'll wake up.'*

So, when Lalita had knocked repeatedly and received no answer, she had used her master key to open the door. Inside, she'd found the bloodstained token and no Sam. And, unable to stop herself, Lalita had screamed.

* * *

She cannot concentrate on her work. Usually the mindless routine keeps her thoughts at bay. Not today.

She's cleaned all the suites assigned to her except Sam's. She's dreading going in there again, but she has no option. It hasn't been touched since the Sharmas' security detail did a sweep of the suite last night and came up empty.

Lalita takes a deep breath and goes in. In just a few hours the suite has already acquired the musty smell of disuse. She decides to tackle the bed first — and its bloodstained sheets. Just the sight of them turns her stomach and makes her worry afresh for Sam.

She's changed the sheets and is plumping up the pillows when she hears a rustling noise coming from somewhere in the room.

It must be a rat, she thinks, the hairs at the back of her neck standing to attention.

Surely, there can't be rats here, in this seven-star resort. Although it's possible, she supposes — the guests are always leaving dirty plates and the remains of meals and snacks for her to clear away.

More rustling.

It seems to be coming from the wardrobe, which is locked.

The rat squeaks. At least she thinks that's what it is, though it sounds more like a human voice. Now she's imagining things, because she has Sam on her mind.

Telling herself to get on with her work, and get out of the room as soon as she can, Lalita nevertheless approaches the wardrobe door and puts her ear to it, listening.

'*Help me . . .*'

Did she actually hear that?

Hands shaking, Lalita fumbles with the lock. Inside, the clothes she arranged so neatly following the discovery of the slashed lehenga are in disarray. Most of them have been pulled off the hangers and are heaped on the floor.

Lalita tuts. The security detail weren't very careful when they searched the room last night.

Louder now, the rustling starts again. It's coming from the back of the wardrobe.

Lalita is afraid to look any further in case the rat leaps out at her. What should she do? While she hesitates, the pile of clothes moves. *That's no rat! It's far too big. There's a person in there.*

She reaches out a hand, even as reason is telling her to desist.

Are you crazy? You've already drawn too much attention to yourself. Get the manager, let him deal with it. You must not get involved.

But she's already involved . . .

Think of the implications. You're here illegally.

There it is again: 'Please help.'

Gingerly, Lalita reaches out and pushes the garments aside.

Right at the very back of the wardrobe, almost hidden beneath a heap of fabric, someone is lying curled up, knees to chin, in a foetal position.

Lalita has found the missing bride.

CHAPTER 55

Now
The resort employee

'I don't know where the lamp is, sir,' Lalita says.
 She knows exactly where it is.
 And she suspects the detective knows too.

CHAPTER 56

The day of the wedding
The resort employee

Lalita didn't want to be involved.

But she is, right in the thick of things, helping Sam to her feet.

How did it happen? How is it possible, when the room was thoroughly searched last night? Sam definitely wasn't there then.

Lalita thinks of Suraj's reaction when he was told Sam had disappeared, his lack of concern. 'If she hasn't turned up by lunchtime, then we'll worry.'

Was it Suraj, then? But why?

Who knows why they do anything, these people? Everything is a game to the rich. Ordinary human beings are nothing but toys, to be played with and then tossed aside.

Lalita has her arm around Sam, who is barely able to stand. How many hours was she in there? There's a swelling on one side of her head, just above her eye. Blood has congealed on the wound. It looks like somebody struck her with something.

Lalita gently leads Sam to the bed. The bloodstained sheets are in Lalita's cleaning trolley, waiting to be washed. Sam refuses to lie down. She sits on the edge of the bed and turns to Lalita, her eyes huge in her pale face. Her grip on Lalita's hand is surprisingly strong. 'I . . . They . . . It was . . .'

She breaks down in tears.

'It's all right. Lie down, that's it, don't try to talk. I'll go and get help.'

Sam struggles to get up again. 'Don't go, please. I'm scared.'

Lalita is gripped by a strong urge to flee. She cannot be involved. But she is. It was she who discovered Sam missing, and now it's she who has found her. She can't remain inconspicuous after this, she's in it up to her neck.

Fool. You should have gone and found the manager right away, when you heard the rustling.

'That cut,' Lalita says. 'You need to see a doctor—'

'Please, don't leave me alone,' Sam implores.

Lalita fingers her walkie-talkie, which she'd forgotten she had. It's normally only used when the manager wants her to do something.

Her hands shaking, she presses the call button.

'Yes?'

'Sir,' she says. 'I . . . I have found the bride. She was in her room.'

'What? How? The room was thoroughly searched last night, and she wasn't there then.'

'I came in to clean, and I found her.' Lalita doesn't mention the wardrobe.

'Well, all right,' the manager says dubiously. 'That's good news, in any case. The wedding can go ahead.'

'She's hurt. There's a bump on her head. She needs to be seen by a doctor,' Lalita says.

'I'm tied up right now. There's an issue with the catering. Let Mr Sharma know, would you?'

'Sir, I—' *Go on, tell him. Tell the manager you think it was Mr Sharma who locked her in the wardrobe.*

'Thanks. Good job finding her.' And the manager is gone.

Now what am I to do? I must get out of this mess before I lose my job.

While she was speaking to the manager, Sam has been crying silently, the tears leaving silvery tracks down her cheeks.

Seeing her, Lalita feels ashamed. *Stop thinking about yourself. This woman is hurt. She needs help.*

'Look, I must go and find a doctor for you,' Lalita says. 'You're safe here. I'll lock the door behind me. No one will come in.'

Sam nods. She looks exhausted, worn out by her ordeal.

'You will come back, won't you?' she says. And her eyes close.

CHAPTER 57

The resort employee

Outside the room, Lalita locks the door — a futile precaution. Whoever put Sam in the wardrobe must have had a set of keys.

This means that she'll need to be quick. But who can she turn to for help? Certainly not Suraj. No, she'll have to disobey the manager. She'll find the watcher, that shadowy figure observing the couple and their embrace.

She knows who they are — it was the way they walked. She doesn't wholly trust them either, but who else can she turn to?

She makes for the room, asking herself every step of the way what she's doing. She stands outside the door for a second, and then, reluctantly, raises her hand to knock.

CHAPTER 58

The bride-to-be

Sam shivers. She dare not go to sleep.

She was asleep when it happened, woken with a blow to her head and dragged across the floor.

This was her punishment, not prison.

Georgie, demanding retribution at last for the harm Sam had done.

She should never have invited Georgie to the wedding. Ever since the death of their parents — murdered by Sam — Georgie had kept her distance, refusing to have any more to do with her.

But Suraj had insisted. There had to be at least one person from Sam's family at the wedding. And to be honest, Sam had wanted her there. The two of them had been close once. She'd wanted her support.

Georgie must have seen it differently. The wedding was nothing but a bitter reminder of everything Sam had taken from her. Being threatened as she got in the limo wouldn't have helped either.

Georgie dragged Sam to her room and shut her in the wardrobe. Lying there in the dark, wondering what was in store for her, she heard someone come into the room. Then a familiar voice. The sound of two people kissing. The creak of the bed as they fell upon it and began to make love. Her sister and her husband-to-be.

Tears squeezed out of her eyes as she tried in vain to shut out the sound.

Then he was gone, and it was just Georgie again. Her sister dragged Sam back to her room, where, locked in the wardrobe, her parents appeared to her in a dream.

'Don't give up, Sam. You need to live.'

'But why? I killed you. Don't you hate me?'

'We love you, sweetheart.'

'You mean you forgive me?'

'There's nothing to forgive.'

'But—'

'You must live.'

Sam heard someone moving about the room. She mustered all her remaining strength and called out for help.

Footsteps approaching the wardrobe . . .

Lalita.

So it wasn't a dream, Sam thought. *My parents brought Lalita to rescue me.*

It means she'll come back. Lalita will bring help, like she promised.

Her parents have forgiven her.

Georgie hasn't. Georgie wants her to die.

And . . . if her sister is sleeping with Suraj, are they in it together?

'I'm not going to die, Georgie,' Sam says to the empty room. 'Mum and Dad told me so. It's not my time yet, they said.'

Perhaps I'm going mad. Perhaps I always have been.

If I were sane, why would I have gone ahead with the wedding, in the face of all those notes, the threats? After all, I've never been comfortable with it — the unwanted attention, all that ostentatious wealth.

Why marry a man I cannot trust?

Sam thinks of what she heard, lying imprisoned in Georgie's wardrobe. The texts. *He's keeping something from you.*

The paparazzi. 'Doesn't it bother you that he's playing away?'

But my sister!

The whole thing has been nothing but a sham right from the start, this whole lavish wedding a front. Well, it's over now.

Sam slides gratefully into darkness, sleep's blind embrace.

CHAPTER 59

The mother of the groom

'Come in!'

Ah, the maid.

'Where are my cucumber slices?' Aru says. 'I know a guest has gone missing, but really. The amount we're paying, I'd expect better—'

'The missing guest is about to become your daughter-in-law,' the maid says flatly.

Not if she's not there for the wedding, she isn't. Aru pictures the headlines. The press will have a field day if the girl isn't found soon. And Dheeraj's reaction doesn't bear thinking about. He can't abide the slightest damage to his precious reputation, and she's not thinking of his myriad affairs. They only enhance his reputation, demonstrate how virile he still is — 'Look how desirable I am, even at my age.'

So far, she and Suraj have managed to keep the news secret, but they won't be able to keep it that way much longer.

Aru has been keeping an eye on the bride and her sister. Ever since she overheard that conversation in the washroom on their flight to the resort, she's been afraid that something might happen, though she wasn't prepared for this.

Aru would like to think that Sam chose to disappear — perhaps she saw sense after all — but why do it like this?

And why the blood?

What is the security detail *doing*, for God's sake? How did they allow this to happen? The minute the girl is found, every one of them is getting the sack. God knows she has little enough influence with Dheeraj, but over the years she's worked out various means of manipulating him, most of which involve massaging his already overinflated ego.

And what about your part in it all? As usual, you're putting the blame on others so as to assuage your guilt.

She dreads to think what her husband will say to his son when he learns that the bride has disappeared. 'You couldn't get even this one little thing right. Surely you could have managed to keep your fiancée from disappearing from right under your nose? What use are you, boy?' The implication being that Aru is to blame. *What kind of mother are you? It's your fault he's like this, all your pampering has turned the boy into a pansy.*

It hasn't helped that this stupid little maid broadcast the news of Sam's absence by screaming the place down — who would have thought the tiny thing had such a strong pair of lungs?

Thank goodness the lodges in this exclusive resort are set so far apart that there's little likelihood of any of the other guests hearing the racket she made. And given that it woke everyone up in this lodge, it was lucky that it was just the core members of the wedding party sleeping here — herself, Suraj, Sam and Georgie.

'Should we, er, call the police?' the resort manager asked, wringing his hands miserably.

Fool. Didn't he realise it was his responsibility to ensure the safety of the guests?

She and Suraj both reacted with a vehement 'No!'

Visibly relieved, the resort manager took out a bright yellow handkerchief and mopped his brow.

'But if she isn't found within twelve hours, we shall have to reconsider,' Aru added.

'She'll turn up, don't worry,' Suraj said.

Aru glanced sharply at him. He sounded very confident.

'She's probably a bit overwhelmed, and has gone off to have some time to herself,' he continued.

The manager opened his mouth and shut it again. Aru knew what he'd been about to say — *What about the blood?*

Suraj noticed. 'If you're thinking about the blood, there wasn't much more than a smear.'

A small whimper sounded from the corner of the room. The maid. Aru had quite forgotten that she was still here. *She must see everything that goes on in this place*, Aru thought.

'She was probably shaving her legs or something and nicked herself,' Suraj said airily.

He seems remarkably unconcerned about it all, Aru thought. *Far too blasé. Does he know more than he was letting on?*

'And I'm sure we have no need to remind you,' Suraj added, suddenly sounding just like his father, 'that no word of this gets out.'

'No, sir,' the manager said quickly, 'not a word.'

'If it does, we'll make sure this resort gets no further business. From anyone.'

'Yes, sir. No, sir. I mean, not a word.'

When they'd finally dispersed, Suraj followed Aru into her room.

He closed the door behind him and stood in front of it, facing his mother.

'I know what you're thinking, but I assure you, I had nothing to do with this.'

'*Beta*, I—'

'I don't know what kind of stunt she thinks she's pulling, but she's hardly likely to miss her own wedding, is she? So relax, Mother.' With that, he left. He didn't kiss her. And he never addressed her as 'Mother' unless he was angry.

Aru spent a sleepless night worrying about Sam, wondering if she and Suraj were doing the right thing in covering up her disappearance. Despite her son's reassuring words, she couldn't shake the feeling that he had something to do with it. Why was he so confident that Sam would turn up? Where was she? Was she all right?

Much as Aru was worried about the girl, she was even more concerned about her husband's reaction.

All she could hope was that if Sam was hiding somewhere, having decided not to go ahead with the wedding, she would let them know she was safe and well. Then Dheeraj would blame Sam and not her.

Like Suraj said, the blood was just a smear, most likely from a cut.

She couldn't have gone that far, assuming she was on foot.

Then why hadn't the security guards found her?

Who are you fooling? You're feeling guilty about your part in it, aren't you? You know you are.

After her sleepless night, Aru woke looking an absolute fright. On her son's wedding day of all days!

So, Aru's first thought was to ring for the cucumber slices.

And instead of bringing them like she was asked to, this slip of a maid is being uncharacteristically cheeky. How *dare* she? Who does she think she is?

Aru takes out all her bottled-up frustration on the little maid. In a voice that could cut glass, she says, 'You will bring me those cucumber slices at once. It's your fault I couldn't sleep, with your screaming.'

The maid's eyes flash.

'And what do I find? Instead of bringing them as you were ordered to, you're giving me mouth. You're sacked. Finished. Now get out of my sight.'

The maid flinches but stands her ground. 'Please, just listen to what I have to say first.'

'What!'

Aru stares at the girl, who looks right back. *What is she playing at?* And then it dawns on her. *Of course, she's blackmailing me. She wants me to pay her to keep quiet about Sam's disappearance.*

Aru opens her mouth to respond.

'I found her,' the maid whispers.

'What?' Aru says again.

While she's relieved that Sam has been found, Aru is wary. *She could still be blackmailing me.* Perhaps this maid and that manager of hers are in cahoots — perhaps *they* took Sam. It would explain why the security guards weren't able to find her — the resort manager and the maid had hidden her away somewhere.

Aru says evenly, 'If that is the case, why come to me? Why not my son?'

If they think she's an easier mark, they have another think coming.

'She's . . . not in a good way.'

The maid appears genuinely concerned. Sam has been hurt. But the question remains, why not go to her son? Does she know something?

The maid gazes at her, twisting her apron in her hands.

'Out with it,' Aru says.

'I . . . You see, I wake up very early, before sunrise, and I usually stand just outside my room. From there, I can see your lodge. I've seen you watching them. You know, don't you?'

Ah. She's right. This unobtrusive, silent little maid sees everything that goes on.

Aru stares at her. *She knows about me as well, knows what I've done.*

'So, what are you going to do about it?' Aru asks.

'Nothing,' the maid says, returning her gaze.

Aru nods. 'Does anyone else know?'

'The manager knows I found her. He said I should inform you.'

'No, no. I mean about . . .'

The girl shakes her head. 'Nobody knows but us.'

'And it will remain that way?' Aru asks.

'Yes.' The maid does not look away.

'Good. I'll go and see her, then.'

The maid waits, still twisting her apron. 'Am I sacked?'

'No,' Aru says shortly. *As long as you keep silent.*

'Do you think you could say it was you that found her?' the maid says hesitantly.

'All right,' Aru says. 'Meanwhile, I want you to watch everyone, observe their reactions.'

The maid's face falls. Obviously, she doesn't want to get more involved than she is already. But Aru isn't about to let her off the hook so easily. After all, nobody asked her to watch the goings-on at night, did they?

'And come to me with anything you find out. All right?' Aru says.

The maid nods.

'So, where is she?' Aru asks.

'In her room.' The maid hesitates. 'She was locked in the wardrobe.'

'But the room was searched,' Aru says. 'She wasn't there then.'

The maid gives a slight shrug. 'Maybe they put her in later, after we'd gone.'

'It was locked, wasn't it?' Aru said.

'Yes.'

'And only Sam and you have the key, right?'

'Maybe she gave hers to someone, I don't know,' the maid says.

'Or they used the connecting door. There *is* one, I presume?'

The maid's eyes widen. Evidently she hadn't thought of this. 'Oh yes, there is. Her sister brought in her make-up trolley that way, on the day of the Mehendi.'

'There you go.'

Perhaps it was the sister. She wouldn't put it past her. And much as it pains her to admit it, she wouldn't put it past her son, either.

Aru marches off to Sam's room, the maid trotting in her wake, looking more than a little relieved.

When she enters, she finds Sam huddled up in bed, crying. She raises her head to look at her, and Aru sees the wound on her forehead, just above the eye. Aru sits on the bed beside her and takes her hand.

Sam whispers, 'Mum?'

Aru blinks back tears. *Dear me, I must have got something in my eye.*

CHAPTER 60

The bride-to-be

Mum. Sam is so grateful to Lalita for bringing her mother.

'Mum,' Sam says, 'I'm sorry. I didn't mean to—'

'Shush now,' Mum says, tenderly stroking her hair. 'It's all right. I'm here. Everything's going to be okay.'

Reassured, Sam drifts back to sleep.

She's awoken by a scream.

'You found her! Thank God she's all right.'

Horrified, Sam shrinks back against the pillows.

Georgie.

Her sister is crying. She takes hold of her hand. Flinching, Sam tries to pull it back. Will she hurt her again?

Now she's here, Sam knows it was definitely Georgie that hurt her. She hadn't been sure at first — the muttered curses, the panting breaths as she was dragged from room to room could have belonged to anyone.

But the feel of Georgie's fingers on her skin is unmistakable.

Your sister hurt you, but you hurt her first, and the hurt you did her was far, far worse. You killed the people you both loved best.

But the guilt she feels is less overwhelming now, because she knows that her parents have forgiven her.

Sam's dream is still vivid in her mind.

'There's nothing to forgive,' they said.

Even if I don't deserve it.

Even if I will never forgive myself.

'Someone call a doctor,' Georgie is saying.

All at once, Sam registers that the room is full of people, all crowding around her bed with expressions of concern.

People who, in reality, care nothing for her.

Suraj. She can't bear to look at him.

And Georgie . . .

The light is hurting her eyes, but before she shuts them, she sees Aru looking at her with a strangely tender expression. She seems to be conveying something with that gentle shake of her head.

Have I been mistaken in Aru?

And what is she trying to say?

People aren't making sense anymore. Everything's upside down — Aru tender, her own sister hurting her. And Suraj . . .

Suraj and Georgie . . .

Sam is still struggling to extract her hand from her sister's grasp, but Georgie's grip tightens.

Exhausted, Sam lies back against her pillows.

When she opens her eyes again, she sees Georgie looking, not at her, but at Suraj.

It *was* him. Suraj, with Georgie. It wasn't a dream.

'Has anyone called a doctor?' her sister says again.

'Yes,' Aru snaps.

'He's on his way,' Suraj says calmly.

Sam shuts her eyes, blanking out the lot of them and the whole mad world. *Come back, Mum, I need you.*

But they won't leave her alone.

The doctor arrives and examines the wound on her head, which he says is not serious. All she needs now is rest. After he's gone, Suraj sits down beside her and, like Georgie, takes her hand. Sam has to fight the urge to pull it away like she did Georgie's.

'My darling, you heard what the doctor said,' Suraj says. 'You're fine. We'll go ahead with the wedding, since everything is set up. My father is due to arrive just before the ceremony, at 7 p.m. He's a busy man, and he'll be upset if it doesn't go as scheduled, as he's due to fly out as soon as we've taken our vows.'

Sam struggles to sit up. 'What?'

'Our wedding, darling. This evening.' Suraj sounds a tad impatient.

Now Sam does pull her hand away.

She cannot believe he's even suggesting this. Marry her, when he's sleeping with her sister? What's going on with him?

'We need to talk,' she says.

'Can't it wait until after the ceremony?'

'No, it can't.'

'Well? What is it?'

'I'd like to talk to you in private.' Lalita and Aru are still here, although Georgie has left.

'You heard what the doctor said,' Suraj continues. 'Rest now. We'll talk later.'

'Suraj, I'm not who you think I am.'

'Nor am I.'

She's surprised he admits it so easily.

'Why do you want to marry me, then?' she says.

'Because I love you.'

'Do you?'

'Listen, Sam. Rest. I'll drop by later, when you're more yourself.'

'I've never been more myself than I am now. I cannot believe I needed to get hit on the head to see things clearly.'

'You're talking in riddles. I'll see you later.' Suraj gets to his feet and makes for the door.

Sam looks at his retreating back. Finally, she's seeing Suraj for what he is — someone who walks off when things don't go his way.

He'll be along later — not to listen to what she has to say, but to make sure the wedding goes ahead, just because his father is coming, and his plans must not be upset. Suraj may act like a spoiled brat, but he'll do anything to please his father.

But Sam will stand firm. She will tell him the truth about herself, and then he will know he cannot marry her, father or no father.

She's hurting, physically and emotionally, but she's also terribly relieved.

CHAPTER 61

Now
Blog post — Starry-Eyed Gal
Who would have thought?

Hello, my lovelies,

It's me again, with updates as promised.

But first of all, thank you, you gorgeous peeps, for all your love and likes and shares and for following in your droves. My posts are trending! Eek! I just cannot believe it! And it's all down to you, my brilliant, wonderful followers! Mwah! Am I blessed or what?

Now, I don't know about you, but when news of the engagement between mega-billionaire Suraj Sharma and ordinary girl next door Sam Reeve leaked, I was blown away. It made my heart swell. Something good, you know, in these depressing times. It gave me hope that the world was not as bad as the newscasters and the doom and gloom prophets made out. It meant that even ordinary people had a hope of happy-ever-afters, billionaire style . . .

But now all that is shattered.

I must admit that despite being an optimist, I feel a little, yes, cynical about it all.

I think that, although we choose to believe the social-media posts and the celebrity magazines depicting the rich living it up in style, we all secretly suspect that their lives aren't as perfect as we like to think. They're just as bad as any of us, if not worse, no matter that they're enveloped in the gilded halo of wealth. And the shocking tragedy at this wedding of the decade proves it.

I told you about my source in the know, didn't I? Well, he said there's been all sorts going on ever since the wedding party arrived at the resort.

There's been a huge cover-up, it appears, and there were warning signs all along, which were ignored.

Reports are emerging of weird and downright scary antics during the Mehendi ceremony, warning threats delivered in the dead of night, bed-swapping — yes, you read that right — and even, wait for it, one of the wedding party going missing the night before the wedding!

Honestly, you couldn't make it up.

The sad truth is that all of this could have been stopped, loss of life prevented, if only those warnings had been heeded.

In any case, who would have thought that the wedding we were all so looking forward to would end up like this?

On that note, I'll say ta-ra, my lovelies. More soon. Watch this space.

In the meantime, please keep following and liking, sharing and commenting, my dearies. You know I always love to hear what you think about it all.

Until next time.

Keep well!

CHAPTER 62

The day of the wedding
The resort employee

Ever watchful, Lalita is keeping well under the radar. Sam is confined to bed, resting in preparation for the wedding, which appears, against all odds, to be going ahead — at least the resort staff haven't been told otherwise. Meanwhile, Georgie and Suraj seem to have no qualms about carrying on their affair. Suraj is still visiting Georgie's room, though it's only a few hours until the wedding ceremony.

Lalita is passing Georgie's room when she hears Suraj's voice.

She pauses. Human nature being what it is, she can't help being curious. She knows just where to stand to eavesdrop on the conversation. There's a small cupboard adjoining Georgie's room, where the staff keep their cleaning equipment. She goes inside, presses her ear to the wall, and listens.

'Well, this is a turn-up for the books,' Suraj is saying. 'I never thought the mouse would have the courage to stage something like this.'

'What do you mean?' Georgie's voice is thick and heavy — they've just finished making love.

Lalita shakes her head in disbelief. *This*, on the very day Suraj is to marry this woman's sister. As long as she lives, she'll never understand these people and the things they do.

They have all the money they could wish for. They could be living their lives peacefully, without a care in the world, yet they persist in creating problems for themselves, never happy, never satisfied with what they have.

She and her fellow villagers had nothing. They survived on whatever the sea saw fit to provide — and sometimes that was nothing. Even when they were forced to go hungry, even if their huts leaked in the monsoons and sweltered in the heat, there was laughter, moments of joy.

They overcame their adversities together, sharing the pain and the sorrow, when it came.

But these people . . . They've made the doctor sign a non-disclosure agreement. Word must not be allowed to get out, their reputation to be preserved at all costs. Only Aru seemed displeased. She was far from happy at her son's insistence that the wedding must go ahead.

Lalita saw another side to Aru in the wake of Sam's disappearance. Of all of them, Aru showed the most genuine concern. Then Lalita remembered what she'd witnessed in the early hours, and realised that Aru, too, was complicit.

What was it, she wondered, that Aru had pushed under Sam's door?

'What I mean,' Suraj is saying, 'is that maybe Sam sensed something was wrong, that I might not be as committed to this marriage as I ought to be, so she staged this disappearing act.'

'What? Who do you think you're kidding? You reckon she's capable of doing something like that?' Georgie cries.

Suraj laughs. 'I can't help admiring her for it. She's actually shown some spirit at last.'

Lalita feels an overwhelming desire to burst into the room and hit him. Poor Sam.

'Oh, come on,' Georgie says. 'Sam wouldn't know spirit if it jumped up and smacked her in the face. *I* did it. *I* hit her on the head and dragged her into my room. I'd asked her to leave the connecting door open — it was easier to get my make-up trolley in that way when I went to do her face for the Mehendi. You know, it would all have been so much easier if *our* rooms were next to each other — we could have gone in and out whenever we liked. Though I suppose that would have made your mother suspicious. In any case, as soon as your security team had finished searching her room, I hauled Sam back again and shoved her in the wardrobe, just in case they searched my room. She's quite a weight, I can tell you. I was worn out by the effort.'

So it was Sam's own sister who had hit her and shut her in the wardrobe! Lalita is amazed, and disgusted. Not only is she carrying on with Sam's fiancé, but she hit her as well, and locked her in a wardrobe . . .

A moment or two of silence follows this bombshell. Lalita pictures Suraj's face as he stares at Georgie. '*What?* Are you telling me *you* did it?'

'I . . .'

Even Lalita, safe behind the wall, shudders at the menace in his voice.

'I . . . I didn't expect them to clean her room. I thought they'd leave it until after the wedding. I only wanted her out of the way until—'

'What? You thought I'd marry you instead?'

'You . . . You said you'd made a mistake, and that you were marrying the wrong sister,' Georgie whimpers.

'And you believed me? You little fool.'

'I . . . You . . .' Georgie stutters, lost for words.

In spite of her dislike of this woman, Lalita can't help pitying her right now.

'I can marry anyone I want. What makes you think I'd choose *you*?'

'You said you loved me,' Georgie says in a small voice. 'And when I told you I was pregnant, just before you took up with Sam, you said . . . You said we would have a child later, when the time was right.'

'Stupid. That was just to make sure you went ahead with the abortion.'

'You lied to me?' Georgie sounds incredulous. 'Lied, so that I'd kill our child?'

Through the wall, Lalita hears Georgie snuffle. She's crying, and Lalita's own eyes prickle.

'You don't love me. You never did. I should have known. I should have realised when you said I was too precious to share with the world. When you told me you wanted to cherish me in secret. It was all lies.'

'Yes.'

'You told me your relationship with Sam was a joke, and you didn't care who knew about it. Some joke. Turns out the fool was me.'

'So it would seem,' Suraj says sarcastically.

'Why pick me in the first place, then?'

'Because, my dear, we're alike. Neither of us has any regard for other people. I saw that in you when we first met.'

'I can't believe I was so flattered when you slipped me your contact card and asked me to call. Funny how hindsight can do that. Right from the start, you wanted to hide what we had.'

'I wanted to see if I could keep at least one of my affairs from the paparazzi.'

'Well, you succeeded there, didn't you? Should I clap?'

'Ah, that's the spirit. That's what I like to see,' Suraj drawls. 'When you told me about your sister, and the way you made her think she was the guilty one, when all the time it was you, I thought I'd found someone after my own heart.'

'But then you made a beeline for Sam.'

'How could I resist? I wanted to meet this woman you'd lied to, who even went to prison to atone for what *you* did. Who took on a whole new identity because of what you made her believe. Here's the perfect wife, I thought, someone who will allow me to do just as I like and still remain faithful.'

Lalita gasps and clamps a hand over her mouth. Sam has been to prison? And . . . did she hear right? She must have mistaken his words, surely. Did he say Georgie fed Sam a lie, and she went to prison for it?

'I'd just told you I was pregnant,' Georgie is saying. 'You told me the timing wasn't right. I didn't realise it was because you had set your sights on Sam. Do you know, Sam called me the day after your date with her, just as I was about to visit the doctor you recommended, to get the abortion? Nice one.'

'Sarcasm doesn't become you, Georgie.' Suraj sounds amused. 'Seems you're happy to play with Sam's feelings, but you can't take the same treatment when it's handed out to you.'

'What do you mean?'

'Remember what happened when you were getting into the limo that brought you here?'

'Oh,' Georgie says. 'You mean that voice? It was — no, it can't have been you. You were inside the limo.'

Suraj laughs. 'Stupid. It was the chauffeur. I paid him to do it.'

'The helpful chauffeur, who supported me when I stumbled,' Georgie cries. 'Who'd have believed it? God, you're so cruel.'

'And you're not, I suppose. Well, I must say I've had a lot of fun stringing you and your sister along.'

'But why marry her? I don't understand,' Georgie says.

Suraj shrugs. 'I have to marry someone. All the other girls I've been with are all the same — dead boring. At least Sam's a bit different. Added to which, she has this big secret hanging over her head. She's so afraid I'll find out about her past that she'll let me do whatever I like. She's easy to manipulate.'

'Just like me,' Georgie says bitterly.

'Yes, but you're high maintenance. She's not. My father has been on at me for ages to settle down and provide him with an heir. I've been looking for someone who won't interfere in my life, preferably without a family of their own to worry about. Sam fits the bill perfectly.'

'She has me,' Georgie says. 'Though you'll make sure I don't get in the way.'

'Exactly. A little more gaslighting and Sam will leave me alone to do as I please.'

'You're horrible.'

'I've never pretended to be otherwise. Whatever I want, I get, and I don't care how. You want an example? Well, there was this one time, back in India this was, when I decided I wanted a certain type of fish. I went down to the beach and asked the fishermen to get me one, but they told me they weren't going out because a storm was brewing. Well, I was determined to have that fish. I asked around and eventually I found one who agreed to risk the storm for the sum of five thousand rupees, which is fifty pounds — a pittance.'

'And? Did you get your fish?' Georgie asks.

Crouched in the cupboard, Lalita has stopped listening. She's back at the side of the road, watching the car disappear in a cloud of orange dust.

CHAPTER 63

India — the day of the storm
Lalita

It's an ordinary day, just like any other. Humming quietly to herself, Lalita is hanging the washing out to dry. There is not a cloud in the sky, though there was a storm in the night. The howl of the wind battering at the hut had woken her and she had lain in the dark for a while, worried in case a branch fell on the hut. She'd half expected Anand to appear — the fishermen don't go out in a storm — but she wasn't concerned. They were probably all in the toddy shop, waiting it out. He doesn't often drink, but once in a while he succumbs, and she doesn't complain. God knows, he's allowed a little enjoyment. She's lucky to have a husband like him, so kind and loving. The things the other women tell her! Anand has never beaten her, never taken one of the women who frequent the toddy shop.

They're saving to move to town. It has good schools and she'll be closer to her mother.

'Our children will study and get good jobs. They won't have to rely on the whims of the capricious sea god to provide for them,' Anand says.

A sudden breeze, tasting of ripe fruit and roasting spices, flings grit into her mouth.

Her son plays peekaboo among the many-coloured saris billowing on the line. Her daughter, lying on the mat at her feet, giggles and claps her hands.

Lalita smiles, unaware of the gathering storm about to burst in and ruin her life. Never again will she experience such moments, never revel in her children's unfettered joy while the sun beats down upon them and the cows low in the fields beyond.

The sound of their wailing reaches her long before she sees them.

The keening is accompanied by heavy thuds — the women striking at their own chests, their foreheads, while the men growl. Lalita pauses. Someone is dead.

Who can it be?

The cries are getting louder.

Now she can hear feet stamping. It sounds as if the entire village has gathered to mourn the departed. Her son looks up at her, his eyes huge. The cries are upsetting him. Her daughter is blissfully unaware, blowing raspberries and waving her hands, while the dog sprawls beside her, wagging his tail.

Lalita stands motionless, listening to the villagers wail. A tremor of fear reverberates throughout her body. They can't be coming here. Can they?

She prays to Varuna, the water god, watching the dark shapes of the villagers emerge, one by one, from the orange cloud of dust their stamping feet have kicked up.

Lalita is clutching her husband's damp lungi, which she was about to hang up. Her grip on it tightens. The sky is cloudless following last night's storm. Perfect weather for fishing, as he would say.

'I'll be back with nets bursting with fish, you'll see. Then we can get you a new sari.'

And she would smile. 'You always say that. Never mind about the sari, the children need new clothes.'

'I'll get those too.'

'Go on with you. No more promises now, you'll be late. And take care.'

'I always do,' he'd answer. 'I know these waters. I know exactly where the currents are most dangerous, and where it's safe to cast my nets.'

'Just don't take any risks,' she'd say. 'I'd rather you came home empty-handed than not come back at all.'

'Oh, I'm always careful,' he'd say, with an airy wave of his hand.

Lalita looks at the sun. He should be on his way home right now. Maybe he's joined the mourners.

She can make out individuals among the advancing crowd, can hear their words, 'Aiyyo, what sorrow to lose such a man, a good man, in his prime.'

She stands as if rooted, the lungi damp against her chest. *I hope it dries, he'll be needing it tomorrow.*

Already, a part of her knows that he won't be wearing it again.

They're here now, the women gathering her children in their arms. 'Aiyyo, you poor, fatherless children.'

No, they haven't come for some non-existent neighbour. They've come for her. They've come to tell her Anand is dead.

The world goes dark.

***

She comes to sitting on the ground, a group of the women bending over her, clucking in concern.

'How . . . ?'

They shake their heads. 'We told him not to go out. The storm . . . the waves were too high. We warned him it was dangerous.'

'No,' she says. 'That can't be right. He was always so careful.'

'That man offered him money. A lot. He couldn't turn it down.'

'Who did?'

'Some rich man. He drove his fancy car right up onto the beach. He didn't even stop for Muthakka's chickens — ran most of them over, and didn't even bother to stop. He gave her a hundred rupees for her loss, but where is she to get good chickens like that?'

Lalita struggles to her feet. 'And then?'

'Well, he wanted us to bring him sardines, fresh ones, just caught. We told him it was too dangerous to go out. "Look at the waves," we said. We brought some from an earlier catch, but it wouldn't do. He said he wanted to see them alive and squirming. "I'm offering a thousand rupees for four or five big ones. Well? Do you want my custom or not?" We all said no, it was too risky. Then your husband offered to go. "A thousand rupees will pay for my children to go to the rich men's school," he said. We told him he was crazy. "Look at the sea," we said. "Look how angry it is. It won't give you anything, it will take you instead. Go home to your wife and children." We thought that was the end of the matter, but then the rich man said, "Okay, two thousand." Your husband shook his head, and then the man said, "Five thousand rupees, and that's my final offer." So your husband went.'

'Where is he?' Lalita asks. 'Where is this rich man who thought my husband's life was worth the miserable sum of five thousand rupees?'

Lalita looks wildly around. 'Is he still there, at the beach?'

'Lalita—'

But Lalita is already halfway across the field.

She reaches the beach just as he's driving away, his tyres churning up sand. Half-blinded, she catches a glimpse of his face, looking back. He's laughing.

'You killed my husband!'

She runs after the retreating car. Runs, until her legs give way and she sinks to the ground. A life lost, three others ruined, all for a handful of sardines.

CHAPTER 64

The day of the wedding
The resort employee

Now Lalita understands why Suraj seemed so familiar. It's him — the man who sent her husband to his death.

Suraj laughs. 'So he set off, into the sea, and was never seen again.'

Georgie is silent.

'And I never got my fish. So annoying.'

'He died out there?' Georgie says. 'Doesn't that worry you?'

'Nope. Not my problem, is it?'

'What about your child? Our child. I suppose that doesn't worry you either.'

'Who knows if it was even mine?' he says.

Inside the room, someone screams. There is a thud. Then another. Then nothing.

Lalita waits, listening.

She hears the muffled squeak of the door opening. Georgie's voice is suddenly loud. 'Oh my god. I've killed him. I've killed him.'

Her footsteps retreating down the corridor are barely audible on the thick pile of the carpet.

For several minutes Lalita remains on her knees in the cupboard, barely able to move.

After a while, she emerges, blinking, into the corridor.

She takes the few steps to Georgie's door like an old woman, and stands there for a moment, out of breath. She pushes the door open.

CHAPTER 65

The bride-to-be

Sam wakes to find Aru sitting on the bed beside her. 'How are you feeling?' she asks.

Sam smiles faintly. 'If I didn't know better I'd think you've been keeping watch over me, just like a mother.'

Aru merely smiles.

Sam is almost sorry it's over. She would have liked to get to know this woman better. She has a feeling there is much more to Arundhati Sharma than meets the eye.

'Well? You haven't answered my question,' Aru says.

'I've been better,' Sam says.

'I'm sorry.' Aru sounds as if she means it.

Sam takes a breath. 'You'll be pleased to know that I'm not going to marry your son after all.'

'Good. You've come to your senses at last,' Aru says. 'You don't deserve him.'

You don't deserve him. The slashed lehenga, the wedding token, both bearing that message . . . All at once, Sam makes the connection.

'It was you. You slashed my lehenga. You left the wedding token.'

Aru's eyes widen, very slightly.

You too, Sam thinks.

All of them — Suraj, Georgie, Aru — have betrayed her in different ways. None of them are who they pretend to be.

You're a fine one to talk, her conscience chides.

CHAPTER 66

The resort employee

Unmoving, deathly still, he lies sprawled on the bed, bleeding from a wound on his head.

Lalita ventures closer and looks down at him. This is the man who killed her husband, who made orphans of her children — after all, she's so far away she might as well be dead to them too.

Lalita bends down and whispers in his ear, 'You've got what you deserve.'

Suddenly, without warning, his arm shoots out and he grips Lalita's hand.

She gasps and tries to pull her hand away.

'Help me,' he whispers. 'Please.'

Lalita hesitates. He's bleeding badly. He'll die if she doesn't help him.

She disengages her hand. 'Why should I?'

'Please!'

CHAPTER 67

The mother of the groom

'And the postcard? The notes? Did you send those too?' Sam asks.

'No,' Aru says.

Sam's eyes are swollen and bloodshot. As if to herself, she says in a whisper, 'So there are two of you.'

Aru doesn't tell her she knows who the other person is. Instead, she says, 'You don't deserve my son.'

Sam flinches.

'You deserve better,' Aru adds.

Sam looks at her uncertainly.

'He was always evil, right from the start,' Aru says. 'And it wasn't just that I spoiled him. When I found I was carrying a boy, I prayed that he wouldn't take after his father. He turned out worse. Once I found him strangling our pet cat. He was giggling while he watched it struggle. He was only seven. When I shouted at him to stop, all he did was laugh at me.' A tear escapes her eye, and Sam watches it roll down her cheek.

'I left those things for you to find because I didn't want you to have to suffer like I did,' Aru continues. 'I knew it would upset you, but nothing else seemed to work. I tried asking you outright, I made sure you overheard the comment I made to Suraj after I invited you to my room. I didn't know what else to do. I'm sorry.'

Now Sam, too, is crying. 'You ripped the lehenga to shreds and then you lent me your sari so that I could attend the Mehendi. Why, if you wanted to stop the wedding?'

'Your determination to go ahead with it took me by surprise,' Aru says. 'To be honest, I didn't think you'd have so much courage. But I didn't change my mind, I just had to find another way. Hence the token through your door with that message.'

Sam frowns, remembering.

Aru points to the cut on Sam's forehead. 'Who did that to you, Sam? Do you know?'

'My sister.'

'Ah.'

'She . . . she and Suraj . . .'

'So you know about that, then,' Aru says.

Sam looks at Aru, a question in her eyes.

'I found out just after we got here. I'm so sorry,' Aru says.

'It's what I deserve.'

'Come now, you're being silly. Of course you don't,' Aru says. 'You—'

'Oh, but I do.'

'What do you mean?'

'I haven't been honest with you,' Sam says.

'I don't see how . . .' Aru thinks of that whispered conversation in the bathroom on the jet.

'I've spent time in prison,' Sam says quietly.

Aru stares at her. This was the last thing she'd expected to hear from this meek and quiet woman. 'What for?'

Sam takes a breath. 'I killed my parents.'

'*What?*'

Her voice shaking, Sam says, 'My parents had been out with friends and I offered to come and pick them up. They said they'd take a taxi but I insisted, even though we were supposed to be going out. I'd just passed my test and I leaped at the chance to drive. I'd been drinking.'

'You said "we". Was Georgie there too?'

'Yes. I didn't mean to drink — I told myself it wouldn't hurt to have just one, but it turned out to be one too many. Georgie had been drinking too, so she didn't want to drive. I should have let my parents take that taxi. What a fool I was. I have gone over it again and again, asked myself why I didn't see sense . . .'

Sam catches her breath in a sob.

'Sam,' Aru says, 'you don't have to go on if it's too painful for you.'

'I want to,' Sam says. 'It's a relief, actually. To tell someone. Anyway, Georgie came with me and we picked up my parents. I seemed to be doing okay, but on the way back . . .' Sam is crying openly now. Aru surprises herself with an impulse to put her arms around the girl.

'I don't remember much about what happened. I only recall seeing the headlights coming towards us and the screech of brakes. I came to in hospital to be told that my parents were dead and that my sister and the driver of the other car were in a critical condition.

'The other driver . . . recovered but lost use of one of his legs. Georgie lives with chronic pain. As for me—' Sam gives a bitter little laugh — 'I got off scot-free. Hardly even bruised. Nothing. Why?'

'Not scot-free. You went to prison,' Aru says.

'But I'm out now. I'm not in pain.'

'Not physically, perhaps.' Imagine what it must be like, to live your whole life regretting one youthful error of judgement. Think of how many teenagers drive after having drunk too much, and get away with it. Aru's thoughts turn to her son. Like his father, he's always on the lookout for vulnerability in others, a chink in their armour that he can exploit. It's why Aru has, over the years, built up a veneer of impenetrability, acting as though nothing affects her. It's why, despite having warmed to Sam, Aru was careful not to show it.

Aru had wondered why Suraj had proposed to this particular girl. Now she knew — he'd picked up on her feelings of guilt and self-accusation, the way she blamed herself for everything that happened to her, and decided it could be used to his advantage.

From the first, Aru had realised that this girl would never be able to withstand the gaslighting, the games the Sharma men played with their women. She knew too that they didn't stop at emotional abuse. Those games, both in and out of bed, often turned violent. It had taken Aru years to construct a backbone of steel. She couldn't bear the thought of another woman having to go through what she'd had to endure. Realising this, she'd hired someone to keep a discreet eye on the girl, just to make sure Suraj did not do too much damage before she could put a stop to the marriage.

She'd had to be clever about it, ruthless too, so as not to arouse Suraj's suspicions. So, when she'd asked to see Sam again, and he'd asked why, she'd answered, 'because I can't understand what you see in her. What about some nice *seedhi sadhi* Indian—'

'No,' her son had said. 'Sorry, Ma, I've made up my mind. It's Sam or nobody.'

Then the games began. He'd bought her that awful yellow dress that didn't even fit her, and had made sure photos of Sam wearing it were splashed all over the papers.

Sam reminded Aru of herself when she first met Dheeraj — young and naive and out of her depth. It was why Dheeraj chose *her*, a girl from the slums, rather than the sophisticates he usually mixed with. He'd used her for his punchbag, a convenient sponge to soak up whatever frustrations he happened to feel on any particular day. Her backbone of steel had been forged on the anvil of his violence.

She'd prayed that Suraj wouldn't follow in his father's footsteps. Then he'd brought this girl home — shy and out of place, in a dress several sizes too small that he'd made her wear for the occasion — and Aru's heart had gone out to her. She was so like Aru had been when Dheeraj first turned the beam of his attention on her — gauche, over-eager to please, making excuses for the subtle put-downs while marvelling that this rich and handsome man could have chosen her.

So Aru had set to work to sabotage the wedding.

She'd arranged for Sam to come to her room at the very moment she told her son that Sam wasn't good enough for him. Her ploy hadn't worked, so she'd resorted to violence — placing the ripped-up lehenga and the wedding token with the message *'You don't deserve him'* in Sam's room. Strategies she'd learned from the master, her husband.

'I . . . I haven't driven since,' Sam is saying.

Suddenly the door is flung open and Georgie bursts into the room. 'Can't you get it into your head? It was *me*!'

'What?' Sam cries.

Aru stares at the woman. Is that . . . *blood* on her clothes?

'*I* was driving,' Georgie is saying. 'You were drunk. Well, I was too. I told you I'd only had a couple of shots, but it was way more than that. But I could hold my drink better and you were so out of it that I decided to drive.'

'I don't understand what you're saying, Georgie.' Sam is staring at her sister, her face pale as milk.

Aru points a finger at Georgie. '*You* were driving. You caused the accident. But you let Sam believe it was her.' She can't keep the disgust from her voice.

'Georgie, is this true?' Sam asks, her voice shaking.

'I—'

'Not only content with that, you sleep with her fiancé as well.' Aru can hardly bear to look at the woman.

'He won't be hers now,' Georgie says. She's swaying on her feet.

Drunk again? No. This is more like shock. And that blood on her clothes . . .

Something cold slithers up Aru's spine. She has a bad feeling about this.

'He . . . he got me to abort our baby—'

'You . . . Suraj's baby?' Sam cannot continue.

'He was mine first.' Georgie sounds like a petulant child. 'I met him at the small business awards where he was the guest of honour. He made a beeline for me, gave me his number. And you . . . You took him away from me.'

'I didn't know you were seeing him,' Sam says softly. 'But Georgie, you just said *you* were driving that day. You mean it wasn't me? But you said *I* killed them. Remember, when I came round. In the hospital—'

'You didn't remember the accident. I kept waiting for your memory to come back, but it never did. And then I told Suraj about the lie I told you, and it made him interested in you.'

Of course, Aru thinks. As soon as her son had heard how vulnerable Sam was, he'd made a beeline for her. Here was someone he could manipulate, just as Dheeraj had manipulated her, a girl from the slums who had nothing but beauty going for her. He'd never allowed her to forget where she came from, and that he could take all that he'd given her away — the wealth, the status — whenever he liked. He kept her walking on eggshells with his comments about her looks, her age. Comparing her to the girlfriends he shamelessly paraded in front of her. Hence the plastic surgeon, the personal trainer, on whom she has come to rely.

Aru often wonders why she's put up with it for so long. The truth is, she's afraid. It's too late to return to the slums. She'd be lost there now. She's traded her world for his, and there's no going back.

She's tried so hard to save Sam from the same fate, doomed to become a pawn in the Sharma games. But what of her? If Sam can be rescued, can't she be saved too? Maybe she owes it to herself to at least try.

Sam is staring at her sister. She looks devastated. 'You mean Suraj knew all along?'

'You know very well that Sam didn't steal him from you,' Aru says to Georgie. 'She didn't know you were seeing him. It was only when you told him how you'd lied to her that he homed in on her.'

'I had the abortion the day after he first took her out,' Georgie cries.

'You expect me to feel sorry for you?' Aru says. 'She wasn't to know, was she? You're a piece of work. You and my son—'

'But you're still seeing him,' Sam says, sounding puzzled.

'We never stopped seeing each other,' Georgie says.

'Even after he proposed to me?'

'I was to be your only guest at the wedding. He warned your friends not to come,' Georgie says proudly.

This is too much for Sam. 'You mean he threatened Edie and Edna, Mr Venables and Mrs Arbuthnot?'

Georgie nods.

'No wonder they lost all their enthusiasm after I handed them the wedding invites. No wonder they kept asking me if it was what I really wanted.' Tears sparkle in Sam's eyes. 'But I still don't understand. Why was Suraj so interested in me when he knew what really happened?'

'I can answer that,' Aru says quietly. 'It's what he does, picks on the most vulnerable.' She takes a breath. Sam might as well know everything. 'It was Suraj who sent you the threatening notes.'

'What?'

'He likes playing games with people,' Aru says gently. *Like father, like son.*

Aru asks herself again why she's put up with it all these years. Sam is vulnerable too, yet she braved all the threats to her and only called off the wedding when she was able to do it on her terms. And it's then that Aru realises something.

Aru is who she is *despite* her husband and his cruelty. There is a small part of her real self that never went away, despite all of her husband's put-downs and cruelty and the veneer of coldness she cultivated to cope with it, and it has taken Sam to understand this, to find it again.

'Oh, he likes playing games all right,' Georgie says bitterly. 'Know what he said to me just now? He asked me if the baby I aborted was really his. That was a step too far.'

Aru feels her heart contract. 'And? What did you do?'

'I think . . .' Georgie swallows. 'I think I killed him.'

CHAPTER 68

The resort employee

He looks so pathetic lying there, helpless.

She'd believed him to be invincible. Laughing as he drove off, the wheels of his car flinging grit in her face.

When he appeared at the resort, she hadn't recognised him. She'd only made the connection when she overheard him telling Georgie about sending a poor fisherman out into a storm. His laugh when he bragged that he always got what he wanted. *Whatever it costs*, she thought bitterly. Even the life of her husband.

And now he's begging for *his* life.

This is her moment.

'You killed my husband,' she says.

His eyes widen. 'What are you talking about? Who are you, anyway?'

Lalita thinks of Anand. So gentle. So kind. The man who showed her how wonderful love could be. She misses him every single day. She thinks of him sinking beneath the waves.

'My husband, a fisherman, didn't know how to swim.'

On the bed, her husband's killer laughs. 'That's rich. A fisherman who can't swim.'

It's too much for her. Incandescent with rage, she picks up the bloodstained lamp still lying on the bed beside him — a nice piece, antique, bronze. Worth thousands. Worth a man's life?

'I'm sorry. I'm sorry. I didn't mean it—'

'You didn't care, did you? You sent him out for the fish you wanted, even though the waves were too high and everyone warned you it was dangerous. He lost his life out there. And you just drove away, laughing.' Lalita tastes the gasoline again, the grit and her grief.

'I'm truly sorry.'

'You're just saying that because you're scared. Well, listen to me. There's a "Do Not Disturb" sign on the door. Your security detail know all about your affair with the woman whose room this is, so they're not going to come in. Meanwhile, you're bleeding out. Looks like I'm your only hope, doesn't it?'

'Please.'

'Why should I save you?'

'I'll give you money. Name the amount and I'll have it transferred immediately.'

Ha, these rich people. Thinking the world turns on money.

But it does. It does. It would mean that her children's future was guaranteed. But she can't accept money from this man. It would be tainted.

'I'll give you anything you want.'

What she wants is to see her children again.

If she allows this man to die, how will she live with her conscience?

In her mind, she pictures the faces of the women in his life. They're watching her: his bride, her eyes bright with suffering; the woman he's sleeping with, hers glittering with rage; his mother, cold and impenetrable.

Why should she let him live only to cause them pain?

CHAPTER 69

Now
The resort employee

'Mrs Anand, I will ask you again. Did you have anything to do with what happened at the cliffs?'

Lalita, her throat dry, swallows with difficulty. The detective's unflinching gaze seems to see right through her, down to her black, cursed soul. 'No, sir.'

'Did you have anything to do with the bloodstains found in the victim's bed?'

She looks at the detective, and all she sees is that man begging for his life. While she . . .

She . . .

'Mrs Anand?'

She keeps her eyes fixed on his. 'No, sir.'

CHAPTER 70

The day of the wedding
The mother of the groom

'What are you saying?' Sam whispers, breaking the stunned silence that follows Georgie's declaration.

Aru can only stare at the two women.

They may be sisters but they couldn't be more different. Sam reacts by retreating, making herself as small as possible. Georgie, on the other hand, goes on the attack, lashing out at whoever is nearest, whoever she can find to blame.

Her son.

Her son, the sadist. Just like his father. Try as she might, she could not change him. Is — *was* there no hope for her son?

Stop, Aru, this will lead you nowhere. Pull yourself together.

Aru musters her resources. 'Where is he?'

'In my room,' Georgie says.

'Take us there. Now.'

'Must I come too?' Sam shrinks back into her pillows.

'Come, Sam. You need to see for yourself.' Aru knows from bitter experience that you have to face up to what life throws at you. Only then can you move on. It has been a hard-won lesson, perhaps the only fruit of a blighted life.

Aru fixes Sam with her gaze, willing her to be strong, even as her heart bleeds for her son. 'Come. We need to deal with it, or there will be consequences.'

If Dheeraj finds out...

Aru shivers. On no account must he find out how his son died.

Oh, Suraj. You played one game too many, went one step too far, with devastating consequences.

Aru is no fan of Georgie, but she wouldn't wish the force of Dheeraj's wrath on her worst enemy.

'Deal with it? How?' Georgie finally seems to be coming to her senses.

'Trust her,' Sam tells her. 'She knows best.' And she gives Aru a wan smile.

'Come on, then.'

Flanked by the two young women, Aru makes her stately way to Georgie's room. She's as upright as ever but each step is an effort, heavy with the burden of her grief.

Reaching the door, she pauses, her hand on the doorknob. 'Ready?'

They nod, their eyes huge and fearful. Suddenly, all their differences are gone, and they are sisters once again.

They have each other, while I will have nobody if Suraj is gone.

Slowly, Aru pushes open the door and gasps.

CHAPTER 71

Now
The resort employee

'Mrs Anand, did you strike Mr Sharma with the intention of killing him?'

'No, sir.'

'Mrs Anand, were you present at the cliffs at the time of the incident?'

'Yes, sir. I went there looking for my trolley.'

'And, tell me, what did you see?'

For a brief moment Lalita imagines herself as a seagull, flying high above the ocean towards home. She's holding her children in her arms, breathing in their warm, sweet smell. 'Nothing, sir. By the time I arrived, it was all over . . .'

CHAPTER 72

The day of the wedding
The bride-to-be

The bed is empty.

Freshly made, as if waiting for a guest to arrive.

Sam heaves a sigh of relief.

She still cannot get her head around what her sister has just told her. How could she have allowed Sam to believe she was a murderess? How could she have left her to do penance for a crime she did not commit?

Sam remembers the dream she had, her parents coming to her and telling her there was nothing to forgive. Was it a subconscious memory of what really happened on that fateful evening when her parents were killed?

She hasn't done anything wrong. All these years she's been living a pitiful existence, convinced that she's a monster.

It's her sister who's the monster. She not only let Sam take the fall for her actions, but has also been sleeping with the man Sam was to marry.

But where is he now, the man who wouldn't sleep with her because his mother wouldn't like it?

The man who slept with her sister instead.

The man who played games with her, probing her, asking what she was hiding.

Who said he hated people who lied.

Who said he believed prison did nothing to reform people, and they should be hanged.

Who caused her to be on tenterhooks every hour of the day, enjoying her discomfort.

Who sent her threatening notes intimating that her past was not secret and that soon the world would know. This is why the notes and the postcard were empty threats, never realised — Suraj had enjoyed playing with her too much to actually carry them through.

Who bought her clothes that didn't fit.

Who made comments about her weight.

Who insulted her friends and warned them not to come to the wedding.

Who played away, knowing she would never complain because of her constant fear that her secret would come out.

Who proposed to marry her just to see how far she would go, how much she would take, before she broke.

But now she's free.

Georgie's voice breaks into her thoughts. 'I don't understand. I hit him. Where's the lamp? It was a heavy, metal one. He dropped like a stone.'

Aru winces.

'He was bleeding — it was all over the sheets.' Georgie stares incredulously at the pristine bedcovers.

Sam cannot process her emotions. Rage at the way her sister has treated her — Suraj too. Hurt, sorrow, disbelief don't even begin to describe what she feels.

Her sister, pregnant with the child of the man Sam loved. Because part of her does still love Suraj, despite all she's learned about him.

Her sister, who locked Sam in her wardrobe while she had sex with that same man. Sam recalls how scared she was, curled up, trapped and bleeding in the dark.

'You probably imagined it,' Sam says, unable to keep the disgust from her voice.

'No!' Georgie yells. 'I'm telling you, it really happened.'

'There must be a rational explanation,' Aru says, sounding composed. 'I'll go and look in his room.'

Sam regards the woman with awe. Her own son might be dead, yet she's so perfectly cool.

After Aru has left, Sam turns to her sister. Suddenly, it's imperative that she knows what Georgie had been planning to do with her. 'How long would you have left me in the wardrobe? Were you going to leave me there till I suffocated and died?'

Georgie looks away and starts to bite her fingernails. It's a familiar gesture, something she did even as a child. Sam recalls how, whenever her sister did something wrong, she would point the finger at Sam, biting her fingernails while she watched Sam take her punishment. How, while Sam was still smarting from the smack she'd been given, Georgie would throw her arms around her and thank her. 'You're so sweet, Sam. I love you so much.'

It was the same when she killed their parents. Sam took the blame, like always.

'How did you know it was me?' Georgie asks.

'I recognised your voice.'

'But I didn't speak.'

'You were grunting, swearing under your breath.'

'You were conscious?'

'All the time. I heard you and Suraj.' Sam bites back tears.

'I tried to get you to break up with him,' Georgie says, 'but you wouldn't take the hint.'

'What do you mean?'

'It was me sending you those texts.'

'What, those ones from an unknown number?'

'Yep. Asking you how well you really knew the man you were going to marry.'

Sam shakes her head, dumbfounded. The texts. The notes. The slashed lehenga. Every member of the wedding party warning her not to go ahead with it. And she, instead of heeding them, had dug in her heels — the more she was warned off, the more determined she became to go through with it.

'How could you allow me to live my life believing I'd killed Mum and Dad, not to mention injuring the driver of the other car, through no fault of his own?'

Georgie bites her fingernails.

So this is why Georgie stayed away, kept her distance. Why she chose a different surname. It was her guilt.

Or is Sam even now making excuses for her?

'We'll talk about it later, Sam. Suraj—'

The door opens to admit Aru. She looks pale, suddenly much older. 'He's not there.'

Sam isn't about to let her sister off so easily. 'When, Georgie? You have to tell me now why you killed our parents and allowed me to take the blame. Why you had an affair with the man I was engaged to. Why you locked me in the wardrobe and left me to die—'

'Oh come on, now you're being dramatic. You didn't die, did you?' Georgie says.

'That's because Lalita—'

And then, along with fury, comprehension dawns, and Sam understands what might have happened.

'What are you saying?' Georgie screams. 'Lolita? Who's she? Where does this Lo—'

Aru catches on immediately, cutting Georgie off. 'Quick, we must find her before my husband does.'

'Will someone tell me who the hell Lolita—'

'Shut up, girl, you're giving me a headache,' Aru snaps.

Georgie stops mid-sentence and stares wide-eyed at Aru.

'You're lucky I'm not your sister, or *you'd* be dead by now.' With that, Aru turns on her elegant heel and marches out of the room.

Georgie's face is a picture of utter bewilderment.

CHAPTER 73

The resort employee

Pushing the cleaning trolley in front of her, Lalita makes her escape.

There is a back way out of the resort that all the cleaning staff use when they need a bit of peace, away from the constant surveillance — human and electronic. One of the other maids, a local girl, showed them where to find it. From this narrow passageway, Lalita emerges onto the clifftop, where the wind catches at her hair and whips it across her face. She has trouble holding onto her trolley, which the wind threatens to tear from her grasp, sending it hurtling down onto the rocks below.

And good riddance, she thinks. That damn trolley has come to stand for everything she hates about this life: Clock up twelve hours a day, if not more. Always do what the guests tell you to. Don't leave the resort without permission. Whatever you do, you must not relax. There is always more work to be done.

What does all that matter now? Now that she's done for.

One unthinking action and everything is ruined. All her hard work, all those months and months of endless slog. Gone.

Just don't send me to prison. Please. Deport me, let me go back to my children. All I want now is to hold them in my arms again.

If she dived into this sea and kept on swimming, would it take her to the Arabian sea? Would she wash up on the beach at home? She's heard somewhere that all the seas join together. Is that true?

The trolley hits a rock and almost turns over. Again, Lalita is tempted to fling it over the cliff.

'*Lalita* . . .' Someone is calling her name, very faintly.

She rubs her eyes. She turns towards where she thinks the sound came from.

Then she sees them. Three figures, coming towards her.

Aru, striding forward in her high heels. Behind her, Sam, hurrying to keep up. And, bringing up the rear, Georgie, stumbling on the rocks.

Like three avenging angels, Lalita thinks.

Lalita throws back her head and laughs.

Do your worst, for I am done for.

CHAPTER 74

The sister of the bride

Georgie wishes someone would tell her what's going on.

She totters after Aru and Sam as they race towards the cliff edge.

Are they mad? Why come up here, away from the safety of the resort?

But she has no choice but to follow them. Not after what she did.

She pictures Suraj, falling backward, blood gushing from the wound in his head. Lying completely still.

If she sticks with Aru and Sam, perhaps they'll find him.

And who the hell is Lolita?

They're following the tracks left by a ... cleaning trolley, of all things.

'She went this way.' Aru increases her pace.

'Lolita!' they call, their voices swallowed up by the breeze. It's so wild out here, so much vast open space. And these treacherous paths, veering too close to the cliffs. From inside the resort, the view seems romantic, with the rocky crags and the sea twinkling below.

But here, outside the safe cocoon of her room, the wind is so strong it almost sends her to her knees. It beats the very trees into submission, and whips the sea against the rocks.

Georgie isn't dressed for this. Her shoes aren't designed for the wild outdoors. She keeps tripping on the pebbles and her heels sink into the mud. She's having trouble keeping up with Aru, who strides forward effortlessly, invincible as always.

A gust of wind flicks Georgie's hair into her face, making her blink. All the trouble she took to get her hair just right for the wedding. Well, it won't go ahead now, if they don't find the groom. If he's even alive after what she did.

And why did she hit Sam and hide her in the wardrobe? Did she think she could make her sister just disappear and she'd have Suraj all to herself? What was she thinking? She wasn't, that was the problem. She never did think when the anger took over, the same old jealous rage. Even after what she'd done to her, allowing her to take the punishment for her crime, Sam was getting what *she* wanted. The Mehendi had gone ahead and Suraj hadn't called off the wedding, despite continuing to make love to Georgie. She couldn't bear the thought of Sam coming out on top, as ever.

Then, when she confronted Suraj, he'd just laughed at her. Right up to the moment when she lashed out at Suraj, she'd believed he would see sense, call it off, marry her instead. When Georgie finally saw that all along she'd been used, the red mist had descended.

Was he dead? He was bleeding badly. When she shook him, he didn't respond.

So she panicked, and did what she always did when she got herself into a mess — ran to her sister.

But where is Suraj now? There wasn't the slightest trace of blood on the sheets. *Am I going mad? Was the whole thing a hallucination?*

Sam's voice is a welcome interruption to her thoughts. 'There she is.'

They've found this Lolita person. Maybe now this madness will end. Suraj is alive and I imagined hitting him. I suppose that means I'll have to get my head checked.

Sam stops and waits for Georgie to catch up. Kind as always. How Georgie hates it. Georgie wishes she hadn't blurted out the truth about their parents, especially after she'd kept that quiet for so long. It was thinking she'd just killed Suraj, and seeing Sam parading her woes before Aru, making everything about her as usual: *I killed my parents, I'm sorry. I'm such a bad person. Me, me, me.*

Georgie knows she's being unfair, but she can't help it. Sam irritates her, she always has.

She really must think about getting help, some form of counselling. It's all got to her, the stress of seeing her man on the point of marrying her plain, colourless sister, who, by the way, is devoid of all personality. She was more fun before the accident, but even then she was the responsible one.

It used to drive Georgie crazy. Why couldn't Sam behave like a proper teenager? She was so sanctimonious, so holier-than-thou, always obeying the rules, doing things by the book. Why couldn't she ever let her hair down? Georgie was delighted when Sam started drinking that day — the day their parents died. Even then, Georgie had to keep badgering her to have another glass.

But, when Sam insisted she wasn't going to go above the limit, Georgie spiked her coke, adding a shot of vodka to it. Sam kept drinking more, thinking it would sober her up, and by the time their parents called, she couldn't even stand, let alone walk straight. When she saw how drunk her sister was, Georgie, who'd been matching Sam glass for glass, offered to drive instead.

'No,' Sam said. 'You've been drinking.'

Georgie almost said, 'And you haven't? Look at you!'

So Sam took the wheel. It was a hair-raising ride. She kept veering over the centre line, and Georgie began to fear they might not make it.

By the time they finally arrived to collect their parents, Sam was looking very pale. 'I think there's something the matter with me. I feel sick and my vision is all blurry.'

'I'll drive back,' Georgie offered. At first, their parents demurred. But they gave in when Georgie told them she hadn't had more than the legal limit, and Sam wasn't feeling well.

They set off, their parents soon falling asleep while Sam slumped in the passenger seat beside Georgie.

The car seemed to come at her from nowhere, its headlights blinding her so that she panicked, and swerved right instead of left.

In the terrible aftermath of the accident, Georgie, suddenly frighteningly sober, had the presence of mind to drag her sister into the driver's seat to make it appear as if Sam had been driving when the ambulance arrived at the scene.

'It was all Sam's fault. She shouldn't have been driving,' Georgie said.

Over the years, she repeated the lie so often that she came to believe it herself.

Fast-forward to the morning Georgie was due to attend the clinic for her abortion. She'd asked Suraj to come with her, but he'd said he couldn't make it. On her way out, Georgie received an unexpected call from her sister. She was about to accept it when her phone pinged with a notification — pictures of Suraj on her social media. With her sister, of all people.

Believing that Sam was calling to gloat, she messaged her that she couldn't talk, she was on her way to hospital. Sam, of course, assumed it was because of Georgie's ongoing pain from the injuries she'd sustained in the accident. Truth was, Georgie had never been in pain. But it suited her to let Sam think she was.

Watching her sister, Georgie feels the familiar sting of jealous rage. If it weren't for Sam, Suraj would be with her now, not lost somewhere with a wound on his head. He liked the fact that she was wild, ruthless and calculating. 'You and me, Georgie,' he would say, 'we're different from everyone else. We go for what we want, and let nothing stand in our way.'

She told him about Sam and how she'd led her to believe that she'd killed their parents, thinking he would approve. And the next thing she knew, Suraj had proposed to her sister.

She tried to break them up by sending those texts, but Sam refused to take the bait. The night before the wedding, something in Georgie snapped. Sam had been a constant thorn in her side, and she wanted her out.

So she hid Sam away, but still she wasn't rid of her.

If only that stupid maid had waited until after the wedding to clean the room.

'Come on, Georgie,' Sam is saying. 'Lolita is just over there.'

Georgie looks at where Sam is pointing.

Oh my goodness — the maid. Whoever named that skinny little thing Lolita? Georgie almost smiles.

Then Sam says, 'I think . . . I think she has Suraj.'

CHAPTER 75

The bride-to-be

Sam has slowed down to wait for Georgie. God knows why. Why should she care what happens to her sister after what she's done?

But seeing Georgie struggling to catch up, her heels sinking in the mud, scrunching her face up like she used to when she was little and didn't understand what was going on but wanted to be part of it anyway, Sam can't stifle the familiar instinct to protect her sister.

'Come on, Georgie,' she says.

Georgie shouts something back, but a sudden gust of wind carries her words away.

Up ahead, Aru is almost upon Lalita, who stands at the edge of the cliffs looking lost, still holding onto her cleaning trolley. Her eyes are wide and terrified, her hair loose around her face.

Sam glances down at the waves crashing against the rocks below the cliff edge. Further along, where the rocks give way to sand, she glimpses movement.

Tiny figures, scurrying about like ants and battling against the wind as they set up a podium. More figures, carrying what looks like — oh, an enormous wreath of fresh flowers. Sam can't make them out from here, but she knows they spell out *Sam Weds Suraj* in red roses against a backdrop of white carnations. Suraj hired a wedding planner to take care of the arrangements. She must be the minuscule person hugging a folder. 'Everything must be perfect,' Suraj said, and the wedding planner smiled confidently.

'Of course, sir.'

They haven't got the memo, don't know that the groom is missing, possibly dead.

Sam shivers.

Is Suraj in the trolley that little Lalita is holding onto so determinedly? She could only have managed to get his ripped and muscly body into it if he was incapable of fighting back.

She turns her back on the sight of those tiny figures on the beach below. She turns her back, too, on her wedding day, and on the man who betrayed her.

But she cared for him. And, to her surprise, finds she still does. Is he there, in that trolley — injured or worse?

Reluctantly, Sam moves towards the small figure with the incongruous cleaning trolley. She shivers, hugging herself, her teeth chattering.

'You're cold. Here.' Sam's sister has caught up with her. She shrugs off her flimsy leather jacket and wraps it around Sam's shoulders.

'B—But you've only got a vest on.'

'I'm all right. You need it more,' Georgie says with a shrug.

The jacket smells of her sister — alcohol and that strong floral perfume she likes so much. Despite all that has happened, it's comforting.

Meanwhile, Lalita is gazing fearfully at the three of them.

Aru asks, in a surprisingly gentle tone, 'Now, Lalita, what's all this about, eh?'

Lalita's face crumples. Through her tears, she stammers, 'He . . . he killed my husband.'

They stare at her. 'What?'

Aru steps forward and takes Lalita in her arms, stroking her windswept hair. 'There, there. It's going to be all right.'

But Sam is eyeing the cleaning trolley. Is he in there?

Lalita disengages herself from Aru's embrace and turns to Georgie. 'I heard him telling you about a fisherman who lost his life at sea because of some fresh fish he wanted. Remember the story? He paid him to go out in a storm.'

Georgie nods. 'Yes, I remember.'

'That was my husband.' Lalita chokes on the words. 'He wanted money for our children's education. The others warned him not to go out, but he was prepared to risk his life for it. For them.'

Aru closes her eyes as if she's in pain.

'He laughed,' Lalita says. 'My husband died, and he laughed about it.'

'Yes, he did,' Georgie says.

'I left my children and came here to support them. It was the only way I could give them the education my husband wanted for them. My children are growing up without parents. All because that man wanted fresh fish, and wouldn't wait for it.'

'I'm sorry,' Aru whispers.

'It's not your fault.' Lalita turns towards the trolley. 'It's his.'

'But where is he?' Georgie asks.

'After you left him—'

'He was dead,' Georgie whispers.

Lalita looks away. Above her, a lone seagull hovers for a moment and then, with a cry, veers away. 'I covered him with the sheets and got him and the lamp onto the trolley. I didn't know what to do, so I just kept on walking. Oh, what have I done?'

CHAPTER 76

The mother of the groom

Aru puts her arm around Lalita's shoulders.

'It's all right.'

But Lalita is inconsolable. 'It's not all right. I've made everything worse. What will happen to my children now?'

'You will get to see your children, I promise,' Aru says. Above Lalita's head, her eyes meet Sam's.

Aru believes Lalita's story. It's just what he would do. Her son never thought of anyone but himself. If he wanted something, he wanted it at once, no matter what the cost.

Yet he's her son, and she can't help loving him.

Slowly, reluctantly, Aru steps toward the trolley.

Then, just as she bends forward to look, the trolley moves. She hears a muffled thump coming from within.

Aru gasps, swivelling round to look at the others. Did they hear it?

Lalita stops crying. Sam is staring at the trolley, while Georgie's mouth is open in a silent scream.

The trolley moves again, closer to the edge of the cliff. Dangerously close.

They watch it, mesmerised.

He's alive.

Aru hears his voice, faint but distinct. 'Let me out at once.'

The tone is imperious. It's her son, all right.

Even as her heart lifts in relief, she thinks, *Someone will be made to pay for this. My son will want his revenge.*

This doesn't bode well. Not for any of them.

Aru glances over her shoulder at the three women standing behind her. Their faces all wear the same expression — dread.

CHAPTER 77

Now
The resort employee

'Mrs Anand. You mean to tell me that when you got to the cliffs, the incident had already taken place?'

'Yes, sir.'

The detective's eyes narrow. In a voice like a butcher's knife, sharp enough to slice bone, he says, 'You're lying.'

How does he know? Is there a camera in that hidden passageway?

Please, no.

Lalita shoots a panicked glance at her lawyer, who merely raises an eyebrow, as if to say, *Well, are you?*

She swallows, her fear bitter as methi seeds.

'Mrs Anand, you do realise, don't you, that if you continue to lie to us, you won't be seeing your children anytime soon. I ask you again, did you have anything to do with what happened?'

Lalita tries to picture her children's faces, but they're just a blur. *Anand!* her heart cries. *Help me.*

'No, sir,' she says. 'I did not.'

The detective sighs. 'Then I'll be handing you over to immigration. I'm sure they'll have something to say about you working illegally.'

Lalita closes her eyes and tries to summon her husband, but all she can see is that monster, rising up out of the trolley, bloody and battered but alive, thirsting for vengeance.

CHAPTER 78

The day of the wedding
The sister of the bride

Suraj is alive.

I didn't kill him, Georgie thinks, both relieved and terrified. Suraj will be angry. Out for blood.

Although she loves him, Georgie is afraid. She knows all too well how cruel he can be. After all, it's what drew them together — that selfish, ruthless streak.

Another thud, and the trolley moves again. If someone doesn't stop it, it will go over the edge.

Hardly daring to take her eyes off the trolley, Georgie darts a swift glance back at the others. Sam's eyes are on stalks. Lolita, or whatever the hell she's called, has finally stopped wailing, thank God. Just like those women in war-torn countries you see on the telly, keening and pulling their hair out over their dead husbands and kids.

Georgie gets it now — Lolita's husband is the one Suraj told her about, the one who died at sea because Suraj wanted fresh fish. Why couldn't he have just gone to a restaurant, for Christ's sake? He was hardly short of cash.

As long as she lives, Georgie will never understand the super-rich. In any case, if Suraj gets out of that trolley, she won't be living much longer.

Suppose they just let the trolley roll over the cliff?

Come on, Georgie, you're not that cold-blooded.

Oh, but I am.

Georgie has absolutely no doubt that Suraj won't think twice about pushing her over the cliffs in his place.

But maybe he won't go after me. Maybe it'll be little Lolita. I mean, it was her who put him in that stupid trolley.

The way it's edging slowly forward, they won't need to do anything, just cover their tracks and pretend they got here too late.

Then Lolita will get the blame. It is her cleaning trolley, after all. And it was her who got him into it and brought him out here.

She has children and all — that's why she came here in the first place. She wanted a better future for them. Well, Aru will take care of that.

If that makes her cold-blooded, fine. If she was like Sam, she'd never get anywhere.

It pays to be clear-headed, especially at times like these.

Aru is inching forward, reaching for the trolley.

'No!' Georgie yells. 'If you let him out, he'll kill Lolita,' she hisses. 'And me. You want that? Our blood on your hands?'

'He's my son,' Aru whispers. For the first time, this woman appears vulnerable, torn.

'He's a murderer,' Georgie says. 'He killed her husband.'

'He—'

The trolley rattles and bounces towards the cliff edge. With a sudden bang, it overturns and springs open. Suraj crawls out just as it hurtles over the edge.

CHAPTER 79

The bride-to-be

Suraj staggers to his feet, bloodied and bruised but alive, staring at Georgie with murder in his eyes.

'You—'

He lunges toward her.

But, weak from loss of blood, he loses his footing.

He flails. Starts to topple.

Backwards, over the edge of the cliff.

'*Beta!*' Aru cries.

But Suraj isn't finished yet. He manages to grapple for purchase, holding onto a rock, his feet dangling over the side of the cliff.

'Ma! Help me,' he cries.

Aru does not move. She gazes at her son, tears coursing down her cheeks.

Sam, too, is weeping.

'Please, Ma!' Suraj calls.

Aru seems transfixed. Her child. And a monster. If she were to save him, he would take his revenge. God knows what he would do to Georgie. Lalita too.

'I love you, *beta*. I always will,' Aru cries.

'Then help me!'

Very slowly, Aru turns her back.

'Fuck you, Ma!' Suraj gasps. His desperate gaze skims over Georgie and Lalita, landing on Sam.

'Please, Sam, help me. I love you.'

'No, you don't. You never did. All you ever did was use me.'

'At first, perhaps.' He moves his hand, sending a flurry of small stones onto the rocks below.

'You got Rohan to sign my book "Maisy",' Sam says.

'Know what?' Suraj says through gritted teeth. 'I had it all planned out. I was going to reveal your secret to the press just as we exchanged our vows.'

He's mad, Sam realises. *This man is a psychopath.*

'I engineered the whole thing,' Suraj says proudly.

'The invite to the book signing and someone to push me when I was there? The press finding out where I worked and lived? Even that scrap of fish and chip newspaper with details of my crime?'

'That was me.'

Sam no longer cares if he falls. She needs to know the full extent of his deception. 'You got someone to follow and threaten me, put a knife to my throat.'

'Control, you see. I wanted you vulnerable and dependent on me,' he says. 'I sensed you were having doubts about the wedding.'

Sam recalls how grateful she was for his offer of a bodyguard. What a fool she was!

'I wanted you to stop working. Those friends of yours, those octogenarians, were the only thing standing in the way of my plan. Simple folk, yet they saw through me,' Suraj says grimly. 'Know what? All my life I've been given everything I wanted. Getting your own way all the time becomes boring after a while, so you start creating elaborate games. The one I played with you was the best yet. You were all alone in the world, apart from a sister who hated you. You were white. An Indian girl would have seen through me. Why do you think I wanted to hold the wedding in Cornwall and not in India? There were too many allegations of rape and abuse doing the rounds in India. I'd bought their silence of course, but the rumours were still there.'

'Why tell me all this now?' Sam whispers.

Suraj glances down, shifts his grip on the rock. 'Because I've had enough of secrets. I'm tired of playing games. I expected to be bored with you within a few weeks, like all the others. But the truth is, I actually enjoyed being with you.'

He sounds surprised, as if he's only just realised this.

'I liked the way we were together. Those evenings we spent sitting on your threadbare sofa watching reruns of *Friends*. I didn't have to put on an act, impress anyone. I could just be myself. It's why I proposed to you. I never meant the game to go as far as it has. But I didn't know how to stop it. Part of me hoped you would save me. It gets tiring, always wanting more, being perpetually on the lookout for new thrills, new possessions. When it was just the two of us, doing something as simple as cooking together, or watching TV, I wasn't bored any longer.'

Tears sting Sam's eyes. At least some of what they'd had together had meant something to him.

Behind her, Aru is sobbing.

'Please, Sam,' Suraj begs. 'Help me. Save me.'

Sam hesitates. Did he say all that just as a ploy to get her to rescue him?

Is he manipulating her again? Playing his last hand? Playing for his life? Admitting that he's been bad but also telling her that she's the only one who can save him, making her believe by admitting what he did, by now telling the truth, that he'll change because of her.

She remembers what he said before. *I had it all planned out. I was going to reveal your secret to the press just as we exchanged our vows.* He *is* manipulating her, still playing with her.

'I love you, Sam,' he says.

She sees through him. She will not be taken in. She takes a deep breath. 'If all that is true, why did you continue playing with me? Because you were, weren't you? Telling me people in prison deserved to die. Asking me if I had something to hide. You liked seeing me squirm. You say you love me, so why were you carrying on with my sister behind my back?'

'I was just stringing her along. It didn't mean anything,' Suraj cries.

Behind her, Georgie takes a sharp breath.

'For God's sake, she was having your baby,' Sam says.

'I didn't want it,' he says. 'Anyway, she got rid of it.'

'You said you wanted children with me. You said we'd be a family, once Sam was out of the way,' Georgie cries.

'What? With you?' Suraj laughs, sending another shower of rocks skittering down the cliff. 'No chance of you having a family now, not with me or anyone else.'

'What do you mean?' Georgie says.

None of the four women seems capable of making a move.

Aru is weeping silently. Lalita has her apron in both hands and is wringing it as if her life depends on it.

Sam stands motionless, as if she herself has become a rock. *Even now*, she thinks, *he's still playing a game, and it's far from over.*

CHAPTER 80

The sister of the bride

The wind whistles like someone's last breath.

Even now, clinging to the cliff face, about to fall to his death, Suraj holds them all in thrall. 'You never thought to check the doctor's credentials, did you?' he says.

'Why should I have?' Georgie says, suddenly seized with a terrible foreboding.

'I arranged the abortion, so you went, like a lamb to the slaughter. Didn't you think it was unusual to be put to sleep for an abortion?'

'I wouldn't know, I've never had one before!'

'You should have asked a few questions, my dear, if what you wanted was a family. You should have asked what the procedure involv—'

'Suraj!' Aru cries. 'Enough.'

But Georgie knows what he was about to say. She recalls what he said before: 'No chance of you having a family now, not with me or anyone else.'

Georgie always knew he was evil. It was why she'd been attracted to him in the first place. Both of them equally proud of their ruthlessness.

But this is a whole new level of cruelty. He not only made sure she got rid of the baby, but he also arranged for her to be sterilised, even though he knew she wanted children, a family, with him. This is a step too far.

Georgie brushes past Sam and goes to stand above Suraj. She looks down on him, making sure that the last thing he sees is the hatred and disgust in her eyes. And then she reaches down and, one by one, loosens his fingers.

CHAPTER 81

The sister of the bride

And then Sam is beside her, grabbing her arm. 'No, Georgie! He's not worth it, not worth sacrificing your future.'

'Why do you care?' Georgie tries to shake her sister off. The wind out here on the cliff edge is biting, relentless.

'Georgie! You and me, we can still have a future together,' Suraj says, pleading for his life, though he must know it's too late.

Georgie laughs wildly. 'You took away my future when you took my ability to bear children.'

'We . . . We can adopt,' he says pitifully.

'You coward. Do you even realise what you've done to me?'

Georgie frees herself from Sam's grasp.

'Georgie!' Sam cries. 'Let him be. Come away now. Let's go home and forget all this. We're young, we still have a life ahead of us.'

Georgie turns to look at her sister. All her life, Georgie has envied her, hated her, pitied her. She has hurt her, betrayed her, and yet . . .

Sam is still by her side.

'Why should you care what happens to me?' Georgie cries, the wind throwing her words back into her face.

'You're my sister, that's why. And I love you.'

Georgie stares at her. 'Even after what I did?'

'It doesn't mean I'm not angry with you,' Sam says, 'with the way you betrayed me. First our parents and then with . . . him.' Sam is weeping now, and so, Georgie realises, is she. What a pair of clowns they are.

'But you're still my sister,' Sam says.

She's braced against the wind, one hand still holding Georgie's leather jacket around her. Her eyes are red and swollen, her face bearing the bruises Georgie inflicted on her. She's a pitiful figure, yet in Georgie's eyes, she is, suddenly, magnificent.

Sam, realising that Georgie is caving, says, 'Come on now. Let's go home.'

Georgie is about to take Sam's hand when three things happen at once.

Turning to go, Sam loses her footing, slipping dangerously close to the edge of the cliff, where Suraj still dangles precariously.

Aru and Lalita both cry out.

Hanging from one hand, Suraj makes a grab for Sam with the other.

But for once, Georgie is too quick for him. She shoves her sister, sending her sprawling to the ground and safety. Then, instead of moving away, she swivels back around and makes a grab for Suraj, intending to push him over the edge. Scrambling to her feet, Sam cries, 'No, Georgie! No!'

But Suraj has taken hold of Georgie's hand, causing him to lose his grip on the rock.

For a split-second that seems to last an eternity, they lock eyes.

As she falls, hand in hand with her betrayer, the last thing Georgie hears is her sister's voice, calling to her.

CHAPTER 82

The bride-to-be

Her scream dying in her throat, Sam steps closer to the cliff edge.

Surely there must be some way to save Georgie?

'No, Sam! Come back.' Aru's voice has none of its usual imperiousness.

Sam turns to face her. She looks frail, worn out, her face ravaged, like her own must be, by what they've just witnessed. Sam can't quite comprehend what's happened, what she's just lost.

My sister. My only family. Gone.

Her heart keens.

'I . . . I'm sorry,' Aru is saying. 'Sorry about your sister. Sorry for what my son put you through.'

Sam looks at her in amazement.

Her son has just died a horrible death, yet her first thought is for me.

Sam wraps her arms around her and Aru collapses into them. Sam beckons to Lalita. 'Come.'

Lalita looks at her with fearful, tear-filled eyes.

280

'Please,' Sam says.

Lalita steps forward hesitantly, and Sam puts an arm around her.

Down on the beach, the tiny figures are still beetling about, wrestling with the marquee, setting up the tables for the wedding feast. The big wreath of fresh flowers that spell out '*Sam weds Suraj*' has just gone up.

Then, further off, the faint wail of sirens heralds the imminent arrival of the emergency services.

The sound spurs Sam to action, shocked out of her grief. She needs to take charge. Aru is no longer the indomitable lady Sam has come to know but a mourning mother who cannot help. Sam clears her throat, getting her thoughts together. 'Now, we don't have much time. We need to decide what we are to say about . . . what just happened.'

Down on the beach, the frantic activity has ceased. People are pointing up at the cliffs.

The news is out.

EPILOGUE

PART ONE

The locals

The locals have gathered at Mr Swain's lookout to chew over recent events. All of them are present except for Mr Stone, whose wife says he's still too upset by what he witnessed.

The women roll their eyes.

Later, as soon as Mrs Stone has gone out of the door, they'll turn to one another, shaking their heads. 'Who does he think he is?'

'Marge tells me he's in a very bad way,' Mrs Devlin, a good friend of Mrs Stone's, will cluck.

'*Tch-tch*,' Mrs Lewes will say, her false teeth clicking. 'Wants attention, he does. Why all this fuss? Nothing happened to him, did it?'

'Not last time I checked,' Mrs Nevis will say drily.

'More than can be said about them lot over at the resort . . .'

'And for it to happen at a *wedding* . . .'

'Death doesn't stand on ceremony,' Mrs Lewes will mutter darkly.

That Mrs Lewes is getting far too sarky in her old age. No romance in her life, that's her problem, Mrs Ramsbottom will think, and then she'll look down at her knitting to hide her embarrassment. She'll think of him, her Swain, saying, 'You'll always be apple-cheeked to me,' and drop a stitch.

Mrs Ramsbottom is resting her ample bottom on a chair that Mr Swain has gallantly pulled up for her. Mr Ramsbottom, who'd arrived panting and huffing behind her and was just about to sit on the chair himself, gives Mr Swain a withering look.

Mr Swain, it must be said, used to be rather shaken by Mr Ramsbottom's 'looks'. Now he meets his gaze full on, before, very deliberately, staring at his hairpiece.

Mr Ramsbottom, much to Mr Swain's surprise, is the first to look away. This has never happened before. Usually, it's Mr Swain who averts his gaze, that is if he meets Mr Ramsbottom's eyes in the first place. Mr Ramsbottom is left wondering whether Mr Swain *knows* that he's wearing a wig. But how? Only Mrs Ramsbottom knows this, and she's not likely to let on, is she? It's a puzzle, that's what it is. A con . . . what is it? Con . . . undrum.

He resists the urge to adjust his hairpiece, settling for scratching it instead.

'Those poor souls who fell—'

But Mrs Ramsbottom isn't allowed to finish her sentence. Mr Kay, who votes Labour and has a chip on his shoulder the size of England, cuts in with, 'Poor souls my a—'

'Language, Terry,' his wife interjects. 'There's children present.'

The teenagers look daggers at her.

'We've heard worse,' one of them mutters.

'Never mind fell. They're saying they might have been *pushed*,' Mrs Lewes says, returning to the matter in hand.

'You think?' someone says.

'I wouldn't be at all surprised. Them rich folks get up to all sorts,' Mrs Lewes says, folding her arms.

'You'd think with all that money, they'd have more sense,' Mrs Ramsbottom adds.

Mr Kay has been waiting for his moment. 'Ah, but you see, more money equals less sense. Less humanity. Less everything.

As I told the press when they came to me for my opinion, I always knew something like this would happen the moment that Tory so-and-so bought the land and announced that he was building a luxury resort on it . . .'

However, the tragedy at the resort is soon forgotten. Soon a new, and much more important, scandal erupts.

'Well I never!' Mrs Lewes, for once, seems hard pressed to find words.

'Right under our noses too,' Mrs Nevis exclaims.

'Poor Mr Ramsbottom, he's devastated.' Mrs Lewes is not silenced for long. 'I took him some of my rock cakes and tiffin bites but he didn't give 'em so much as a sniff. Not like him at all.'

'Did you know he's bald as a duck egg? I would leave him too, in her place. Swanning about in a wig . . .' Mrs Devlin's voice peters out under Mrs Lewes's severe gaze.

'Lost at least a stone in weight, poor man,' Mrs Lewes adds.

'I shouldn't wonder. How could she?' Mrs Kay shakes her head, envy radiating from every pore of her plump body.

'Mr Swain of all people. I thought he had more sense.'

'Eloping, at their age,' Mrs Kay says wistfully.

As ever, Mrs Lewes has the last word. 'Whatever next!'

PART TWO

Blog post — Starry-Eyed Gal
How the Mighty Fall

How the mighty fall, eh? I know it's a bit of a cliché, but it's appropriate in this case, don't you think?

The resort has closed its doors in the wake of a scandal even those who pull all the strings cannot fail to ignore.

The string of lies finally toppled like dominoes, one after another, as the arm of the law descended, bringing an end to the reign of one rule for one, one for another. Now the politicians and administrators, the top-tier police commissioners and justices who fell over themselves to brown-nose the Sharmas, are distancing themselves from the shambles.

It wasn't just the Sharmas, either. It transpired in the course of the investigations that the resort administration had been cutting corners, employing illegal immigrants and treating them despicably. They paid these workers less than half the minimum wage, made them work long, back-breaking hours and accommodated them in bunks, three to a room tinier than the box room in my own little house.

While the guests were guaranteed absolute privacy, their servants were subjected to round-the-clock surveillance, their employers making sure they squeezed every drop of labour out of them.

I managed to interview one of the workers, who spoke to me in strict anonymity. 'They had someone monitoring the cameras, noting the times we went into the rooms to clean them, and when we came out. Then they would lecture us on how to improve our timing without compromising the standard of cleanliness.'

'Did they adjust your pay accordingly? Did you get more the quicker you worked?' I asked.

'You must be joking. We thought ourselves lucky not to be sacked, or reported to the authorities. They had the threat of deportation to hold over us, you see.'

So now you know.

You suspect the truth about people, but you can't help believing that at heart they're better, don't you? At least I do, eternal optimist that I am.

And on that optimistic note, I have a bit of good news to pass on to you. Three bits, to be precise.

You remember me mentioning a friend of mine at the resort, who's been keeping me up to date on the latest developments? Thanks to him, I've been able to keep you abreast of events before they hit the mainstream media. As a result, my blog has now gone viral.

Well . . .

The first bit of good news is that I've been offered a book deal. And it's all down to you! I'm ever so grateful to you for spreading the word about my blog. The book is an exclusive, no-holds-barred account of what really happened, told from the point of view of someone who worked at the resort at the time it all happened. I am, of course, dedicating the book to you.

Which brings me to my second piece of news. I can now reveal the identity of the friend who gave me the story. You've probably guessed by now that he's more than just an informant — well, the truth is we're engaged! His name is Harry

Lewes, sous-chef at the resort, and now my partner in crime. He helps run the blog and will work with me on the book. He's taken advantage of the reporters and their hangers-on that are inundating the village, and has opened a café behind his mum's shop. What's more, they all love his food so much that he's thinking of launching a restaurant!

Now for my third piece of good news.

In a bid to salvage his reputation, the owner of the resort has, as a gesture of goodwill, donated the land and buildings to the local community — amid plenty of fanfare, as you can imagine. The council has decided to turn it into a leisure centre, since it has all the amenities in place (I'm talking several swimming pools, spas and a gym). The council says it's going to add a library, function rooms, a music venue and bandstand. Plus a restaurant, to be run by — you guessed it — my very own Harry Lewes!

But never fear, good peeps, despite all these goings-on — the book and the wedding — I will not be giving up my blog.

I'll tell you all about the wedding (yippee, can't wait!) and I'll cover it here. It won't have the pomp of the Sharma wedding, but at least it will happen. And it will end happily ever after.

So there, I've finished on a positive note.

Until next time, my lovelies. Keep well!

PART THREE

Lalita

The dust road that leads to her village is just as she remembered it. At this time of the afternoon the sun is at its zenith, and everyone is asleep. The rumble of the rickshaw fills the still, silent air, churning up clouds of red dust, while in the distance the waves can be heard tumbling onto the sand. The noise they make is gentle and reassuring, so different from the wind-battered Cornish sea.

The road rises almost imperceptibly. Lalita knows it's coming but still she gasps in wonder at the sight of the sea, her sea, blue-green and capped with white.

The sea that watched her grow up. On its shore, she met the love of her life, before it took him from her.

She thinks of all the dark days she spent in Cornwall trying to summon the image of her husband, the feel of him holding her, his kisses. Endlessly going over every detail of the last hours they spent together. It was a comfort to her during the long, barren years of her exile.

She took a rickshaw rather than a taxi because she was afraid of being dubbed one of 'those' people. People who considered themselves superior just by virtue of having been abroad. Her fellow villagers will never know what those years have cost her, and if she tried to tell them they wouldn't believe what she was saying.

As they near the village, the *tuk-tuk* of the rickshaw wheels alerts the village children, who gather by the side of the road, staring at Lalita, rubbing sleep from their huge, round eyes.

'I'm one of you,' Lalita wants to cry, but she knows they're eyeing the suitcases, her shiny new clothes, and they'll conclude that she's not.

They're wearing nothing but rags.

The rickshaw passes Duja's little store. It's unchanged, still selling its boiled sweetmeats from the front, while its real business, the dispensing of illicit arrack, is conducted out of sight at the rear. In the ditch by the back entrance, covered in flies, the drinkers still sleep off its effects.

The air, even in the shade of the coconut trees, is hot and humid.

Heedless of the perspiration soaking her back, she searches the children's faces. Are her children among them?

Will she know them if they are? Will they know her?

* * *

The deaths were ruled accidental.

It was agreed that Suraj must have tripped, and Georgie tried to save him and went down with him.

The trolley was never found, and neither were the blood-stained sheets or the lamp. In the absence of any evidence, the detectives were forced to admit defeat, and no one was prosecuted.

As for the blood on Georgie's bed, his mother claimed that Suraj suffered from severe nosebleeds whenever he undertook any 'strenuous activity'. Sam backed her up, leaving the detectives to infer what 'strenuous activity' meant in this case. Suraj's father insisted that this was a load of rubbish. *His* son never suffered from a single weakness, and certainly not nosebleeds. How would he know, Aru countered, he was never around to see.

Lalita knows exactly where the trolley containing the bloodstained sheets and bloodied lamp is, of course. She hopes it has been washed far out to sea by now.

Aru, Sam and Lalita. Three women from three different worlds, bound together by a secret they will never reveal.

Aru insisted that Lalita address her by her given name. 'I won't hear of you calling me "ma'am", and I'm certainly not Mrs Sharma — I've left my husband, thank God. I'm not even Arundhati Goel anymore — that girl is dead.' She smiled sweetly at Lalita (Yes, the woman who never even looked at the 'help'. Who would have guessed?). 'Now I'm just Aru. I refuse to be defined by either my ex-husband or my father, and don't you forget it.'

She sued for half of her husband's wealth — and got it. He paid up, *and* agreed to a quick and quiet divorce after she told him she'd go public with his abuse. When he'd arrived at the resort to find his son dead, he'd taken out his rage and sorrow on his wife, who had recorded it and threatened to show the media the photos of the damage he'd inflicted.

Her divorce out of the way, she went straight to Lalita and apologised. 'I'm sorry you had to face those detectives and their interrogation all alone.'

They'd honed in on Lalita in the absence of any other culprit. Aru had the best legal team money could buy on her side, and Dheeraj made sure Sam was just as well protected. Dheeraj was no fool. He'd strongly suspected that his wife's version of events was far from the truth — hence the beating he gave her — but he cared too much for his reputation to risk the fallout that might ensue if she were to go public.

Which left Lalita to take the brunt.

'I am so sorry I wasn't there to help. I was too busy fending off that bastard Dheeraj.' Aru's lip trembled.

Aru had changed beyond recognition. The cold, aloof demeanour she had so carefully cultivated had been discarded, never to return.

'But you did help,' Lalita said, 'as soon as you could.'

It was true. She had.

Lalita didn't know the nature of the agreement Aru had negotiated with the detectives and lawmakers, but she was the reason Lalita was not in prison right now.

'Come on,' Aru said. 'Call me Aru. It's not that hard.'

Having forsaken all her expensive beauty treatments, Aru looked older, more real. Without the Botox, her face was expressive, revealing all the weight of her years, all the hardship those years had contained. Lalita thought her beautiful.

'I still can't think of you as anything but "ma'am",' Lalita said. 'What do the English say? "Old habits die hard."'

'Well, work on it,' Aru said. 'You need to teach your children not to be subservient. If they face the world as if they own it, they will.'

'But how can I teach them? They're half a world away.'

'That's why I'm here.'

'I don't understand,' Lalita said.

'I have a debt to repay, on behalf of my son. I think you know what I mean — your husband's life.'

Lalita said nothing. After all, Aru was right.

'Here.' Aru handed Lalita a cheque.

Lalita couldn't believe her eyes when she saw how much it was made out for.

'I know it's a poor recompense for the loss of your husband,' Aru said.

'But it's so mu—'

Aru raised her hand in a gesture that brooked no argument. 'That's just part of it. I've instructed my lawyers to settle bursaries on your children. Their studies will be paid for as long as they remain in education. And there is another for you. You need to study further, my girl.'

'But—'

'Here's what I'd like from you. Finish your degree and then come and work for me. I have an idea of what I'd like to do with my ex-husband's billions, his "blood money" as I call it.' Aru smiled. 'I'm thinking of setting up a number of charities to assist the underprivileged — the hungry and the destitute. And particularly those who have no option but to resort to working illegally, far away from their homes and families.'

Lalita felt the prickle of tears behind her eyes.

'And when you're qualified, I will need you to help me run them.'

Now the tears could no longer be contained. She'd never, in all her wildest dreams, imagined that she herself might have the life she'd envisioned for her children. *Oh, Anand! If only you could be here to see it.*

But you brought it all about, by sacrificing yourself. You wanted your children to have a better life, which is why you went fishing in the storm that day.

Perhaps you're smiling from wherever you are now.

Aru laughed. 'I wouldn't mind seeing Dheeraj's face when he hears of it. God, will he be angry.'

'Good for you.' At least, that's what Lalita thinks she said. But perhaps she said nothing. Her throat was too full of the taste of salt, and gratitude.

'And, here.' Aru pressed an envelope into Lalita's hands. 'It's some cash to tide you over until the cheque clears.'

'But—'

'I refuse to take no for an answer,' Aru said with some of her old imperiousness. 'You can repay me by working extra hard when you come to help me run the charities. Now, off with you. Buy yourself a ticket and go home.'

Go home. Words as sweet as jalebi, as the taste of gulab jamun on her tongue.

'Give those kids a hug from me.' Aru's eyes shone. 'And make sure you keep in touch. Sam and I expect to hear all your news.'

'Thank you,' Lalita managed through her tears. 'And, please, come and visit.'

Aru nodded, unable to speak, and threw her arms around Lalita.

And, encased in those bony, jasmine-scented arms, Lalita felt free at last. She imagined the look on her ma's face when she got the letter — she did not have a phone — after weeks with no contact and no money from her daughter, telling her that Lalita was coming home . . .

* * *

The rickshaw rolls to a stop by the fields. Lalita turns to the group of village children who have followed them here. 'Would you please help me carry my suitcases over to my house? I'll pay you for it.'

As soon as he hears the mention of money, the rickshaw driver abandons his sullen air and begins unloading the cases, knocking against Lalita in his eagerness to earn a few rupees. He shoos the children away, insisting that he'll carry the cases himself.

Lalita gets down and stands for a moment, breathing deeply, inhaling the scent of brine and spice that means home.

Home.

She worked herself to the bone for this, dreamed of it while never believing that she would see it again.

She still can't quite believe it.

Soon, she will see her children.

She will hold them again. Kiss their innocent heads, breathe in their smell, feel them against her. Only then will she know that this is not all a dream.

Lalita remembers waiting for her husband to cross this field on his way home. She remembers going about her chores — drawing water from the well, stoking the kindling and boiling a pot of water for the children to wash in. Grinding spices and grating coconut ready for their meal of the fish he would be bringing. Carefully picking stones out of the rice. Soaking it, ready to cook with the curry. Lalita would do all this while listening out for his approaching footsteps, keeping one eye on the copse of fruit trees from which his beloved figure would soon emerge.

She'll never hear those footsteps again. Never see his face light up when he sees her. Never see him smile when she shouts at him.

The loss of him overwhelms her all over again.

It's why she accepted Aru's money.

Nevertheless, she's determined to repay it. Once her children are grown up and independent, she'll work for Aru until she's repaid every single rupee.

This does not mean that she wants to be free of Aru. They are bound together by their shared secret. Sam, too, who came to say goodbye to Lalita just before she left for home. Sam called her 'sister'. They are closer now than Sam ever was with Georgie. The three of them are open with one another in a way they can never be with anyone else.

The two suitcases Lalita has brought home with her are crammed with presents from Sam. 'Don't think you're getting rid of me that easily,' Sam said. 'One of these days I'll turn up on your doorstep.'

'I don't want to get rid of you, ever,' Lalita said. Both of them were crying. Lalita swallowed. 'I know I'm a Hindu, but I've come to appreciate some of your people's customs. There's one I like very much.'

'Yes?'

'My children . . .' Lalita twisted her blouse in that habitual gesture she couldn't seem to discard. How would Sam take what she was about to ask?

'Go on,' Sam said.

Lalita cleared her throat. 'You see, since their father died, I worry about their future. My mother is old, and when she's gone they'll only have me. I . . .'

'What is it, Lalita?' Sam said gently.

'Well, my friend Magda said that when her parents died, her godparents brought her up. You're a good person, you're kind. If anything happens to us, my mother and me . . .'

'Now I get it,' Sam said. 'You're asking me to be your children's godmother. Is that right?'

'Yes.'

Sam threw her arms around her. 'It would be an honour.'

'Are you sure?'

'Of course I'm sure. I'm humbled. Once you're settled in, I'll be on the first flight out. I want to meet my godchildren.'

'Thank you . . . my friend.'

Despite their shared secret, this was the first time Lalita had dared to call Sam 'friend'. It was hard to shake off centuries of colonialism and accept that they truly were equal.

'I'm not sure I'm worthy of it,' Sam said.

'No one is more worthy than you,' Lalita said firmly.

'Okay,' Sam said through her tears. 'Here's what I'm going to do. I'm giving you a week to settle in, and then I'll come and meet my new godchildren.'

Lalita couldn't quite believe that Sam had agreed so easily. 'You do realise that if anything happens to me—'

'Nothing's going to happen to you.'

'But if it does, you will look after them?'

'I will. I promise,' Sam said.

Now Lalita can meet her children with an open heart, happy that their future is secure.

Jalajakka and Muthakka, who are Lalita's nearest neighbours, emerge from their huts. Muthakka is rubbing her sweaty face with her sari pallu while Jalajakka wipes her hands on her sari skirt, wet from washing clothes beneath the mango trees by her well. There is a story about this well. It was infested with rat snakes, requiring the assistance of a snake charmer, who had to climb down, right into the well, and remove them one by one — hundreds of rat snakes and their babies. The entire village gathered to watch.

Now, Muthakka and Jalajakka watch the rickshaw driver approach, bearing the suitcases on his head. Muthakka stands well away from her sister-in-law, keeping her face averted. It looks like they're fighting again.

The two women are married to brothers who live side by side in huts built on land inherited from their father. Their marriages took place almost simultaneously, and as soon as the festivities were over, they divided the field into two compounds of equal size. Ever since, each has remained convinced that his brother has more than his fair share of the land. The well is situated in Jalajakka's compound, and Muthakka gets to use it in return for (grudgingly) sharing produce from the fruit trees growing on her side of the compound. Digging their own well would have meant giving up some of the land, along with the fruit trees on it, so Muthakka has to put up with the situation.

Each of them is so intent on looking anywhere but at her sister-in-law that neither sees Lalita approach.

'Hello,' Lalita says.

They stare at the well-dressed stranger who has addressed them. In that instant, the two sworn enemies look so similar they could be taken for twins.

'La—' Muthakka begins.

'Lalita, is that really you?' Jalajakka says.

'Of course it's me. Didn't Ma tell you I was coming?'

'I don't think she knows,' they both say at once, and glare at each other.

'But I wrote . . .' Lalita's voice trails away.

'You know what the post is like here,' Jalajakka says.

Lalita forgot. If the postal van is stuck in the Ghats, or if the monsoon wind has felled a tree, if the road is flooded, or if there is no excuse at all, the post doesn't make it.

At the resort, Lalita would wait eagerly for letters that arrived only sporadically, if at all.

'I see you've become a foreigner now, forgetting our ways,' Jalajakka says, showing her envy by spitting into the hibiscus.

Muthakka sniffs. 'A few months away and your head has already been turned.'

The sisters-in-law look at each other and shake their heads, briefly united in their resentment.

'It's been more than a few months,' Lalita says mildly. *You try staying away from your beloved children for months on end, missing out on all their milestones. You don't know what I've sacrificed to get here — the greatest sacrifice of all. I've sold my soul to the devil.*

The thought of what she was forced to do transports Lalita back to that nightmare moment when he begged her for his life.

'Help me. Please.'

Lalita thought of her children, growing up thousands of miles away, fatherless and with a mother they didn't know. She thought of her husband, the love of her life.

And she made her decision.

Lalita shuts her eyes, but still she hears him cry, *'Please!'*

'Help you? Pah! You don't deserve anyone's help, most of all mine.'
And all Lalita's accumulated rage and sorrow rose up within her. She picked up the lamp.

She hasn't told anyone what she did that day. Not even Sam and Aru know. Lalita guesses that Sam thinks she was covering for her in the mistaken belief that it was Sam who hit him. Lalita still wonders if perhaps Aru suspects there's more to it than that, but she hasn't said anything.

But Lalita will never forgive herself for the satisfaction it gave her to see him cower, to hear his pleas.

Lalita struck him twice, only coming to her senses when he fell back and lay still. But before he lost consciousness, he seemed to smile at her, as if to acknowledge that they were complicit, that when it came to it, she was no better than him.

Summoning all her remaining strength, Lalita hauled him up onto her trolley, along with the sheets and the lamp, and pushed it out of the room. All she could think of was getting away. Outside in the corridor, she remembered the hidden passageway and headed for it at a run, with little thought of what she would do once she was out of the resort.

Dismissing the memory, she smiles at Jalajakka and Muthakka, who are still staring at her. 'Nice to see you again. Now I must get to my children.'

Beckoning to the rickshaw driver, Lalita strides away from her curious and envious neighbours.

The hut waits for her, unchanged beneath its canopy of mango and jackfruit trees.

Lalita breaks into a run. That tiny hut contains the people she loves most in the world. Only one is missing, and he's never coming home.

She remembers the first time she caught sight of her new home. 'Look!' Anand said proudly. 'We'll have nobody around to bother us, we'll live in peace for the rest of our lives.'

Happy ever after, Lalita thought as he picked her up and twirled her around, the stray dog that had followed them erupting in a frenzy of excited barking. Lalita glanced at the little animal and noticed her swollen teats. So she too . . . Giddy with happiness, Lalita leaned against her husband and told him her news. Anand whooped with joy and kissed her, the dog nipping at their heels, eager to join in.

The dog is long gone, but one of her offspring runs up to greet her, barking at this stranger.

Her mother calls out from inside the hut. 'Who's there?' There is a new tremor in her voice, and when she peers out through the sari hung across the doorway, her face is lined with wrinkles that weren't there when Lalita last saw her. Her mother looks tired, careworn.

She shouldn't be caring for children at her age. She should be resting.

It's my turn to look after you now. And I'm going to make sure you never have to lift a finger again. Just as the thought passes through her head, the sari curtain is pushed aside and a little girl skips out.

She stops in front of Lalita and puts a finger in her mouth. 'Who are you?'

Her heart breaking, Lalita squats down in front of the child. She hears her husband's voice, stroking her bump when she was heavy with this child.

Do you know what I wish for? I wish for this one to be a little girl who looks just like you.

Well, his wish came true.

I know. I can see her . . .

Then her mother appears beside her, her hand on her heart. 'Lalita? Is that really you?'

'Lalita?' Her daughter casts an uncertain backward glance at her grandmother.

At that moment, she hears a cry from behind her. 'Ma!'

He's grown. He's a proper little boy now.

His face, an echo of his father's, is lit up with joy.

'Ma!'

Lalita had forgotten how he glowed.

Her little girl is standing with her face screwed up in puzzlement, a finger still in her mouth. 'Ma? Our ma, who lives in . . . far away?'

'Yes! Yes!' Lalita's boy shouts. 'You were only little when she left, so you don't remember her. But *I* do.'

His chest swells with pride.

Swallowing the lump in her throat, Lalita opens her arms wide.

Her boy flings himself into her embrace, while, not to be outdone, her daughter follows suit, elbowing her brother aside. 'Move over. She's my ma too.'

Oh, how she has longed for this moment! Over their precious heads, she sees her mother leaning against the doorframe, watching them, beaming through her tears. And the dog jumps around them, and butterflies flit among the hibiscus like scattered blessings, and the rickshaw driver sets the suitcases down and waits, scratching his crotch, for the promised tip.

Up, amid the swaying fronds of the palm trees, her husband looks down upon his family and smiles. *We're all together again.*

Already, Lalita's rotten, wounded heart is beginning to heal.

PART FOUR

Sam

'So. Are we going to India next week?' Aru asks Sam. 'We should visit Lalita. It's about time you saw your godchildren . . .'

'Well, yes, I—'

'That's settled, then. I want to set up a branch of our foundation in India, to support women and children in need, and I thought I might as well do it in the community where Lalita lives. It'll do you good to get away for a bit too.'

After the terrible events of the wedding, Sam had a breakdown.

Aru saw her through it.

In one of her darker moments, Sam cried, 'I'm all alone in the world.'

'Well, thank you very much,' Aru said. 'Here I am, spending all this time with you and you tell me you have nobody.'

'I'm sorry, Aru. I—'

'You're not alone, Sam,' Aru said softly. 'I'm with you, and I always will be, as long as you need me.'

Sam was so touched she burst into tears.

'Could you please, just for once, turn off the waterworks?' Aru said, smiling. Then, she put her arms around Sam and hugged her.

Sam promptly burst into tears all over again.

'I'm so sorry,' she said when she could speak. 'Here you are, having lost your son, separated from your husband, and it's me who's crying.'

'Well, I certainly don't miss my husband,' Aru said grimly. 'As for my son . . . I tried so hard to change him, but all to no avail.'

'I know,' Sam whispered.

'It's better this way,' Aru said, but her voice shook. 'I hated the things he did, but I couldn't help loving him.'

'I know. I couldn't help loving him either. He did have his moments.'

Aru smiled gratefully at Sam. 'You know what the best thing about not being with my husband is?'

'What?'

'I can be my age.'

Sam grinned. 'Embrace those wrinkles.'

They smiled at each other.

Sam never expected that she and Aru would be friends. What's more, Aru received the seal of approval from her friends at the charity shop. Even Mrs Arbuthnot, who declared that Aru was 'not bad for someone from new money,' agreed that she passed muster.

Her friends were sad to hear that Sam was leaving her job at the shop.

'It's my fault,' Aru said. 'I'm starting a foundation to help women and children in need, and Sam is going to be my partner.'

Sam recalled the moment Aru had first put it to her. 'But I've no qua—'

'You don't need a college degree.' Aru's eyes had twinkled. 'I presume you *are* literate. What I need is someone I can trust.'

Sam had tasted the words on her tongue. 'Someone I can trust.' She, who had lied to everyone, lived under false pretences in the belief that she'd committed murder. It was a miracle.

'We will miss you,' her friends said. 'The shop won't be the same without you.'

'Although the new manager is rather dishy,' Edie and Edna simpered.

Mrs Arbuthnot rolled her eyes at this. 'Common.'

Addressing Aru, Mr Venables said rather pompously, 'I think I speak for all of us when I say that you've done very well in choosing Sam to be your partner. And I must say, personally, I can't think of anyone better.'

Edie and Edna clapped and Mrs Arbuthnot nodded. Aru glanced at Sam, noticed her tears, and rolled her eyes.

Breaking in on her thoughts, Aru says, 'So, shall I book our flights for late next week? That suit you?'

For a brief moment Sam recalls having hoped to visit India with Suraj after the wedding, and spending their honeymoon there.

She hears him laugh. *Ha! You wish.*

He's been haunting her dreams recently. She keeps seeing his eyes, his lips twisted in a cruel smile. *Okay, you didn't kill your parents, but you're still evil. You wanted to kill me.*

Sam sees herself pushing him with all her strength, pushing until he disappears from her life for ever.

She wakes up gasping.

But I didn't!

Only because your sister got there first, he taunts.

'I couldn't do it,' she whispers.

Oh yes you could. You're just as much a monster as I am, he says. *And you know it.*

'Sam!' Aru says, startling her. 'Stop thinking like that.'

'Like what? How do you know what I'm thinking?' Sam asks.

'I can see the look in your eyes. You're doubting yourself again. You're a good person, Sam. We all have murderous thoughts sometimes, but that doesn't make us bad people.' Aru takes Sam's hands in hers. 'Look at me, Sam. You didn't do it. All right?'

Sam doesn't know whether Aru is referring to her parents or Suraj, but she nods.

'It's over,' Aru says softly.

Sam touches her stomach, which is already starting to swell. No, it's not over. Not by a long shot.

Suraj's child is behaving just like he did when Aru was carrying him. 'He never liked me, even when he was still in my womb. He kicked me, he made me ill.'

I'll have my revenge yet, Suraj whispers inside Sam's head.

She tries to love this child but she cannot do it. It's impossible with these evil thoughts churning and festering in her head. When it comes down to it, she's a monster, just like him.

What sort of mother doesn't love her child?

THE END

ACKNOWLEDGEMENTS

Thank you to my amazing editor, Jasmine Callaghan — you are the absolute best, so passionate and committed, and I am incredibly lucky in you.

A huge thanks to all the wonderful team at Joffe for helping shape my book and make it the very best it can possibly be, and for making it travel far and wide.

Thank you, Anne Derges, for the wonderfully thorough edit. I'm so very grateful and lucky.

Thank you, Cat Phipps, for your eagle eye and wonderful suggestions during copy edits for this book. A huge thank you to Kate, for coordinating the edits, and Tia, for your wonderful and tireless marketing efforts for the book.

Thank you to my lovely author friends, Angie Marsons, Sharon Maas, Debbie Rix, June Considine (aka Laura Elliot), whose friendship I am grateful for and lucky to have.

A huge thank you to my mother, Perdita Hilda D'Silva, who reads every word I write; who is encouraging and supportive and fun; who answers any questions I might have on any topic — finding out the answer, if she doesn't know it, in record time — who listens patiently to my doubts and who reminds me, gently, when I cry that I will never finish the book: 'I've heard this same refrain several times before.'

I am immensely grateful to my long-suffering family for willingly sharing me with characters who live only in my head. Love always.

And last, but not least, thank you, reader, for choosing this book.

THE JOFFE BOOKS STORY

We began in 2014 when Jasper agreed to publish his mum's much-rejected romance novel and it became a bestseller.

Since then we've grown into the largest independent publisher in the UK. We're extremely proud to publish some of the very best writers in the world, including Joy Ellis, Faith Martin, Caro Ramsay, Helen Forrester, Simon Brett and Robert Goddard. Everyone at Joffe Books loves reading and we never forget that it all begins with the magic of an author telling a story.

We are proud to publish talented first-time authors, as well as established writers whose books we love introducing to a new generation of readers.

We won Trade Publisher of the Year at the Independent Publishing Awards in 2023 and Best Publisher Award in 2024 at the People's Book Prize. We have been shortlisted for Independent Publisher of the Year at the British Book Awards for the last five years, and were shortlisted for the Diversity and Inclusivity Award at the 2022 Independent Publishing Awards. In 2023 we were shortlisted for Publisher of the Year at the RNA Industry Awards, and in 2024 we were shortlisted at the CWA Daggers for the Best Crime and Mystery Publisher.

We built this company with your help, and we love to hear from you, so please email us about absolutely anything bookish at feedback@joffebooks.com.

If you want to receive free books every Friday and hear about all our new releases, join our mailing list here: www.joffebooks.com/freebooks.

And when you tell your friends about us, just remember: it's pronounced Joffe as in coffee or toffee!

We built this company with your help, and we love to hear from you so if pleased or not please do let us know at feedback@joffebooks.com

www.ingramcontent.com/pod-product-compliance
Ingram Content Group UK Ltd.
Pitfield, Milton Keynes, MK11 3LW, UK
UKHW020038290425
457968UK00004B/157

9 781805 731009